—————————— ——————————

Sweete, playing the receptionist-nurse, opened her mouth to reply. But before she could do so, on the other side of the partition Janis Mahafey let out a shriek that made everybody in the room jump.

She staggered back from the gurney, almost knocking Raddell down.

"He's dead!" she cried. She held up one of her hands. Something bright red and glistening had gotten smeared all over it when she began her make-believe examination. "I mean," she yelled, "he's *really* dead!" And keeled over.

—————————— ★ ——————————

"Mr. Miles does keep you focusing on the events, compelling you to uncover the murderer."

—*Rendezvous*

"An excellent ear for the way the elderly talk to one another."

—*The Boston Globe*

JOHN MILES

MURDER IN RETIREMENT

WORLDWIDE®

TORONTO • NEW YORK • LONDON
AMSTERDAM • PARIS • SYDNEY • HAMBURG
STOCKHOLM • ATHENS • TOKYO • MILAN
MADRID • WARSAW • BUDAPEST • AUCKLAND

MURDER IN RETIREMENT

A Worldwide Mystery/July 1997

This edition is reprinted by arrangement with
Walker and Company.

ISBN 0-373-26243-4

Printed in U.S.A.

MURDER IN
RETIREMENT

ONE

BRACING HERSELF for a murder, Laura Michaels drove up the narrow gravel road toward Timberdale Retirement Center at 7:45 a.m. Wednesday. A chill Oklahoma wind out of the northwest swirled small storms of fallen oak and willow leaves across the hillside, threatening colder weather. Timberdale stood pale in the early sunlight. It was a curious architectural cross between Georgian and contemporary that somehow managed to work.

Pulling her car into the retirement center's west parking lot, Laura felt glum. Today it started—preparation for Timberdale's first "mystery weekend"—and on Friday an actor's body was supposed to hit the Timberdale floor, highlighting what Laura's boss termed "all the planned fun."

More than six weeks ago, back in September, Mrs. Judith Epperman had swooped down on Laura's office and gushed the previously secret plan.

"Laura! I have wonderful news, dear girl!"

Laura had looked up cautiously, trying to gauge her boss's meaning. The redoubtable Mrs. Epperman removed her small gold reading glasses and let them free-fall to the end of their thin gold chain, where they plopped onto the considerable bulk of her breasts. Laura couldn't read her expression, but it looked uncharacteristically gleeful.

"Well?" Mrs. Epperman prodded. "Aren't you going to ask me what it is?"

"What?" Laura had lost the thread. When Mrs. Epperman descended on her like a panzer division, this frequently happened. "Ask what *what* is?"

"Ask me what *it* is!" Mrs. Epperman demanded. "What the wonderful news is!"

Laura took the path of least resistance: "What is it?"

"Well! You *know* we've been under some pressure from the board of directors to find better ways to promote Timberdale—attract new residents to fill those vacant apartments, get things moving, beef up the bottom line. And you *know* our occupancy percentage certainly hasn't been helped any by having no less than five residents decide to die on us this summer! It's just been a dreadful string of bad luck, wouldn't you say, dear? I mean, I *know* the old darlings didn't die on purpose, but they couldn't have died at a more inopportune time, in terms of our cash flow. You would think they'd have more loyalty—take better care of themselves for *our* sake, if not for their own. Don't you agree?"

"Sometimes people are really thoughtless," Laura said carefully.

Mrs. Epperman blinked and glared, as if almost aware there was an irony here somewhere. "Eh?"

"I was just agreeing with you," Laura told her. "Please go on."

Mrs. Epperman went. Several weeks earlier, she said, while pondering many a quaint and curious volume of accounting sheets overflowing with red ink, it had come to her that what Timberdale needed was an *event*—something wonderful to draw media attention, show Timberdale for the truly neat and fun place it was, and cheer up the residents, pick them up out of their autumn blues, all at the same time. Didn't Laura agree? Didn't Laura—as a graduate student in social work as well as Timberdale's assistant to the manager and the outfit's resident shrink without portfolio—*agree?*

Laura agreed.

Well, then. The inspiration Mrs. Epperman had come up with was a really fun mystery—one of those staged events more often played in a dinner theater, or at a weekend resort where people registered to witness the "crime" and try to dope out whodunit. After some heavy-duty channeling (Mrs. Epperman claimed to have regular psychic contact with two women whom she believed to be Cleopatra and Queen Victoria), she had examined the idea and pronounced it good.

At that point she had uncharacteristically started arranging the event on their own, rather than delegating all the work as she usually did. The result: She could now announce a signed contract with the traveling dramatic troupe of the Redwine Players for a mystery weekend starting on Friday, November 8, and climaxing on Sunday, November 10, six weeks hence. Wasn't it *exciting,* dear girl?

Laura had dutifully said yes. In reality she thought it was a dumb idea. And it never occurred to her—then or now—that the murder might turn out to be a real one.

Despite her blissful optimism, however, she felt grumpy and depressed as she locked her battered little Japanese car and hurried toward the canopy-sheltered front entrance of the retirement center, fighting to keep her skirt somewhere below the level of her neck. She knew Mrs. Epperman meant well, but the idea of having a staged murder melodrama here didn't feel right to her. The median age of the hundred-plus residents was well over seventy; it had been a rare month lately when someone didn't die, even though Timberdale was a retirement community, very much like a luxury residential hotel, so when people got really seriously infirm they weren't allowed to stay any longer. Still, there had been too much death recently; the residents, almost all of whom Laura really had strong feelings for, did not need any more reminders of mortality.

And besides, Laura thought, murder-mystery weekends were *dumb.* They were always phony and hokey and amateurish and awkward, about as truly dramatic as one of those charity plays put on by the Junior League or other groups of charitable ladies looking for an excuse to strut around onstage in tights.

It was too late to try to head it off now, however. At the moment, she had quite enough to cope with, trying to keep her skirt down.

Grabbing her hem with one hand and her flying hair with the other, she happened to glance upward at the ranks of unit windows across the front of the building. The draperies were pulled open in a second-floor room near the center, and something glinted, catching her eye. She caught a good glimpse of him before he ducked out of sight: a gray-haired man, stocky, with a bullet-shaped skull and the shoulders of a lightweight boxer, staring down at her with a pair of ten-power binoculars. Ken Keen. At sixty-three, the youngest male resident of the place, and the most persistent lech. *Dammit, next he'll have a 300-millimeter lens up there to take pictures.*

Grateful for the shelter, Laura ducked in under the canopy and pulled the front door open. She had the briefest glance at her own reflection in the heavy glass door as she entered, and except for her wind-tossed hair she looked nice: trim, quick, neat. She had worn heels and hose and one of her prettiest red dresses today because she had a midterm exam at the University of Oklahoma in Norman at 6:30, and then a late dinner with Aaron...unless something awful happened to make him work overtime at the sheriff's department, where he was a deputy. She hoped not.

Especially after the brisk wind, the atrium Laura entered now had an effect of quiet and elegance. Three floors tall, open to a silvery skylight roof, it was surrounded by white railed balconies that circled the vast emptiness. Doors of individual apartments faced the open halls. White wood trim and ivory-colored walls soared. On the main floor, scattered large Persian rugs formed conversation areas with traditional chairs and sofas, mahogany tables, and heavy lamps. A larger-than-usual number of residents was already standing around and visiting while they awaited the eight o'clock opening of the dining room. But because they were all old, and so had a concept of politeness, the atrium seemed almost as quiet as if no one at all were in it.

Smiling and waving to some of them, Laura hurried behind the curving reception counter at the front left of the area. Stacy Miller, the college coed who usually worked night shift on the desk, had some time off. Her substitute, a girl named Browning, was so new on the job that she hadn't even left any

wrecked pizza or drooled Diet Coke on the counter. There was
no mess at all. Of course there was no Browning at all, either;
she had apparently bugged out already.

Laura checked the recorder behind the desk for messages,
found none; glanced at the incident sheet from overnight,
found nothing; and went down the short corridor behind the
reception desk area to her own tiny cubicle. Mrs. Epperman's
office remained dark, and the other bane of Laura's existence,
sex bomb Francie Blake, would be late as usual. That gave
Laura five minutes on her own to try to get a brush through
her hair and check the day's schedule of events.

It looked to be a quiet day at Timberdale. The only business
item penciled on Laura's desk calendar was the notation
"Mystery actors arr. today." She wished that note weren't
there. It was, though, and there would be no getting around
it.

Walking back into the atrium, she found the crowd of residents a bit larger and a tad more tense, as the entire small
crowd seemed to be drifting into a tighter clot near the double
doors to the dining room, like filings to a magnet. Nobody
was saying a word, of course, but the nervousness could be
felt. *What if I don't get in there before all the prunes are
gone?* Forty percent wouldn't eat once they did get in and an
equal proportion would bitch about the menu no matter what
it was. Of the remaining twenty percent, fifteen would com-
plain there wasn't enough per portion, two would eat quietly
and politely, and the other three wouldn't remember where
they were long enough to be tallied. But the morning ritual
was in full cry: Jostle and jockey to be among the first through
the doors when they opened, but for heaven's sake pretend it
isn't happening.

Actually, this doorway demolition derby was often one of
the high points of the day for some of them. That, Laura
thought, made it not so funny.

She drifted onto the edges of the crowd and started saying
hellos. Angry Ellen Smith, Timberdale's resident artist, hurried over, squash-blossom necklace and ten pounds of other

Indian jewelry tinkling furiously. She was wearing a paint-spattered white smock over her buckskin dress. "Laura!" she gasped, eyes shooting sparks. "It's two minutes after eight!"

Laura glanced at the towering grandfather clock in the nearest corner. "The clock says it isn't eight yet, Ellen."

Smith drew herself up to her full height of five and a half feet. "Balderdash! That clock is never right!" She thrust a veiny arm at Laura, rattling eight or ten silver bracelets. "Look! Just look! This is a fine Casio watch I paid almost twenty dollars for at Service Merchandise!"

Laura found the watch in the silverware. Its digital readout said 8:02:14. She glanced at her own wrist. "I really think you might be fast, Ellen."

"I can't be fast! This watch is guaranteed to be accurate within five seconds a year! Now look, Laura, you have *got* to get this place shaped up. I've already set up in the crafts room for my day's work. My oils will begin to thicken unless I proceed within forty-five minutes."

Laura glanced at the handful of other residents gathered around her, wondering what feelings lay behind their carefully opaque expressions. "It will be only another minute or two, Ellen, I'm sure—"

"No one appreciates the artist's life! This kind of delay and worry is terribly destructive to the artistic vision. I fully expected to have a wonderful day of work on my barn painting. Now, with *this* unforgivable inconvenience, I may lose the entire color scheme I had in mind."

"I—"

"It's *terrible!*" Smith's eyelids flew up and down like venetian blinds under attack by a cat. "Inspiration is a fragile thing. No one seems to appreciate that around here!"

A bear-shouldered old man, bald head gleaming, made a muttering noise at Laura's elbow. Judge Emil Young, ninety-two, straightened the sleeves of his brown tweed sport coat. "To the contrary, my dear lady. The insightful character of aesthetic articulation is at times paramount among the subjects adumbrated by certain of your institutional peers."

Smith whirled, blinking furiously. "What?"

"In a word," Judge Young rumbled, "you have my most empathic commiseration." He adjusted his ivory-headed cane from his left hand to his right and fixed her with eyes narrowed with malice. "On the other hand, my dear, your cheap watch is clearly wrong."

"Well! I never!" Smith stormed off, managing to get nearer the dining room doors in the process.

Tiny Maude Thuringer, seventy-three, wearing, as usual, a diaphanous floral silk dress and thick-heeled black shoes, tugged at Laura's sleeve. "Today's the day!"

"Good morning, Maude. Yes, it is."

"Day for what?" Mrs. Stoney Castle chirped. She and her husband had been standing by, looking like geriatric twins in their matching red Nike sweats. "It isn't time for the Social Security checks."

"No, no, no," Maude shot back impatiently. "It's the day the mystery-melodrama acting troupe arrives."

Stoney Castle studied her with watery pale-blue eyes. He looked like Jack Nicholson might if he lived another forty years—that is, like a very old lizard waiting to pounce. "Can't say that it's anything to have a hemorrhage over, Maudie."

Thuringer drew herself up to her full height, sixty inches. "It's the biggest thing that's happened around here in a month of Sundays."

Castle squinted in disbelief. "Just yestiday you were saying this Redwine feller ain't worth the powder it'd take to blow him to hell."

"Of course." Thuringer returned fire. She pointed at her own chest with her index finger. "*I* am no fool, Stoney Castle, and don't you ever forget it. I've read every mystery that's been published in the last hundred years, and some of them twice. I'm a *student* of intrigue and suspense, if I do say so myself."

Castle cocked his head. "What's *that* got to do with anything?"

"I know about J. Turner Redwine. He's no spring chicken,

you know. He's been doing these mystery things for years. I've read about them. I'll watch everything like a hawk and it won't even be a challenge for me. I'll solve the mystery before anybody else even knows there is one.''

"Then why," Castle demanded, torn between irritation and puzzlement, "did you just say we ought to be excited about it?"

Thuringer looked stunned. "It's better than nothing, isn't it?"

"Well, I don't know, you danged fool. You just talked like it ain't."

"Stoney..." Mrs. Castle murmured, cringing.

"Well? She *did*. You just stay out of this, Opal, dammit."

Mrs. Castle looked hurt. Maude Thuringer looked angry. Stoney Castle looked triumphant. Judge Young appeared to be sleeping on his feet. Laura was about to interrupt. But the doors of the dining room began to open, salvaging everything.

After an initial soft surge, the residents calmed down and formed two orderly lines past the food—scrambled eggs or Egg Beaters, bacon, hash brown potatoes, toast, biscuits, grapefruit, cereal, bran muffins, take your pick. Part-time college boy workers stood by to dish things up, looking uncomfortable in their white linen jackets. Two of the kitchen helpers bustled around, serving coffee or tea to the ones first through the line and already at the table. Laura drifted, saying hello to people. Beyond the side windows, the bitter wind hurled leaves and bits of debris across a flagstone patio with scattered pots of desiccated petunias and geraniums. Laura learned that Davilla Rose, Timberdale's poet, had a corn; Col. Roger Rodgers (U.S.A., Ret.), was mightily sick and tired of the effete sissy Frenchified chow the new chef had been shoving at them every night, and he intended to write a letter to the board of directors about it if Laura didn't get it squared away ASAP, as in pronto; Sada Hoff was expecting a visit from her daughter next weekend; the Wilcoxes and the Harrisons weren't playing bridge any more because the Harrisons wouldn't stop using all these tricky new bidding conventions, and it gave them an unfair advantage, and the Wilcoxes just liked to have a nice friendly game, and it wasn't even nice; Ken Keen thought she looked hot.

The dual kitchen doors in the back of the room swished open again, as they had been doing throughout the breakfast hour for helpers to run errands, but this time the person who put in a grand appearance was none other than the subject of considerable gossip, speculation, and equal parts praise and condemnation, Timberdale's new chef, Pierre Motard. Towering over six feet six, his height exaggerated by his eighteen-inch white cook's cap, Motard certainly looked the part of a chef. And he had decreed that "chef" must be his formal title, when Laura and Mrs. Epperman interviewed him to replace the last head of the kitchen, Margaret Knott, who had been merely head cook.

Motard's slightly bulging eyes scanned the room, found Laura. He raised a hand and snapped his fingers: *Report to me instantly, wench!* Laura got up from the table where she had finally started to have some coffee. She told herself to be nice; finding a new cook had been tough, at the wages Timberdale paid.

"Hi, Pierre. Nice breakfast. What's up?"

Motard held out a sheet of paper filled with Mrs. Epperman's back-slanted, loopy handwriting. "What is meaning of such a bother thing as *this?*"

"What is it?"

Motard glowered. He smelled of garlic. "You are assistant manager this place and you do not be aware of it?"

Laura held on. "No. What is it?"

"Is memorandum, Mrs. Epperman, saying kitchen staff is assign prepare special meals for all acting troupe. This is an outrageous! Nothing was ever say, special menu, when you of me hire."

"Pierre, I'm sure something can be worked out. Part of our agreement with the Redwine Players was that we would put them up here during the time they prepare and put on their show. Mrs. Epperman must just want to make sure they get nice meals.''

"'Nice meals'?'' Motard stood taller, outraged. "You say, 'nice meals'? Pierre Motard *always* does 'nice meals'! Every meal done by Pierre Motard is *exquisite* meal, meal of grandeur!'' He slapped the paper with the back of a large, hairy hand. "I refuse! I will not prepare unusualness for these actors. They will eat what residents are prepare, the finest. You will tell Mrs. Epperman this for me.''

Laura eased in a deep breath. It was starting out to be a lovely day. "I'll inform Mrs. Epperman, Pierre. Thank you for calling it to my attention.''

Getting her coffee cup from her abandoned table, she made her way out of the dining room, back across the atrium, and to the office area behind the reception desk. In her mind she ticked off her plans for the day, already awry. Her daughter, Trissie, would ride to elementary school in Norman with their neighbor, who regularly helped watch over her while Laura worked or attended night or weekend classes at the university; after school, Mrs. Barker would pick Trissie up, along with her own daughter, and take her to the Barker apartment, where she would stay until Laura collected her late this evening. Laura had intended to handle a dozen routine job details she was behind on, do some paperwork, meet with her ten o'clock informal therapy group here, attend to whatever problems might arise with the arrival of the actors, steal two hours (or more, if at all possible) to review for her test tonight, grab something sinful at Dunkin' Donuts on the way to the campus to hold her over, take the test, and then meet Aaron for that late el cheapo dinner she was so much looking forward to.

Pierre Motard's dudgeon would require a bit of time to fix, however. Mrs. Epperman would want to hold a meeting about it. And unless Laura missed her guess, Ellen Smith would make a big thing of her allegation that breakfast had been late. Mrs. Epperman would want to have a meeting about that, too; she loved meetings. If anything else went wrong, Laura's plans to steal study time would go straight down the tubes.

But maybe nothing else would go wrong.

The telephone on the reception desk was blinking and ringing persistently. Through the back glass, Laura could see lights ablaze in the manager's office, but Mrs. Epperman's bulky figure was hunched over her desk, making no move to answer the call.

Laura hurried around the desk to answer. "Timberdale Retirement Center, Laura Michaels speaking. Good morning."

"Laura? Hi. Glad I caught you."

She felt a distinct warmth in her belly. "Hi, Aaron. What's up?"

He sounded gloomy. "I'm afraid there's been a complication."

"Oh, shit. What?"

"Ameringer just called in sick, so I'll have to take his shift tonight in addition to my own."

"Dammit. No dinner then, huh?"

"I'm afraid not. I'm really upset about it. We haven't seen each other for two days."

"Tell me about it," Laura said glumly.

He paused a beat, then: "Well, look, honey. I'm going to get out there to Timberdale in the morning to see you if nothing else in the world gets done. Okay?"

Seeing him here, with a hundred eyes looking on, was not her idea of fun. She looked down at herself, the dark hose and pointed little pumps. *Oh, well, hell, Laura. You'd probably wear black bikini panties and this damned uncomfortable garter belt to take a midterm anyway, right?* "Sure, Aaron. No problem."

"Well..." He sounded miserable, the darling. "I'll call you later, okay?"

"Sure."

Another pause. Finally: "Hey."

"Yes?"

"I love you, babe."

The warmth spread all over her. "I love you, too." She hung up.

Well, nothing else could possibly go wrong.

She walked into the office area and past the manager's door. Mrs. Epperman looked up. "Laura. A word, please?"

Laura went in.

A newspaper lay spread across Mrs. Epperman's desk. It was turned to the crossword puzzle. Mrs. Epperman, bulky in a military-cut suit complete with epaulets, peered up at her over her reading glasses. "Everything is fine, dear? Good. Let me ask you one." She glanced down at her puzzle. "Four letters. 'Victim of feudalism.'"

"Esne," Laura said.

"What?"

"Esne. E-S-N-E."

Scowling, Mrs. Epperman wrote it in. "What kind of a word is that?"

Laura smiled. "The kind you learn when you do puzzles all the time." She might have added "during a divorce," but she didn't.

"Have you heard anything from our actors yet today?"

"Not yet."

"Are all the old dears simply gaga with excitement?"

"Oh, yes. Pierre—"

"I want you personally to be in charge of their convenience, dear girl. Nothing is too good for them. I'm awfully busy today, so the first thing I want you to do is run and make sure their rooms are all ready and everything is shipshape. Will you do that right away, please?"

"There are a couple of things we need to talk about, Mrs. Epperman."

"Well, they can wait, they can wait. I'm busy here. Run along, child. We can talk later." Mrs. Epperman bent again over her puzzle.

Laura left the office. All she needed was the added chore of checking on the guest rooms. *Now* things couldn't get worse, she thought.

She was still thinking that around ten-thirty, when the arrival of J. Turner Redwine, whose card identified him as a "renowned thespian," proved her wrong again.

TWO

WHEN SHE HAD first been told about Mrs. Epperman's "wonderful idea" about a mystery weekend featuring the Redwine Players, Laura had gone to the university library at first opportunity—good M.S.W. candidate that she was—to try to find out something about this Redwine character. She had located two magazine entries, one in a very old *Time* and a more recent short mention in *People*.

In neither case had Redwine rated much more than a footnote, but Laura had been able to glean some information nevertheless.

Apparently he had been a busy character actor in Hollywood in the 1950s and early 1960s. He had been in more than two dozen pictures, mostly second-feature thrillers involving vampires, werewolves, and aliens from outer space. Once he had managed a walk-on in a Basil Rathbone Sherlock Holmes adventure. He had also done summer stock, evidently, and had played minor parts in touring companies of the old *Mr. Roberts*.

It seemed Redwine had started his own acting troupe around 1974, evidently to do some kind of performance with a circus. Later he was involved in a nasty lawsuit alleging failure to pay his actors. In 1982 there had been a bankruptcy, followed closely by a divorce that rated two lines in the *Los Angeles Times* and another lawsuit alleging fraud of an unspecified type. He had remarried—an actress, a bit player—in 1983.

In 1985, *People* had mentioned the Redwine touring group as "one of a dozen or so marginal groups that pop up periodically to try to scare people at summer resorts."

Laura had not been very encouraged.

"Are we sure," she had diffidently asked Mrs. Epperman, "that this troupe is reliable...and everything?"

"We've got to look at the bottom line, dear," the redoubtable manager had replied with heavy sarcasm. "We can hardly afford John Barrymore!"

"I think," Laura observed meekly, "he's dead."

"Of course he's dead, you silly child! I channeled to him only a month or two ago. He said he misses the California sunshine."

That had been it as far as pro forma protests were concerned, and now the grand event was about to move forward. Laura found herself dreading it more than ever now that the big day of arrival had finally come.

She had just returned to her office from a routine check on the walk-in medical clinic, and was thinking about some of this, when the commotion started in the atrium.

First came a sharp, startled female scream—a yelp, really, quickly extinguished. Then, before she could get around her desk to investigate, Laura heard something crash out there, followed by a stentorian male voice declaiming something she couldn't make out.

Mrs. Epperman had gone to the bank and some kind of meeting. Francie Blake seemed to have taken the day off again without prior notice. That left Laura nominally in charge. Fuming, she hurried out past their darkened offices and out to the reception desk.

Paula Burwell, the woman who worked the day shift behind the desk, was on her feet and staring, her handsome, middle-aged face wearing a stricken expression. Laura was aware of some scurrying around on the upstairs balconies as residents hurried to spot the source of the commotion.

Out in the middle of the atrium, she saw, some of the furniture had been shoved out of position; four people stood there beside a small pile of luggage. What looked like a large wooden easel and poster of some kind had toppled over, taking a large porcelain lamp off a table as it fell. The lamp—evi-

dently the source of the crash Laura had heard—seemed to be
in about nine hundred pieces.

The only one of the four people Laura recognized was tall,
lanky Still Bill Mills, Timberdale's gardener-maintenance
man-chauffeur and resident philosopher, who stood there in
his tattered old bomber jacket and bib overalls with his lantern
jaw hanging in shock. One of the others was a tall, very young
and very well endowed girl with blond hair halfway down her
bare back; she wore a silver sundress, a mink stole, and five-
inch spike heels. Down on his hands and knees, frantically
fiddling with the collapsed easel and poster, a thirtysomething
flower of a little man without much hair, wearing factory-
faded Levi's and a black sweatshirt, seemed to be accomplish-
ing nothing. The fourth person, towering over all of them in
a grand theatrical pose, had to be J. Turner Redwine himself:
at least six foot four, far over two hundred pounds, with flow-
ing grayish hair that reached the shoulders of his crimson-lined
black cape.

"Lout!" he thundered, pointing the length of his arm at
Still Bill. "Incompetent! Have you never set up a theatrical
poster before? I shall see that you recompense us in full for
this damage!" His voice echoed all over the atrium, and might
have rattled the skylights.

Laura hurried over. Still Bill had started to say something,
but Redwine threw one side of his cape back over his shoulder
and didn't let him continue. "Apologies will garner no for-
giveness! This is inexcusable! Where is Mrs. Epperman? I
demand—" He turned at Laura's arrival and stopped dead.
"Mrs. Epperman? My dear lady, I—"

"I'm Laura Michaels. The assistant manager. I—"

Redwine's head shot back. "Summon Mrs. Epperman at
once. This is not a situation for a mere underling."

Laura kept her voice quiet and calm, which wasn't easy
when his yelling had already set her ears ringing. "Mrs. Epperman is out at the moment, so I'm afraid you'll have to deal
with this mere underling, Mr. Redwine. —It is Mr. Redwine,
isn't it?"

"Of course." He put a hand inside the dark suit coat underneath the cape and whipped something out. "My card."

Laura took it but didn't look at it. "What's going on here?"

Redwine rolled bulging eyes at Still Bill. "Upon our arrival moments ago, this—this *personage* met us at curbside. He was instructed to bring in our luggage and assist my associate, Mr. Vanlandingham, with the installation of the poster announcing our impending dramatic presentation. The fool clumsily tipped over the easel, as you can see, doing damage to our poster and this lamp as well."

The small, prematurely bald man on the floor raised up, face twisted with worry. "It's all right, Reddy. Be calm."

"Quiet, George," Redwine snapped. He turned back to Laura. "Your name, again, is...?"

"Laura Michaels."

"Laura. Does this person work for your establishment?"

"Yes. Bill is—"

"Dismiss him. At once."

Laura turned to Still Bill Mills, who had been standing there with a baffled expression on his long face. "Bill, what happened?"

Redwine thundered, "I have already made the issue clear. I—"

"Be quiet a minute, for heaven's sake," Laura snapped at him.

Redwine's beefy face went blank with shock. "*What* did you say?"

Laura turned again to Still Bill. "Bill?"

Mills removed a toothpick from between his teeth and looked dispassionately at the mess on the floor. "Brang in the stuff. Set up the tripod. Nut missing on the back leg, there. I told him she was shaky, but he said set 'er up, so I did. Then I started to put the poster on, and that back leg went right over, just capsuled, and she pitched over." Mills thoughtfully reinserted the toothpick. "It just proves what they always say. Haste makes the devil's workshop."

"Well, Bill," Laura said, stifling a smile, "I think it was nice of you to try to help."

One of the old man's eyebrows tilted. "Well, I offered even though I knew right off I would be skating on thin water, trying to help dramaturgicals. Ordinary, I don't even help Miz Smith with her canvases any more if I can get out of it. I just don't like to get myself in a sub-serpent conflagration, if you know what I mean."

George, the little man on the floor, tried nervously to set the tripod up again. The back leg instantly collapsed, pitching the wood contraption over.

"Bill," Laura said, "can you fix that thing?"

The toothpick came out again. "Sure. Right nut ought to cost three cents at Ace Hardware in Norman."

"Could you get one and fix it?"

"I probably got one in my toolbox. I always believe in not throwing anything away. A stitch in time saves an hour, right?"

Laura tried to figure that one out for a few seconds, then gave up. "Go ahead and fix it then, Bill, okay?"

"Who pays? I mean, hardware don't grow on a bush."

"Tell Paula to pay you the three cents out of the petty-cash drawer."

"Okey-dokey." Mills turned and shambled toward the desk.

Redwine stared at her with angry, bulging eyes. "You *refuse* to dismiss that incompetent?"

"Mr. Redwine, I seriously doubt that we could keep Timberdale running without that 'incompetent.'"

He straightened majestically and scowled down the length of his nose. "Mrs. Epperman will hear of this, I assure you."

"Well, until she gets back, what do you say we get the rest of your things brought in?"

The old actor scowled. He had a thousand graven lines in his face, and if his hair hadn't been too long, his efforts to present his Barrymore-esque profile too persistent, and his gestures too grandiloquent, Laura thought she might have felt pity for him. In this moment of repose he suddenly looked very tired.

He said heavily, "Very well, then. Allow me to present my associates." He extended a hand toward the blonde who towered over Laura in her spike heels. "My production assistant, Deena Sweete."

Sweete wriggled and gave Laura a flash of large white teeth that could have blinded someone in bright light. "Hi! Gee! This is a cute old-folks' home, it really is. Real neat!"

"And," Redwine went on, "our business manager and also, I might add, the accomplished author who has thoroughly revised a script to make it totally compelling for the audience here at Timberlake: George Vanlandingham."

"Timberdale," Vanlandingham fretted, scrambling up off the floor.

"Eh?"

"Timberdale. Not Timberlake."

Redwine waved airily. "Whatever. Why do you always have to be such a prissy prig, George?"

Vanlandingham fussed, wiping small pale hands on the front of his shirt, then offered one to Laura. "Hello. Please excuse Reddy—it's been a trying day already."

"There is no need to apologize for me, George," Redwine intoned.

"Are the rest of your people still outside?" Laura asked.

"They have been, ah, unexpectedly delayed. However, we anticipate their arrival no later than noon tomorrow, which will provide adequate time for rehearsals in situ and opening of the drama on schedule Friday."

A voice behind Laura squeaked, "I know you!" She turned.

Maude Thuringer, dark floral silk dress aswirl, rushed up and seized Redwine's hand. "J. Turner Redwine, right? The constable in *The Hound of the Baskervilles,* right? The one who caused trouble for Chester Morris in two Boston Blackie movies, right? I saw your company in Branson, Missouri, once. Wow. You've really gotten old since I saw you last."

Redwine stared down the long slope of his nose. "And who is *this?*"

"Thuringer," Maude chirped. "Maude Thuringer. You must remember me. I'm the one who wrote you that long letter after Branson, telling you how to fix the holes in your plot."

"Yes…" Redwine turned to Laura for help. "I believe you mentioned assistance with the remainder of our cargo?"

Maude turned on Deena Sweete. "Just don't think you can get away with it!"

Sweete's eyes shocked wide, dislodging several pounds of mascara. "What?"

Maude stabbed at her with a bony finger. "I know you're the murderer! I know how the Redwine company master script works! I just want you to *know* that I know!" Triumphant, she pulled a small gray notebook out from under the belt at the back of her dress. "You see this, all of you? This is my clue book! I'm putting down every clue in this mystery, starting right now. I intend to be the first one to figure it all out, and I just hope you've made it more complicated than it was the last time I saw you. I figured *that* one out in about six minutes." She wheeled on Redwine. "I know from my vast experience that this child is going to be the murderer, but I won't tell anybody else. I'll play fair. But the minute I dope it out from the clues, I'll let you know about it. I might even be willing to let you have my clue book, so you can improve your script. Of course I'll have to charge for that. Don't worry. We can negotiate."

"Lady," Vanlandingham growled, "are you sure you don't need to check your medications?"

"Sticks and stones," Maude snapped. "Sticks and stones!" She turned and rushed away.

Laura went back outside with the trio. A white, block-long 1982 Cadillac with a California plate that read REDYN completely blocked the front driveway. Fighting the chill wind, she helped them carry in six suitcases, two duffel bags, four attaché cases, a laptop computer and printer, and two battered cardboard cartons seemingly loaded with lead bricks. Vanlan-

dingham consented with bad grace to move the road hog to
the side parking lot. Laura followed Redwine and Sweete back
into the atrium.

By this time, the bustle in and out had attracted a generous
gathering of the Timberdale faithful. They hovered in the conversation areas, watching with intense interest. Laura saw that
Still Bill Mills had the easel on its feet again, and was cranking
at the defective leg with a screwdriver and pliers. Tossing his
cape back over his right shoulder, Redwine strode around the
small mountain of piled-up baggage and stood scowling at
Mills's work. Vanlandingham rushed in the front door,
blowing on his cupped hands and dancing up and down lightly
in his loafers. Redwine strode back to Laura. ''You may accompany us to our quarters now.''

She took them around the loose-knit crowd in the center of
the atrium, past the doors to the dining area, and into the
corridor that led to the back elevator. They rode up to the third
floor in silence, Redwine frowning into space.

Timberdale's east wing was its least popular. In winter the
rooms never seemed to get quite warm enough. Also, the
building design inexplicably put 2E and 3E farther from an
elevator than it did the apartments on the west. One entire
short leg off the main hall was vacant up here at the moment,
and Mrs. Epperman had decreed that members of the acting
company would use these one-bedroom efficiencies.

Redwine didn't like being on the third floor. He also did
not like the size of the efficiency apartments, the wall colors,
the sparseness of the furnishings, the lack of a soft-drink vending machine on the floor, the absence of telephones in some
of the rooms, the temperature, the dustiness, the size of the
closets, the lack of built-in-desks, the failure to provide a fax
machine, the distance to the building copier, and the quality
of the linens. Sleeping on sheets with a thread count of less
than 200, he informed Laura, was tantamount to reclining on
a bed of nails.

Laura made notes, promising to pass everything along to

Mrs. Epperman and wondering if she could possibly get away with calling in sick the rest of the week.

Still Bill Mills hustled up from the first floor, bringing mountains of luggage and paraphernalia on each of three trips. Redwine scowled. Sweete examined her nails, and then went away, announcing she had to potty. Vanlandingham rolled his eyes to the ceiling when Mills put down one of his cosmetic cases rather hard.

"Come, come," Redwine said. "Surely Mrs. Epperman has returned by now. I insist on lodging my complaints with her personally, and at once."

Laura took them back downstairs.

The crowd in the atrium had changed positions. More than two dozen residents had now moved front and center, where they stood staring at the easel. Laura walked that way with her guests, and saw that Still Bill Mills had gotten everything shipshape. The playbill was in place:

J. Turner Redwine presents—
A Mystery Thriller!
MURDER IN RETIREMENT

"Excellent," Redwine pronounced. "The dolt surprises me. Now all it lacks is the montage of photographs of myself in some of my greatest roles."

Laura's last glimmer of hope went out. Too late now to turn back, she thought glumly. The play—darn it—was going to go on.

THREE

FROM MAUDE THURINGER'S MYSTERY JOURNAL
Wed morn—Redwine arr. Big Boob, Blondie named Sweete (!), sweetie named Vanlandingham. Others tmrw. Maybe clue in busted tripod for poster? Can't be too careful, he's sneaky. Maybe clue in lunch—tapioca??? Yuk.

JUDITH EPPERMAN BLEW in with a few autumn leaves immediately after lunch hour, a tactic she often used to avoid the Timberdale food. Spying Laura standing in the middle of the atrium with J. Turner Redwine, his two assistants, and several residents, she screeched a happy greeting and chugged right over, hands extended.

Redwine's scowl put a stop to the hilarity at once. "Madam, would that you had been here upon our arrival, as your correspondence and telephonic communications clearly implied."

Mrs. Epperman handed Laura the results of her shopping, a plastic bag from B. Dalton containing the latest bestseller by an actress who had been Dante's Beatrice in one of her earlier lives. "Is there a problem?"

"There have been nothing but problems! First that dolt you call a general handyman virtually destroyed our easel; then this young woman here ensconced us in rooms that are totally inadequate. I have just spoken with your so-called chef concerning food service to our accommodations, and he has been highly insulting."

Mrs. Epperman, who sometimes resembled Babe Ruth when puzzled, now looked ready to hit one out of the park. "Insulting? How, insulting?"

"He informed me in the bluntest and most disrespectful terms that no service to the rooms is available."

Old Judge Emil Young, leaning ponderously on his cane among the bystanders, seemed to rouse himself. "If I may offer a modest word, sir, supplementary victuals may be procured in the canteen and coffee cubicle, located—"

"I'm not talking about candy bars, you old fool!"

The judge flinched visibly. Sada Hoff, standing next to him, straightened up, fiery-eyed, to her full height of slightly over five feet. "That's a bit uncalled for, Mr. Redmond."

Redwine's face flushed. He leaned close to Mrs. Epperman. "Can we discuss this matter with some semblance of privacy and decorum? You *do* have an office, don't you, madam?" He jerked a finger in Laura's direction. "Even this little twit seemed to have a cubicle of some kind."

A small brilliance flashed. Laura turned and saw Maude Thuringer excitedly fussing with an automatic camera. She had a cassette recorder slung over her shoulder, and a notebook on a clipboard stuck precariously under her arm.

"No photos without prior permission," Redwine told her.

Maude made a face at him. "I'm collecting clues."

"There are no clues yet, you silly woman. The presentation doesn't start until Friday at noon—the day after tomorrow."

Maude crouched, looking crafty. "Oh, sure, that's what *you* say."

"Come, come," Mrs. Epperman fussed. "Let's continue this in my office."

Redwine straightened with massive dignity and turned to follow her. George Vanlandingham, his close-set eyes black with bitterness, followed. Deena Sweete started past onlooker Ken Keen, who had been watching her with eyes like airplane landing lights. Laura saw Keen move fractionally as Sweete's opulent backside swished past him. Sweete stifled a yelp of shock and jerked forward before whirling on him.

"You old fart!" she gasped.

Keen's eyebrows did a Groucho imitation. "Admit it, you loved it."

Mrs. Epperman glared at Laura. "Are you coming, dear?"

Laura hung back. "The Breakfast Club meeting was post-poned this morning. We're supposed to start right away in the activity room—that's why some of these residents are waiting here."

The Epperman breasts rose and fell again with saintly patience. "Laura," she explained grimly to Redwine and his crew, "is a graduate student in social work down at Norman. She meets with some of our dear people individually and in groups, doing her little therapy things. Go ahead, dear. Have your little meeting. I'm sure no one would want to postpone your practice for something as unimportant as Timberdale business."

LAURA LED her charges into the larger of the two activity rooms off the atrium. A dozen straight chairs had been arranged in a rough semicircle in the center of the barren, par-quet-tiled area. Sliding glass doors with pale-green drapes shot fully open looked out onto an interior courtyard with brick decking and small flower beds choked with dead petunias, dying chrysanthemums, and a half-dozen wind-whipped azalea bushes. A dusty baby grand piano occupied one corner, and at the far end of the room some year-old magazines were piled high on a never-used yellow Formica coffee-and-snack counter. Her regulars began to seat themselves, fussing with the metal chairs and making scraping sounds on the tiles.

They had dubbed themselves the Breakfast Club more than a year ago, when Laura first succeeded in getting more than three of them together each Wednesday morning to talk about whatever might be bothering them. She had nervously hoped for a kind of therapeutic group interaction because (a) she already knew that aging was not easy anywhere, and especially in a place like Timberdale that could be lonely, and (b) she needed the practical work for a graduate project credit. Since that opening session—devoted exclusively to complaints about the food and other residents' rudeness—membership had ebbed and flowed. Right now she had seven regulars.

She sat down in front of the half-ring of unreadable expressions, crossed her legs, and opened her notebook on her thigh. A latecomer appeared in the back doorway. "Hi, Colonel. Come on in. Will you please close the door behind you? Thanks."

Colonel Rodgers strode up to join the group. Tall, ramrod-straight, his gray hair cropped in a military burr, he wore tight maroon double-knit slacks and an equally form-fitting black T-shirt. Muscles bulged in his shoulders and bare arms, showing the effects of his constant workouts, which he seldom let anyone forget. He glared and sat down on the end of the row.

"Now," Laura said, smiling encouragement. "Who would like to start today?"

Ken Keen leered. "I wouldn't mind starting with you, babe. You look extra hot today."

Beside him, Ellen Smith twitched a cacophony of silver jewelry. "That's disgusting!"

Keen looked sincerely befuddled. "What is?"

Maude Thuringer fluttered a tiny hand. Laura looked vainly for someone else to call on, then gave in. "Yes, Maude?"

Maude's eyes sparkled, as she held up her clipboard. "I think I'm on to whodunit."

"You're talking about the mystery weekend play, Maude?"

"Sure Mike!"

"It isn't going to be done until sometime Friday, Maude. So I don't think—"

"Yes, but maybe we've already been given the clues! That's what would make it clever instead of the same old thing, don't you see? I mean, everyone is asleep at the switch, and the play has already started *even though the cast won't be here until tomorrow*. Wouldn't that be neat?"

"Yes, it certainly would, Maude. Does anyone else—"

"See, Redwine is mad about the rooms. Sweete is mad at him about something—I don't know what, but I heard them yelling at each other in her room when I was eavesdropping a while ago—and Vanlandingham, well, I figure he's not very happy, either. So when Ken, here, patted Sweete's fanny, it was a clue to make Redwine jealous—it's obvious she must be Redwine's girlfriend, I mean, he calls her a production assistant, but the only thing *she's* smart enough to produce is a hot flash—so I figure she and Vanlandingham are going to kill Redwine. He always has to star as either the victim or the detective.'' She paused, eyelids fluttering sixty miles an hour. ''So it was a big clue when Ken patted her a while ago.''

Ken Keen blinked. ''I did what?''

THERE WERE TIMES when the group meetings went well—which is to say, genuine pain suddenly came into the open from someone, and some of the others shared similar feelings or offered suggestions that proved a real caring. Like true group therapy, however, the Breakfast Club could never be wholly controlled, nor could results—or the lack of same—be predicted. When Laura closed this session an hour after it had begun, she noted the glumness on some regulars' faces. It hadn't been a productive hour.

Colonel Roger Rodgers stayed behind as Laura cleaned up her notes and others drifted out.

''Something else, Colonel?''

''Miscalculation,'' he snapped. ''Tactical error of the first water.''

''Sir?'' There was something about him that made people say ''sir.''

''I didn't realise who this crook was until I got a glimpse of him leaving the lobby a while ago. Do you know what a criminal he is?''

''You mean Redwine?''

Rodgers's jaw worked with anger. ''I had forgotten his name when you first announced this stupid mystery thing. Of course it was almost ten years ago when his criminality cost me twenty-five thousand dollars.''

''It did *what?*''

The old military man's jaw jutted, but his eyes looked suspiciously as if they might have extra moisture in them. ''The prospectus said the company planned to produce television shows featuring senior citizens. Offered stock in the firm. It said six shows had already been produced. I invested twelve thousand five hundred. Then, after a personal letter from this...this *man*,, I bought another twelve thousand five hundred.''

Rodgers straightened, jaw jutting harder as he avoided her eyes. ''Months passed. No reports. Investigation followed. Had to hire a lawyer just to learn what happened. No shows ever produced. No scripts. Nothing. Company took bankruptcy. Returned nothing. Fraud. Right from the start.''

''Colonel,'' Laura breathed, ''I had no idea. You're sure it was this same Redwine?''

''I'll never forget that damned Shakespearean profile. How did I fail to recognize the name? Maybe like combat fatigue. Wipe things out of your mind. *Want* to forget.''

''Colonel, if he cheated you, we might still call—''

''No.'' Rodgers's lip quirked with bitterness. ''Pursued all that. No charges could be filed. Legitimate business failure, they ruled out there in California.'' His eyes finally came to Laura's face, cold as wintry mountain rock. ''But I know it was a scam. I won't forget again. And by God, that man had better hope he doesn't get left in a dark hallway with me while he's staying here. For two cents, I'd—I'd—'' He stopped, swallowed, and turned abruptly away. The heels of his spit-shined loafers clicked on the tile.

''I JUST THOUGHT you should know,'' Laura said.

Mrs. Epperman waved a hand over the small crystal ball she had been consulting at her desk when Laura interrupted. ''Why am I not surprised? Each of us has problems in our lives, my dear girl. I'm sorry Colonel Rodgers lost money on a Redwine enterprise years ago. But I have plenty of problems of my own with the dreadful man.''

''I thought you admired him,'' Laura said.

Mrs. Epperman's reading glasses hit the end of their thin gold chain and plopped to rest on her bosom. ''Admire him? Did I ever say anything of the kind?''

Laura sat down. "What's happened?"

"What's happened—and this is strictly between us, dear girl—what's happened is that the beastly villain just almost doubled his bill for this performance."

"He can't do that. You signed a contract with him for the show. I saw it."

"Of course it isn't quite double," Mrs. Epperman fumed. "From seven thousand five hundred to thirteen thousand isn't double, actually."

"But he can't do that," Laura repeated.

Her boss spoke through stiff lips. "The contract—which, I was assured, was a standard artistic agreement—allows the acting company to make 'cost adjustments,' in the agreed-on fee. Perfectly legal. Nothing we can do about it, if we want to have the show."

"I'd cancel the show."

"And forfeit the seven thousand five hundred we've already paid?"

"We paid in advance? Why did we do *that?*"

"I was assured it was standard."

"How in the world did he try to justify almost doubling the fee?"

"Added expenses."

"Like—?"

Mrs. Epperman tossed a long typed sheet across the desk.

Laura glanced over some of the items. "He should have planned most of these alleged expenses. I'd call our lawyers, Mrs. Epperman."

"Who do you think I've just been on the phone with? That dreadful man has us by the yin-yang. He's a beast. I wish he was dead. Instead, I had to write him a check for the remainder of the fee, payable up front, or he threatened to walk out and give us no performance whatsoever."

"That's blackmail."

Mrs. Epperman's lip curled. "No, dear. Apparently that's show biz. I wish I had never let you talk me into this horrible mystery weekend idea in the first place."

"It wasn't my idea!"

"Then you should have talked me out of it, you dreadful girl."

The telephone on Mrs. Epperman's desk began blinking. She picked it up, magically filling her voice with sugar. "Judith Epperman, how may I be of service?" She listened. "Right. I'll tell her. "Thank you, Paula." She hung up and glowered at Laura again. "The horrid man is at the reception desk. Asking for you."

J. TURNER REDWINE had at some point changed clothes, and now wore a khaki safari outfit, complete with a soaring, wide-brimmed cloth hat. He had either patted on after-shave or had a drink: His cheeks glowed pink.

"The larger activity room," he said, snapping his fingers at Laura. "I will inspect it as a possible drama site. I believe you have the key?"

Laura was thinking how long it had been since anybody around here had had a raise. With simmering anger, she took the large key ring out of the desk drawer beside Paula Burwell's chair and led Redwine across the atrium, which now stood silent and vacant during afternoon nap time.

She unlocked the shuttered glass double doors and swung them wide for Redwine, who swashbuckled in before she could find the light switch on the wall just inside. As the fluorescents buzzed to life, Redwine strode to the center of the large area and turned twice around, taking in everything.

The big activity room had not been used since the pre-Christmas gala. Roughly twenty-five by forty-five feet, it had a small conversation area—a couch and two chairs—at one far corner. Otherwise it was empty at the moment; Still Bill Mills and his crew had removed all other furnishings in order to shampoo the expanse of lime-green indoor-outdoor carpet. The draperies at the side windows were closed, as was the solid wood door at the back of the room, which led to the seldom-used rear service corridor.

"Perfect!" Redwine proclaimed, turning around twice more. "I assume that back door can be opened?"

"Yes, but—"

"Then this will be the place for the emergency-room scene. I must find George at once. He and Deena must see this. It is ideal. At last something has gone right in this awful place."

"I'm so glad for you," Laura murmured, starting to move out of his way.

Redwine's sudden burst of enthusiasm seemed, however, to carry over into everything. Laura's first warning was his sudden pause in flight, followed by a loud gasp of either thespian passion or stomach gas. He stared at her, eyes bulging with interest she didn't like at all.

Then, before she could move to defend herself, he had taken one giant stride and snaked a thick arm around her middle, jerking her close. His hot breath poured over her. "And perhaps, my little beauty, other parts of my visit can be made equally enjoyable, eh?"

Laura started to wonder if it was Charles Laughton he was doing, or maybe Charlton Heston, but then she didn't have time to wonder anymore because he bent down, trying to kiss her. My God, he was *strong!* Panicked, she twisted her face away from him.

"It's all right," he mumbled, getting one thick, powerful arm around her neck, starting to hurt her. "No one can—"

She hammered her high heel down on his instep.

He grunted with pain and staggered backward, hopping ponderously on one foot. For an instant he had a really frightening, crazy light in his eyes. "Bitch. You'll regret that." It was not his usual voice.

Laura wanted out of there. She started for the door.

"Oh, I say!" he called out behind her, his normal voice suddenly returning. "Just a friendly gesture! No harm intended!"

Baffled and a little shaken, she hurried on through the doorway. A brilliant flash half-blinded her. Through the dazzled sparks in her vision she made out Maude Thuringer standing there with her camera in hand.

"Hey!" the old woman chirped. "That was exciting!"

FOUR

WHEN AARON LASSITER called her after ten o'clock that night and said he had one hour off for a coffee break, Laura felt it was the first good thing that had happened all day. She asked how fast he could get to her apartment, and he said about as fast as her coffeepot could heat.

Actually, he beat the coffee. They sat at the kitchen table, waiting for the maker to finish its cycle, and she told him about her day.

"The guy actually tried to put the moves on you?" Lassiter demanded, anger pulling his eyebrows close.

"Oh, it was a fun day from beginning to end." She got up and went to get the coffee.

Behind her, Lassiter muttered almost to himself, "That's damned strange!"

Laura turned. "That somebody might make a pass at me? Thanks!"

Startled, he shook his head. "I was thinking about something else."

"What?"

"Never mind." He seemed to shake himself mentally. "Maybe I ought to just go over there and beat him up a little."

"No." She poured.

"No?"

"No." She returned the pot to the maker and returned to the table and sat opposite him. "Beat him up *a lot.*"

He grinned at her. He had the nicest grin in the world, she thought. Tall and athletic—his conditioning was evidence of the minor-league baseball career he had had after college—dark-haired and dark-eyed, he would have made any television commercial look better. She loved his crooked, self-

deprecating smile. She loved the wrinkled-brow look of concern he got sometimes when she spoke of problems at Timberdale or of raising a bright-eyed eleven-year-old daughter
alone.

There was an awful lot she loved about him, actually.
Maybe it was really going to go somewhere, like to the altar,
if she could just stop having something that resembled post-
traumatic stress disorder from her divorce...and if he ever got
up the courage to broach the subject.

"What did your boss say when you told her about it?" he
asked now.

"I didn't mention it to her."

"What? Was that wise?"

"Maybe I overreacted, Aaron. Oh, he scared me for a second, but he's an actor, after all. Maybe all actors are kind
of...nutty. He probably didn't mean anything by it, just sort
of got reality and fantasy mixed up for a second."

"Well, I still think you should have told someone."

Laura smiled. "Since Maude Thuringer apparently saw the
whole thing, I'm sure by now most of the residents have heard
all about it, in three-D and Panavision."

His scowl deepened. "I'm going to have to talk to him."

"No, Aaron."

"No?" His forehead furrowed.

"Not yet, anyway. I think he probably learned his lesson. I
bet that will be the end of it. Let's just not make any waves—
try to get through this damned silly weekend deal as smoothly
as possible."

He thought about it, that endearing John Wayne frown per-
sisting. "If he gives you any more trouble—"

"You'll be the first to know."

"Good. Also—" He stopped abruptly.

"Also?"

"Nothing."

"You started to say something more. What is it? Are you
holding back on me?"

"No. Forget it."

They sipped coffee in silence. Somewhere a mile or two away, a train sounded its horn for a crossing, a lonely call in the night.

"I wish," Lassiter said after a while, "I didn't have to go right back to work tonight."

"I do too," she said with feeling.

His dark eyes studied her. "Trissie went right to sleep, sounds like."

"Yes. I looked in on her. They had a spelling contest at school today. She hung in there almost to the final round. It kind of wore her out."

He scowled down at his coffee cup, turning his spoon in it. "I hate to leave you when you're even a little shook up."

"I'm fine. Really. It was no big deal."

"Sure. But if I didn't have to get back on duty, we could watch some TV, maybe."

"Yes." They had spent many evenings doing that. Both of them knew every episode of "M*A*S*H" backward and forward, but they still watched them anyway.

Head down, he kept fooling with the spoon. "Maybe," he muttered, staying at the topic like a bulldog, "have some hot chocolate."

She saw where he was headed now, and hid her smile. "I suppose."

His eyes swept up suddenly to hers. "Maybe mess around."

She fought to show nothing, to tease. "Maybe."

He looked down and heaved a sigh. "Damn."

She poured more coffee. What a lovely, lovely man.

"If Redwine gives you any more grief, you *will* let me know?"

"Yep. You can count on that."

"Good. I'll be on another eighteen-hour day tomorrow, I reckon, but I'll be out in the car a lot. I might drop by."

"I'll be fine, Aaron. Really."

"Well, I might have other business. Or it might wait till Friday afternoon when I'm officially off. I guess I'll be out there a lot both Friday and Saturday."

"Great. Why?"

"Had a call this afternoon from a guy named Vanlandingham. One of the company?"

"He's the writer."

Lassiter nodded. "They want somebody to play a law officer after they stage the murder. In uniform. I told them I'd do it."

"Wow."

"Why 'wow'?"

"It doesn't sound like the kind of thing you'd agree to do."

His left eyebrow tilted. "They're paying me a hundred bucks."

Laura almost blurted it out, but stopped herself in time. When she had glanced at the revised expense sheet in Mrs. Epperman's office earlier, one of the items that had leaped out at her was "Local law officer—$500." She wondered if all the expenses were equally exaggerated.

Lassiter stayed only another twenty minutes or so. She told him her impressions of Deena Sweete and George Vanlandingham, and about Colonel Rodgers's bitter experience with Redwine. When she got to the part about Redwine jacking up the charges for the weekend show—but not mentioning his— Lassiter shook his head in dismay.

"Mrs. Epperman picked herself a loser, Laura."

Laura sighed. "I guess we'll just have to see how it turns out."

He stood, hitching up his gun belt and reaching for his broad-brimmed deputy sheriff's hat. He seemed to be pondering something. "Well, maybe I ought to go ahead and tell you."

She looked up sharply. "Tell me what?"

"Your guy Redwine?"

"Yes?"

"We got a missing persons report yesterday out of Dallas. Seems like he filed it. Seems like his wife is supposed to be missing."

"*Redwine's wife?* My gosh, he didn't even mention it!"

Lassiter shrugged wearily. "Might be just a domestic problem. But it strikes me a little funny, he files a missing-persons
report and then shows up here as if nothing had happened—
and puts the moves on the first pretty woman he sees."

Laura thought about it as her surprise sank in. "Aaron, I'm
not sure I like the way this makes me feel."

An eyebrow cocked. "That's why I almost didn't tell you.
But you've already given me enough codependency lectures,
thank you, so I mentioned it after all."

"Well, I'm glad you did."

"Just watch your step around him. And if anything weird
happens, let me know pronto."

She took a deep breath. "I will. Right now, I just want the
whole mess over with. The cast arrives tomorrow, we've got
TV people coming in to shoot some stuff about them, and then
comes the play, starting around noon on Friday. There's stuff
going on all day Saturday, and the final payoff is at Sunday
breakfast. Then I just want them *out* of there, and things back
to normal."

Lassiter hugged her at the door. "It'll be over before you
know it."

"Don't I wish!"

But after he had gone, she found herself oddly edgy and
disturbed by what he had said. She tried to attribute her vague
feelings to nerves in the wake of tonight's midterm, which had
been a bear. She hoped it was only that. She could not be at
all sure. J. Turner Redwine had managed to antagonize almost
everyone he had come in contact with today. He had a history
full of what sounded like fraud. His crude, sudden pass at her
had been too ridiculous to be more than momentarily frightening, but it showed the kind of vulgar directness he was capable of. Maude had said she'd overheard him and Deena
Sweete shouting at each other earlier. Was there serious trouble between them? Had he lunged at Laura in some kind of
reaction to that? Now the missing wife; what did *that* mean?

Feeling a chill, she rubbed her upper arms and found them
covered with goose bumps. She decided she was getting as

silly as Maude. But the gut-level feeling—a vague sense of unfocused dread—would not go away.

At Timberdale Retirement Center, the vast atrium lay silent and deserted, the only dim light coming from the desk lamp in the reception area. At the desk, night clerk Stacy Miller munched on a chunk of Domino's sausage-and-onion pizza while turning the pages of a sociology textbook some previous student had thoughtfully highlighted for her. Everyone had gone to bed long ago, or so it seemed.

In the back hallway of One East, however, Maude Thuringer was wide awake.

Crouched behind a huge plastic ficus plant, Maude had been in hiding for almost an hour, and her bent knees were killing her. But she was collecting some really good stuff. She was glad J. Turner Redwine had had such a hissy fit about his third-floor accommodations that Mrs. Epperman had caved in and moved him and his aides to the larger vacant apartments strung along the east section of the first floor; it made surveillance less physically taxing, and management had placed much more plastic greenery down here, which meant better places for Maude to hide.

All of which was wonderful, assuming she would be able to get her throbbing joints to straighten out when she finally decided to get out of here.

Right now, however, she had no intention of going anywhere, pain or not.

Her potted plant gave her an excellent view down the hall from the little alcove. She had found it intensely interesting earlier, when this vantage point allowed her to see George Vanlandingham furtively depart from his own room, sneak down the hall to the room Deena Sweete had been assigned, rap furtively on her door, and hurry inside when she opened it for him. Vanlandingham had been wearing only a frayed flannel bathrobe and the kind of floppy slippers once called Romeos.

At that point Maude had instantly started imagining nifty

sexual perversions. Only two minutes later, however, the Sweete door opened again and Vanlandingham hurried right back out, slippers scuffing on the hallway carpet as he returned to his own room.

Almost at once Sweete had opened her door yet again, coming into the hall in a floor-length black peignoir and spike-heeled mules with fuzzy black stuff on the toes. Maude itched to get a picture of *that,* because the gown was essentially transparent and would make a great exhibit when she showed how she had solved the crime. But she resisted, because a flash would have betrayed her position.

She watched as Sweete went to the nearest door in the hallway, the one to Redwine's apartment. Sweete tapped softly, persistently. The frown on her face did not suggest nifty perversions in the offing.

The door opened. Redwine, a pipe in one hand and a brandy snifter in the other, appeared in a royal-blue velvet smoking jacket over dark trousers. He did not look happy. Sweete spoke softly but urgently. Maude discovered that her corner hiding place was a natural hearing booster. By straining, she could make out every word.

"Reddy," Sweete said in a near whisper, "I want your *promise.*"

"We've already discussed it, Deena. Go to bed. You'll be paid when I receive the check. All will be well, I assure you."

"Dammit, you've 'assured' us before! This time you're going to pay us everything you owe us, or else."

"Or else what, Deena? Don't make a bigger fool of yourself. Good night." Redwine started to step back and close the door.

A talon-hand leaped out and grasped the shiny lapel of his jacket. "You're *not* going to put us off again!"

"Unhand me, you little bitch!"

Sweete started to swing at him. "I'll—"

"No!" Redwine caught her hand in midair, twisting her arm backward so that she made a sharp moaning sound.

"Let me go," she sobbed.

He released her wrist, but in the same movement slipped one arm around her waist, jerking her close against him. She was a big girl, but she seemed powerless in his grasp. The next words were lower, but Maude managed to catch them:

"You know how much I care about you, Deena."

"Do you? Do you really? Oh—you haven't acted like it lately.... I don't know what to think anymore—"

"We'll all be paid after this performance. How could I deceive you, of all people on earth, about that?"

She seemed to wilt, melting against him. "Oh, Reddy..."

He stepped backward with curious grace, almost like a dancer, and drew her with him inside the doorway. The door closed. Everything fell silent.

Oh boy, oh boy, oh boy. Knees screeching, Maude stayed in place and scribbled in her notebook.

At this point, the far door—Vanlandingham's—opened again. Dressed as before, but now carrying a liquor bottle, the rail-thin little man tiptoed down the hall again and reached Sweete's door as before. Leaning close, he tapped softly, waited, and tapped again.

Too bad, little boy, Maude thought.

Vanlandingham tapped yet again. The blank look of puzzlement on his face began to change to one of anger. He waited, whiskey in hand. Nothing happened. He turned from the door to stare down the hall—seemed to look directly at Maude behind the plastic plant—then riveted his attention on the nearest door. Redwine's door.

The look that crossed his face then was one that made Maude again yearn for a photo. Such a combination of surprise, disappointment, pain, and bitterness. Such intensity, visible for the briefest few seconds.

Then he turned and hurried back up the hall to his own room, closing the door silently behind him.

Thoroughly delighted, Maude stayed in place for another thirty minutes or more. Nothing else happened. She began to get chilled. Her knees sent up additional distress messages. Finally giving up, she clambered to her feet in a crescendo of darting aches and pains, and limped softly away in the direction of her own apartment. Oh, this was great! she thought. This was wonderful. It was all just like in *Epitaph for a Spy*, where Ambler had everyone lying to everyone else, but good old Roux saw through the whole bloody mess. Or *Murder in the Wind*, where John D. MacDonald had used a character named Flagan, if she remembered correctly. An awful man just like J. Turner Redwine, no class at all.

Mind riffling the murder-mystery file cards that filled her brain, Maude went around the corner of the hall, nearing her own unit.

Maude seldom missed anything. But she did not see the far door open in the hallway behind her, nor did she see George Vanlandingham take a half-step out into the hall to peer after her, his face a wreckage of anger.

FIVE

"I SUPPOSE YOU HEARD," Ellen Smith said excitedly, Indian jewelry clattering.

"Heard what?" Laura said. It was mid-morning Thursday.

"Maude Thuringer is in the clinic."

"What for?"

"How should I know? I'm an artist, not a doctor."

Laura went to the office area. Mrs. Epperman had gone to an emergency meeting with the auditor, probably about the extra payment to Redwine. Laura found gorgeous Francie Blake, Timberdale's alleged social director, perched on Laura's desk, mile-long legs crossed, applying eight centimeters of fresh lipstick to a mouth that had already maddened far too many strong men and destroyed far too many weaker ones.

"Laura! Hi!" Francie uncoiled those legs and batted incredible eyelashes. "I *hate* to bother you, hon, but have you got Poison or Opium or anything like that around here? Dirk just called to say he wants to stop by for coffee with me, and I really need a touch-up. He's *such* a dear. I think he's going to ask me to go to Mexico City with him next week. I know you're more the White Shoulders type, but if—"

"Francie," Laura cut in, "listen for the phone and keep an eye out front for a few minutes, okay? Maude seems to be sick or something—I hear she's in the clinic and this isn't regular checkup time—and I want to run down and look in on her."

"Do you have any nice perfume, like I said?"

"I'm afraid not, Francie. All I have is a little Charlie in my purse."

Francie—tall, model-slender, stunningly blond, with electric-blue eyes and a complexion out of heaven—giggled and wriggled. "That's so cute! 'A little Charlie in my purse'! It sounds like a commercial, doesn't it!"

"I'll be back as soon as I can."

Hurrying, Laura was mildly winded when she reached the door of the clinic in One West. Lights shone inside the glass enclosure. She tested the door, found it unlocked, and hurried in. The tiny front waiting room stood vacant. She saw more lights in the back hallway, and heard familiar voices. She went back.

"Ouch!" a shaky female voice cried out. "Ow! You're killing me!"

Laura turned into the first examining room door on the right, the source of the complaining. She found three people in the small enclosure: Maude Thuringer, perched on the edge of the examining table with her skirt hiked halfway up skinny legs purple with multiple varicose veins; LPN Kay Svendsen, grimly starchy white and hanging on to both Maude's hands for dear life; and Dr. Fred Which, Timberdale's regular consulting physician, bending over one of Maude's knees with a vicious-looking hypodermic needle in his hand. "Hi, Laura," Kay Svendsen said with a quick, nervous smile.

Dr. Fred Which raised his lean face for a moment. "Good morning. Have you come to see the fun?" He held the needle poised as he spoke, and a droplet of silvery-clear liquid dropped from the wicked tip.

"Laura!" Maude Thuringer groaned. "They're doing me in!"

Which stood straight. "We can stop right now—not put the cortisone in. But the painkiller will wear off in an hour or two and you'll be right back here, saying you can't stand it."

"What's going on?" Laura asked. "Is it serious?"

"Maude," Which replied, "seems to have spent too much time praying last night, or something." He bent down with the needle again. "Both these cute little knees have just about as nasty a case of joint inflammation as I've seen in a long, long time." He plunged the needle into an indentation in Maude's right knee, making her jump and Laura flinch in sympathy.

"Oh, God," Maude groaned, "I'm dying."

"I'm relieved," Laura admitted, turning away so she didn't have to see any more. "I thought it might be bad."

"If it was any worse I'd be at the Mayo Clinic," the old woman moaned, tears bright in her eyes. Which slightly moved the hand applying the long needle to her joint, and she stiffened spasmodically. "Ow! Ow!"

"Ah, good," Which soothed. "We've located the primary inflammation site."

The telephone started ringing in the outer office. Kay Svendsen, dutifully struggling against Maude's wriggles, threw Laura a despairing glance.

"I'll get it," Laura said, and hurried out front, glad to escape the scene. She picked up the extension phone. "Clinic."

"Laura!" It was Francie Blake, and she sounded hysterical. "There's a big van parked out front, and these *weirdos* in the atrium! What do I do?"

"I'll be right there, Francie." Laura hung up and ducked back into the examining room. "Gotta run. Glad it's nothing worse, Maude."

"He's killing me," Maude wept. "I feel like poor Brad Smith in *Breakfast at Wimbledon*. Do you remember how Jack Bickham had the poor man's knee give way on him in the big match, and then the doctor shot him full of that painkiller stuff that burned like fire?—Ow!"

Laura fled thankfully.

The scene that greeted her in the atrium was not totally unexpected. As Francie had reported, a large Dodge van seemed to be blocking the front driveway. On its side was emblazoned the blue lettering *Redwine Players*. A handsome young man with blond hair was unloading piles of suitcases and steamer trunks out of the side doors. At the reception desk, Francie Blake stood batting her eyelashes nervously at a tall, middle-aged man wearing tight, factory-faded Levi's, a white sport coat, and an Australian-style safari hat with a floppy brim; a striking young brunette in shorts cut off at the crotch and a leather jacket that appeared to have made it through fifty missions over Germany; and an older woman with white-blond hair whose Native American suedes and jewelry were sure to send Ellen Smith off on a jealous run to her latest Smithsonian catalogue.

Laura went over.

"Oh, Laura!" Francie cried with relief. "Here you are at last! These are some of the other actors! I thought"—she went a pretty pink with embarrassment—"I don't know *what* I thought!"

The middle-aged man turned, head going back, to stare at Laura. Wavy gray tresses flowed out from under his floppy hat, and two long gold earrings bobbled in his left earlobe. An eighteen-inch cigarette holder jutted out of his teeth. He slightly resembled pictures Laura had seen of the old movie actor Errol Flynn.

"Madam?" he intoned.

"Hi. I'm Laura Michaels, assistant to the manager."

He extended a hand missing most of the middle finger. "Franklin Pierce Lord. You will pardon my hand—an old war injury. May I introduce my associates, Janis Mahafey, on the right, and the lady you undoubtedly already recognize, the famed Freddie Filmont, former star of one of the longest-running soap operas in television history, 'Tomorrow Is Another Day'."

Laura glanced at Mahafey, whose vivid green eyes and wide mouth made her even more striking close up. Before they could speak to one another, Filmont reached out and grabbed Laura's wrist in a death grip. "You mush tell ush at once. Hash the dear woman been located?"

Better to play dumb. "'Dear woman'?"

Filmont's eyelids slammed up and down like semaphore signal lights. "Rebecca! Surely you know—"

Lord murmured, "This is unnecessary, Freddie. You're drunk."

Filmont's inch-long fingernails, painted silver, dug into

Laura's wrist. "Rebecca! Mrs. Redwine! Surely you've been informed—"

"We haven't heard any news of her," Laura said.

Filmont's talons relaxed. Tears gushed. "It's sho terrible! Rebecca ish so dear to all of us!" She dove into a large shoulder purse, revealing a small silver flask and a pack of Chesterfields, among other things. "Which way to the restroom? I must collect myself. I am devastated!"

Francie Blake nervously headed off to show her the way. Lord peered around the spaciousness of the atrium and pronounced it good for their purposes. Janis Mahafey asked where Reddy was. The fourth member of the troupe staggered in with two armloads of baggage. Tall, golden-blond, bronzed as Tarzan and with a body to match, he introduced himself as Tad Raddell, whom Laura surely recognized—he gravely told her—from his roles in *Surfer Boy* and *Texas Bloodbath Bonanza.* Laura said she had somehow missed both of them. He told her they would be available soon on videotape.

Mrs. Epperman chose the moment to arrive. She seemed impressed by Lord, especially, and volunteered to show them to their rooms on Three East. Francie came back with Freddie Filmont, whose eyes appeared brighter. Francie whispered to Laura that Filmont had had a belt from her flask in the powder room. Laura caught a glimpse of Maude Thuringer spooking around behind a king-sized dieffenbachia as they all loaded into the back elevator.

When they reached the third floor, Mrs. Epperman led the way down the hall. "I know you'll enjoy the rooms. They're representative of our smallest efficiencies. Residents normally provide their own furnishings, of course, but we've taken furniture out of storage to make them comfy for you."

She unlocked the door to the room to be shared by the two women.

Janis Mahafey stepped inside, pretty legs twinkling.

Janis Mahafey went ballistic.

"You call this an *apartment?*" she demanded shrilly. "You expect two of us to share this—this *cell?*"

Mrs. Epperman's round face turned putty-colored with shock. "It's really a very nice standard efficiency. The sofa opens into another bed, you see—"

Mahafey stamped her foot. "Did Reddy say you could screw us around like this? I bet he did, the—"

"Now, now, Janis," Lord put in, patting her shoulder. "I'm sure a bit of room-sharing for a night or two won't hurt anyone."

"That's easy enough for you to say, you old queen. You've been wanting to move in with Tad since the first time you laid eyes on him."

A stentorian voice came from the hallway behind them all: "Do I sense some difficulty in the ranks?" J. Turner Redwine, wearing black trousers, black sweater, and Birkenstocks, swept into the apartment, which had begun to feel claustrophobic.

Mahafey grabbed at his arm. "Reddy—"

"I heard, I heard, my dear. Surely you don't mind sharing rooms for two nights."

Mahafey's emerald eyes sparked. "Is *your* room up here on this back hallway?"

"Actually, to facilitate production of the drama, George and Deena and I are housed on the first floor. But—"

"I won't share a damned cell with Freddie or anyone else."

Redwine sighed heavily and turned to Mrs. Epperman. "For the sake of maintaining peace and equilibrium in my happy little company, can you open additional rooms, madam?"

"I suppose so," Mrs. Epperman said glumly.

"Done, then." Redwine turned to the others. "Mr. Raddell will have his own room, and so will Janis, Freddie, and Franklin. They will be adjacent here on this third-floor hallway? Excellent. Is that satisfactory, everyone?"

The actors looked unhappy, but no one spoke.

"Good. I have asked George to join us here at once. He has been hard at work, as usual, preparing a special script to incorporate these surroundings as a vital part of the drama we will present. All of you should be receiving—"

He was interrupted by George Vanlandingham's hurried entry. The thin, harried little man had a small armload of stapled copies which included a good number of dark-green insert pages just run off on the first-floor photocopier. Without a word, he thrust one sheaf at Redwine and began passing the other sets to the other members of the company.

Redwine flipped the pages. "My speaking part will have to be expanded, George."

Vanlandingham's tired, bloodshot eyes narrowed with resentment, but he said nothing.

Mrs. Epperman edged nervously toward the apartment door. "We'll arrange to open the other units right away."

Scowling at the printed pages again, Redwine didn't answer.

Laura and Francie escaped on Mrs. Epperman's heels. As they started down the hall from the room, Janis Mahafey's shrill voice followed them:

"This isn't a new script, Van! When are you going to stop retreading the same old shit?"

In the elevator, Francie dabbed at her eyes with a darling little lavender handkerchief. "I hate conflict like that."

"Now, now, little girl," Mrs. Epperman said soothingly. "It'll be all right."

Dab, dab. "But I'm already so busy, planning the Sunday bridge circle and next week's piano recital by Mrs. Miller, and—"

"That's all right. Laura will take care of getting the rooms changed around and everything else. Won't you, dear."

"I have my group at one-thirty."

Mrs. Epperman found her reading glasses in the mountainous terrain out front and popped them on. "It would not be the end of the world if one of your little groups had to be canceled one week, Laura. Remember, that was our agreement when I first agreed to let you practice your therapy thing on the old dears here: It must never interfere with your *real* obligations."

THE LUNCH HOUR witnessed mild chaos in the dining room, as most of the residents hovered around the actors, asking nervous questions and offering books, napkins, and stationery for autographs. The Redwine troupe seemed to enjoy that. After lunch, Mrs. Epperman had a brief meeting with Colonel Rodgers and developed a migraine that sent her home for the afternoon. George Vanlandingham rushed around with still more replacement pages for his script, and somehow managed to jam the copy machine. J. Turner Redwine went off somewhere in the big Cadillac. Deena Sweete ushered Lord, Raddell, Mahafey, and Filmont into the large activity room, where loud voices could be heard declaiming behind locked doors. The playbill easel in the front of the atrium fell down again, and Still Bill Mills resorted to duct tape. The two Oklahoma City television stations that had scheduled visits for five P.M. both called and rescheduled for Friday. It seemed there had been a prison break at the state penitentiary at McAlester. Laura suggested that they might come around eleven tomorrow, do whatever interviews they had in mind, and then stick around for lunch and the start of the drama itself. The two news directors seemed to think that was a grand idea. Laura devoutly hoped her acting company and Mrs. Epperman would think so too.

Late in the afternoon Redwine reappeared, scowling. Laura caught him near the reception desk.

"Mr. Redwine, could we have a word?"

His bulging eyes rolled. "My dear, if this is in reference to yesterday's unfortunate momentary misunderstanding in the activity room, please allow me to assure you I meant no harm. Now I must prepare for the arrival of the TV crews—"

"That's what I wanted to tell you. They've had to postpone until late tomorrow morning."

"Damn!" His face suddenly looking a decade older, Redwine mulled over the news. "Well," he said at last, sighing, "we can manage. The performance does not begin until noon."

Laura hesitated, then let her curiosity get the better of her. "I understand your wife is missing."

He recoiled. "Who told you that?"

"Does it matter? I'm awfully sorry to hear about it, and wondered if there's anything we might possibly do."

The old character actor drew her into the office corridor, where he lowered his voice to a near whisper. "I had no desire to inflict my personal tragedies on you or anyone here at Timbermont."

"Timberdale."

"Whatever. I have just been to the fair city of Norman, where I consulted with the sheriff as well as a gentleman from the city police department. They are fully cognizant of all details. If there are any developments, I have provided them with this telephone number. I trust you will make certain I am notified at once if any such call comes in?"

"Of course. How long has Mrs. Redwine been missing?"

"A few days."

Laura watched him keenly, searching for whatever feelings lay beneath the surface. She could not read him. "You must be worried sick."

His lip shook, and he looked very much as if he might break down. "Rebecca is a dear, wonderful woman—means everything to me. Only my dedication to the art, as well as my record of never having broken a contract, gave me the strength to come here for this performance."

"As I said, if there's anything I can do—"

"Yes." He patted her on the shoulder. "Thank you, my dear." The distant echo of the actors' voices, still in the activity room, caused him to turn, distracted. "If you will excuse me, I must go to my people." He turned, took a step, and turned back. "Fear not. The show will go on as scheduled, starting around noon tomorrow."

Laura watched him hurry out into the atrium, then turned and went into her own office. The next week's menus had appeared on her desk for approval, along with paperwork from Kay Svendsen in the lab, some bills for maintenance and supplies, five letters from potential new residents, and proofs from the printer on the new and revised price lists for various sizes of units. She pitched in.

It was very much like running a small hotel, this job. Timberdale was not a nursing home, but a rental apartment facility that offered extra amenities such as the part-time clinic, planned activities, and local transportation in the small Mercedes bus driven by Still Bill Mills. Residents were billed by the month for a total package including meals. Each unit had a small kitchen of its own in case a resident did not wish to use the dining room. Leases were on an annual basis, and no one had to sign over their life savings or pledge something to a church in order to get in.

Laura thought it was a decent, humane way to run a place like this. She cared about the people. She liked working here. She had felt extremely lucky a year ago when she found the job, which dovetailed so nicely with her work toward an M.S.W. It had come at a time when finding a job—any job— was mandatory; the divorce decree had just come down, and her lawyerly ex-husband had screwed her for the first time in quite a long time, somehow finagling a court order that granted her monthly Jell-O money for child support along with the legal right to continue payments for three more years on a small imported sedan with sick exhaust headers.

She spent some time on the paperwork, losing herself in it. Then a small sound at the office door caught her attention and she looked up. Deena Sweete stood there, hair messy and makeup askew.

"Yes?"

"Has anyone heard from Reddy?"

Surprised, Laura glanced at her watch. "He got back almost an hour ago. I think he might still be in the large activity room. I thought you were in there, too."

"I've been in the back, helping Van work on some more script changes." Sweete started to turn away, then turned back. "Had Reddy heard any news? I mean—about anything?"

"I know about his wife being missing," Laura replied. "No. He hadn't heard anything new."

Sweete's ample breasts heaved. "I probably shouldn't say

this, but it's just like that awful woman to toot off someplace and worry him half to death.''

Laura was on the alert. "He seems very devoted to her."

Eyebrows shot up. "He didn't say that, did he?''

"I just got that impression."

"He's an adorable, loyal man. He would—he *would* put on a good front, and act like she's wonderful.''

"She isn't?"

Sweete's bright eyes narrowed vindictively. "She's the awfulest bitch in the world, that's all.''

"I'm surprised," Laura murmured.

"If you ask me," Sweete said, starting to turn away again, "the best thing that could happen for us would be for her to *never* show up again.''

"'Us'?" Laura repeated quickly.

The big eyes glazed. "Did I say 'us'? I meant all of us in the acting company, of course. She's always been, well, nothing but trouble. She was never an actress, you know.'' Her lip turned down. "Unless you consider it *acting* to take your clothes off at stag parties.''

Laura thought it wise not to say anything.

Sweete fidgeted, nervous. "I'd better go find out where he is.''

"Yes."

The leggy blond flurried out of sight. Laura looked down at her papers, but found it hard to concentrate again right away. She tried to tell herself all of this was silly; nothing but a—what was the word Maude would have used?—a botheration. But something instinctive in her sensed a deep undercurrent, a darkness that made chills rise again on her arms. She felt vaguely scared.

It was a premonition: Something bad about to happen. She seldom had premonitions—didn't believe in them.

You're being awfully silly, Laura Lynn Michaels, she lectured herself.

She hoped so.

SIX

FROM MAUDE THURINGER'S MYSTERY JOURNAL
Fri morn. Big day. Knees killing me. Last night, late, big doings: heard Vanland. having big row with Redwine in R's room—something about money. Then Vanland. went to 3, stayed in Filmont rm a long time, came out real mad. Mrs. Redwine missing in real life! Vy inter. caper so fr. Watch Laura—may be in cahoots with them.

LAURA MADE IT a point to get to Timberdale early Friday morning, and she was glad she had. The place was in a tizzy.

She had expected most of the residents to take Mrs. Epperman's "grand idea" in stride, and perhaps even smirk at it. Much to her surprise, they seemed to have gotten into the spirit of things. A few people were already milling around outside the dining room when she arrived before seven-thirty, and by breakfast time the din of voices made Timberdale sound more animated than it had in a long time.

Even Judith Epperman showed up on time.

"It's going to be a wonderful experience for everyone!" she proclaimed.

Members of the acting troupe were late for breakfast. Freddie Filmont, hair undone and heavily lined face shockingly old without makeup, put in a shaky appearance at 8:45. She sat alone at the long corner table reserved for the cast and crew, setting a new indoor record for consumption of orange juice. One of the college-boy servers asked if he could bring her a plate. "God, no!" she croaked loudly enough to turn heads.

Breakfast hour was normally from eight to nine; residents departed a few at a time until the room was vacant at 8:55

except for Filmont, who sat alone with her head in her hands; one of the college servers; and Laura and Mrs. Epperman standing near the entry doors.

"I guess they aren't coming down for breakfast," Laura said.

Mrs. Epperman scowled with worry. "He said they would."

"Redwine?"

"Yes. He called me in the office more than an hour ago, demanding room service. I told him that was impossible. He was really very crude about that."

Redwine, Laura thought, seemed to have a knack for antagonizing everyone. "Maybe—"

She got no further, because at that moment the great man himself, in a rumpled royal-blue jogging suit, appeared in the dining room doorway. Pale and puffy from sleep, or the lack of it, he scowled across the nearly vacant room and strode toward the table where Filmont sat alone. Gaunt George Vanlandingham, in tweed coat and Levi's, came in behind him, followed closely by Deena Sweete, wearing paint-tight silk pants and a bulky white sweater. As Redwine neared the cast table, Franklin Pierce Lord walked in, Janis Mahafey and Tad Raddell close behind.

Mrs. Epperman looked at her wristwatch. "Oh, dear. Pierre is going to be furious! He's such a prig about observing the meal hours. Laura, you'd better—"

Across the room, Redwine's loud voice interrupted. Glowering down at Filmont, he pointed a finger. "You missed the morning meeting."

Filmont raised bloodshot eyes. "Don't feel good."

"Have you been drinking again? I *told* you what would happen if you were caught drinking again!"

Filmont mumbled something and put her head down on the table. Redwine swelled up with indignation. Vanlandingham edged closer to him and whispered something in his ear. Redwine listened, visibly gritted his teeth, and made his shoulders slump. He turned and gestured imperiously at the others. "Be seated, everyone." He turned toward the remaining college boy, hovering uncertainly in his white coat and cap. "Garçon!"

The doors of the kitchen flung open. Pierre Motard, tall white chef's hat wobbling from the violence of his movements, charged in. "Zee hour of breakfast, she is concluded!"

Redwine drew himself up, imperious, and made a sweeping gesture in the direction of the clock on the far wall. "It is three minutes before the hour. We demand service."

Motard folded his arms across his chest. "You will receive nothing!"

Mrs. Epperman edged nearer the doors. "Laura, take care of this situation, dear girl. I have an important telephone call."

"But—" Too late. Mrs. Epperman's sturdy black orthopedic shoes clumped on the parquet floor beyond the doors as she rushed away.

Redwine and Motard were nose-to-nose by now, exchanging loud insults. Thoroughly disgusted, Laura hurried over, pasting a big, dumb grin on her puss. "Hey, guys! Isn't there some way we can work this out?"

"My colleagues and I require sustenance," Redwine intoned. "Yet *this* cretin insists—"

"Hours of meals, they are established," Motard cut in coldly.

"Well, look," Laura said. "I know we've got cinnamon rolls and some fruit still out, Pierre. And there's always a lot of coffee left over. Let's let these people go through the line and see what they can serve themselves."

Redwine huffed. "Go through the line? Go through the *line*, like commoners at a cafeteria?"

Motard held his arms up to heaven. "Give me strength! Did I accept zis position for to serve fast-order snacks to sluggards? I am not a short-order cook! I am an artist!"

Laura clung to her temper. Motard's artistry last night had resulted in franks and beans and Jiffy corn bread. "Pierre, they'll go through the line. Have Harley over there, bring out enough dishes and silverware."

"I protest zis—"

"Pierre: Shut up."

The Frenchman stopped, mouth hanging open. "Eh?"

"Service at table," Redwine began, "is the minimum—"

"And you shut up, too," Laura snapped. "I mean it." She angrily scanned the gaping faces along the table. "You guys want coffee and a roll or something? That's all you're going to get, because you're late. Sorry. If you want that, please line up over there at the serving table." She turned. "Pierre, move it, dammit!"

Motard pointed at Redwine. "I will have my revenge."

"You—"

"Shut up," Laura repeated sharply. "Pierre, *move it.*"

To her surprise, Redwine shut up. Motard turned and flung himself back into the kitchen. Another of the college boys showed up, bustling out with plates, cups, and silverware. Chairs scraped as cast members got up to head for the line. Freddie Filmont looked around and groaned. Laura stepped back to referee if necessary. She caught a movement in the atrium doorway and spied Colonel Roger Rodgers standing there, ramrod-straight, bitterness sparkling in his bright blue eyes. He was watching Redwine with an expression of pure, killing hatred. Seeing Laura's gaze, however, he turned and vanished.

As the members of the troupe returned with laden plates and began settling down to eat, Laura crossed the room and returned to her own table, pretending to study the newspaper over more coffee. It was not a happy group across the room from her. They mainly kept their voices low and she missed a lot of their talk, but there was constant argument.

Janis Mahafey seemed to be complaining to Vanlandingham about lack of lines. He snapped at her, but then Redwine leaned close and said something that made the little man go white with rage before he reached into his coat pocket for a notebook and pencil. Tad Raddell, the surfer boy, got into a brief, whispered squabble with Deena Sweete. Filmont started to leave, but Redwine yanked her back down and whispered furiously in her ear. Franklin Pierce Lord, wearily trying to stay above it all, said something about paychecks. Laura was unable to hear Redwine's reply, but she saw the look of hatred that flared briefly in Vanlandingham's bloodshot eyes. Raising his voice slightly, Redwine said all would be paid as soon as he received the company fee.

Laura found this particularly interesting because she knew the fee had already been paid. She thought it likely that Redwine had taken it to a bank yesterday, when he vanished for an hour or two. He had the money to pay his actors. How did he manage to cheat his own people like this and keep the troupe together?

After breakfast, members of the company made themselves very visible indeed at various places around the center. Seeing the repairman leave the copy room, Vanlandingham rushed in with a few more pages to duplicate. Meanwhile, Redwine took Sweete and Raddell into the large activity room, where they slammed the door and then could be heard pushing furniture around. Filmont, after staggering upstairs and vanishing for a while, came down looking brighter-eyed and walked around the atrium, passing out single-sheet playbills to anyone who would take one. Janis Mahafey strode back and forth on the third-floor balcony, gesturing to the heavens and silently rehearsing. Lord energetically shoved some of the dining room tables into new positions, which brought another diatribe from Pierre Motard. Laura intervened again. Lord explained that the table locations were necessary for the first scene, scheduled to play during lunch hour. Motard protested. Laura ruled. Motard pouted. The tables stayed moved.

Some pounding in the large activity room brought Mrs. Epperman out of hiding. She rushed over, used her master key to open the locked door, went inside for what seemed a long time, and came out shaking her head and muttering under her breath.

"They say no one is to enter and see the set they're arranging," she grated bitterly to Laura. "They put me out! Of my own place. Took the first-floor master key right out of my hand. Now the doors are locked and I can't even get in there myself.''

"You mean they kept the key?"

"Yes. No one enters except them, until the scene begins. They said no one must interfere with their art. Oh, that *terrible* man!''

Redwine appeared in the atrium, issuing instructions to Tad Raddell and then hurrying around the large area, putting an envelope on one end table and a crumpled cigarette pack on another. Still Bill Mills shuffled over to collect the cigarette pack in his trash sack. Redwine's voice boomed loud enough to break windows: "Don't touch anything I leave, you fool! I am distributing clues for the play."

Looking disgusted, Raddell moved two chairs in one of the conversation areas near the front of the atrium. Muscles bulging in a tight red T-shirt, he made the heavy chairs look like toothpicks. "Ooh," Francie Blake almost moaned, standing beside Laura behind the desk. "He's really cute, isn't he!''

"Young," Laura replied.

"Jiminy, wouldn't you say he's about my age?"

"Probably, Francie, but I thought you preferred older men."

Francie's lower lip pouted and her vivid eyes never left Raddell's moving figure. "Well, sure. That's because older men have more…you know…resources. But he's a hunk! And being an actor, he's probably got as many resources as anybody, wouldn't you say? If I wasn't ready for a trip with Dirk, gee…''

A number of residents milled around the lower level. Maude Thuringer darted out of the crowd, clipboard in hand and camera flying on its tether. "I think I've already got it cracked!''

"Maude, it hasn't started yet. It doesn't start till noon."

"That's what you think!" Maude turned and charged off.

A LITTLE BEFORE eleven o'clock, the crew from Oklahoma City Channel Nine appeared on the scene and began setting up lights, moving chairs, and generally creating a commotion.

Everything else stopped. A crowd gathered. Redwine and all the members of his company magically reappeared, most of them dressed for the roles they were to play in the murder mystery. George Vanlandingham hustled around, handing out playbills.

Laura grabbed one from him. "You're a busy man, Mr. Vanlandingham. You seem to do a lot to keep the operation moving."

His bitter expression became startled. "Someone noticed, anyway."

Laura carried the sheet in to Mrs. Epperman.

"What is it, dear girl?"

"A list of cast and characters."

"Let's have a look at what I'll be helping to pay for out of my salary for the next three years."

Laura handed it over and they read it together:

J. Turner Redwine presents
The Redwine Players
in an original mystery theater production:
MURDER IN RETIREMENT

Dramatis personae:
Harrington Abercrombie...J. Turner Redwine
James J. Miller....Franklin Pierce Lord
Mary Miller.........Freddie Filmont
Martha Miller.........Janis Mahafey
Brick Abercrombie.......Tad Raddell
Special guest star:
Elizabeth Abercrombie....Deena Sweete
　　　　Original script by George Vanlandingham

Mrs. Epperman looked up hopefully. "It better be good. That's all I have to say."

"Let's hope," Laura said.

Mrs. Epperman consulted her watch. "And oh, my, it's almost time. We must hurry to the dining room. We don't want to miss any murders, do we, dear?"

SEVEN

BOTH TV CREWS on the scene had decided it would be nice to stay for a free lunch and tape the first incident in the murder drama. When Laura walked into the dining room, she found it packed—every resident had decided to show up for *this* to-do, and the presence of the TV people and their cameras on tripods against the front wall made things more exciting.

None of the Redwine Players were in evidence.

Laura found a place at a table with Colonel Rodgers, Ellen Smith, and Fred Which.

"I can't believe they declined my offer to paint dramatic backdrop posters!" Smith said bitterly, dabbing at the front of her buckskin vest where a bit of red sauce had dribbled out of her sloppy joe.

"*I* can't believe this damned menu Motard has set up," Which commented. "Is this supposed to be French? How high do you suppose the fat and cholesterol are in these sandwiches?"

"I suppose," Rodgers grumbled, "Redwine will be the detective."

"It doesn't say on the playbill," Laura pointed out.

Colonel Rodgers glowered. "I wish he could be the victim. But in actuality."

George Vanlandingham, twittery-nervous and dressed in a drab sweater and slacks, poked his head in from the atrium.

"Uh-oh," Which grunted. "It starts."

"No," Smith said. "He isn't listed in the cast."

"You can't believe that paper," Rodgers said. "Redwine wrote it."

Vanlandingham vanished, but not before every head in the room had turned, and an eerie silence momentarily fell.

The clock on the wall said 12:20.

Suddenly everyone stirred and began turning toward the doors again. Conversation rushed up for an instant and then dropped to zero.

Into the deep quiet, at the far atrium door near a spot where two tables had been rearranged to create an empty space, a figure appeared. For a few seconds Laura did not recognize him: a tall man, but bent far forward from the waist, obviously very old and moving with pain. He had long gray hair that fell past the collar of his old-fashioned black suit, and he moved shakily using a cane. Only as he teetered farther into view and turned partly her way did Laura recognize J. Turner Redwine.

Redwine—she consulted her list of characters: Harrington Abercrombie—shuffled feebly to one of the tables moved and left vacant for the show. He pulled the chair out, removed a large handkerchief from his hip pocket, dusted the chair, and sat down with exaggerated agony. He heaved a sigh that could be heard all over the silent dining room.

A few seconds passed. Laura could hear Colonel Rodgers's stomach growling. Or maybe it was Stoney Castle, at the adjacent table.

More movement in the doorway: Another elderly man, wearing a dark velvet bathrobe and slippers, came slowly into view. He moved with the same exaggerated painfulness that ''Abercrombie'' had displayed. Because of his enormous false gray beard and sideburns, he was halfway to the Abercrombie table before Laura recognized him as Franklin Pierce Lord, playing ''James J. Miller.''

Right behind Miller came Freddie Filmont—''Mary Miller''—gotten up in a Victorian-era dress complete with high-button shoes and a parasol. Her stage makeup, designed to make her look ancient, made her face a sickly white.

Lord faltered closer to the ''Abercrombie'' table. ''Abercrombie'' finally looked up from deep meditation, saw him, and gave a violent start.

ABERCROMBIE (very loud): *You? Here*, of all places? Have you no decency, sir?

MILLER: Speak not to me of decency, you swine! I have made my decision, and Mary and I are going to move into Timberdale Retirement Center whether you like it or not.

There was a mild ripple of enthused interest across the room at mention of the retirement center. Redwine boomed over it.

ABERCROMBIE: But I already live here at Timberdale Retirement Center! You can't believe the Millers and the Abercrombies can live under the same roof!

MILLER: My wife, Mary, here, and I have discussed it.

MRS. MILLER: Yes, Mr. Abercrombie, we have.

MILLER: We want you to pay your old debts to us. Then there will be no more reason for bitterness between our families.

MRS. MILLER: After all, your son, Brick Abercrombie, and our daughter, Martha Miller, are deeply in love. We must end this old rivalry, Mr. Abercrombie! You must pay us what you cheated us of, and then we can all live here…you and Mrs. Abercrombie, James and I…in peace and harmony at last.

ABERCROMBIE (getting shakily to his feet and pointing): Fools! Knaves! I owe you nothing! I will see you in hell before I pay you a dime! Now you will excuse me, as I see my wife approaching. We will go at once to find the manager, Mrs. Epperman, and demand that you be barred from residence in this wonderful retirement center!

Another character teetered in. Deena Sweete—"Elizabeth Abercrombie"—wearing a long black wig and an old-fashioned outfit that must have come out of the same trunk that furnished Filmont's, hurried over to "Abercrombie" and grabbed him by the shoulders.

ELIZABETH(shrilly): Oh, Harrington, my husband, I just heard they were here. I hurried to try to warn you.

ABERCROMBIE: No problem, Elizabeth. You are a good wife to want to warn me, but I can handle people of this ilk. Come. We must find Mrs. Epperman and block their residency here at Timberdale Retirement Center.

MILLER(extremely loud): You insist on this old vendetta? I could kill you for this!

ABERCROMBIE(laughing): Try to fight me, and I shall take whatever it is you have left, you fool.

The ''Abercrombies'' moved slowly to the door in an impressive silence, and were gone. ''Mr. and Mrs. Miller'' remained onstage at the table.

MILLER: After all these years! I'll get him for this!

MARY: There, there, James my darling. Perhaps there is another way…a way to solve our problem with him.

MILLER: Another way? Another way? Tell me!

MARY(taking his arm): Let us go outside, where we can be sure no one overhears our conversation.

The ''Millers'' turned and exited through the doorway.

In the lingering silence halfway across the room, Maude Thuringer chirped like a monster mockingbird: ''Wow! That was great! Do you see what's coming, Esther? Did you have your hearing aid turned loud enough, Judge?''

Somebody else walked in through the doorway used by the actors. Then someone else. Janis Mahafey (''Martha Miller'') and Tad Raddell (''Brick Abercrombie'') were dressed more neatly than normal, but otherwise they were instantly identifiable.

Hand in hand, they hurried to the table area just vacated by the other actors. Mahafey turned to Raddell and threw her arms around his neck. He bent forward and they kissed passionately.

A slight murmur of amusement and surprise went around the room.

''Miller'' and ''Abercrombie'' kept kissing. The murmur

became a general buzzing. Someone—probably Ken Keen—whistled.

The actors broke the kiss but remained in each other's arms.

MARTHA:Oh, Brick, what can we do to make them understand?

BRICK:It's all my father's fault. I could kill him myself!

MARTHA:Everyone hates him. I, too, wish he were dead. If he were gone, you would have your inheritance and we could be married.

BRICK:Someone has to do something. This can't go on!

MARTHA:Break with him! Marry me now! We will be poor, but—

BRICK:Are you crazy? I could never do that!

MARTHA:Sometimes I hate you, too. You love his money more than you love me! (Slaps him with a sharp crack that carries through the room.)

BRICK:I won't take that from you or any person! (Turns, charges out.)

"Martha" burst into tears, remained a moment, then hurried out the same way "Brick" had gone.

Everyone in the dining room waited. It stayed very quiet. a minute or so passed.

Then George Vanlandingham walked in. "Ladies and gentlemen," he announced, straining his squeaky voice, "this concludes Act One. You will see further developments soon. Thank you." He turned and walked out as scattered applause began.

EIGHT

Deputy Aaron "Salt" Lassiter was standing near the radio console desk in the Cleveland County sheriff's office when the woman walked in.

He walked to the counter, noting that the visitor was tall, fortyish, with long red hair and a lined face that must have been extremely attractive once, before time and bad luck had done too much roadwork on it. She was wearing a wrinkled, linty black cloth coat over an expensive-looking blue summery dress, and her white legs were bare. She snapped her eyelashes up and down at him with obvious agitation and impatience.

"Can I help you?" Lassiter asked politely.

"Yes. I want to report a non-missing person."

Lassiter leaned closer. "I beg your pardon, ma'am?"

"I just heard on my car radio that I'm supposed to be missing. I'm not missing. I don't know who told somebody I was missing. I'm right here. Did my husband do this? Do you know where the rotten man is? I know he's in this area someplace. Damn him! I go to visit my children for a couple of days and he *vanishes*—all of them just bug out for Oklahoma without me and think I'm not smart enough to track them down. Then somehow I get listed as missing. I'm not missing! He's the one who's missing, but I'm going to track the cur down, and when I find him I may kill him."

Lassiter pulled an incident pad over between them. "Slow down, ma'am. Just slow down. You say you're listed as missing?"

"Yes. Do I look like I'm missing? That bastard!"

Lassiter felt glad he was not the lady's husband. "Let's start at the beginning. Your name?"

"Redwine. Rebecca Redwine."

SEEING J. TURNER REDWINE, still in costume, rush into the rear elevator in the east wing, Maude Thuringer raced up the fire stairs after him. By the time she reached the third level, the fire stairs were appropriate because her knees were burning up and her heart was sounding an alarm. But she cracked the door and darted behind a potted plant just in time to see Redwine leave the elevator and catch Freddie Filmont, who seemed in an unholy hurry to reach her room not far away.

"Freddie! A word with you."

"Not now." Filmont fumbled at her door lock.

Redwine angrily grasped her arm and tugged. He did not pull very hard, but Filmont staggered and almost fell. He had to catch her.

"Lemme alone," she mumbled.

"You've been drinking. Damn you! I thought I detected the signs during our first act downstairs."

Filmont shook her head and pulled away from him. "You're crazy."

"Why are you in such a hurry?" Redwine demanded. "Can't wait to get inside to your bottle? Freddie, I warned you—"

"What are you going to do?" she spat. "Not pay me?"

Redwine's face worked. "Everyone will be paid as soon as—"

"Liar!"

"What?"

"You've already been paid for this job."

"Where did you ever get that outrageous notion?"

"Never mind. I know it's true."

Redwine's voice softened, became cajoling. "Freddie, old friend—"

"What do you plan to do, you cheater? Hold back, and then pay us part and say they didn't make good on the contract payment here? Is that what happened in Fort Worth, too?"

Redwine's voice lowered further. "Now, now, Freddie. Just stay calm. I plan to get into a bank later today—in just a little while, actually—and convert her check into cashier's checks for all of you."

The actress's eyes shot venom. "You did that yesterday."

"Nonsense! You have to get hold of yourself, Freddie. We have a performance to do. Everyone will have their money before day's end."

She turned to the door again. "I'm going to tell everybody."

"There's no need for that, Freddie! Let me assure you—"

"I don't believe anything you say anymore. You said I could get my career moving again. You said I could make two thousand a week. If I need a little drink to keep going, whose fault is it but yours, you—"

She was cut off then, wincing as he seized her arm roughly this time, spinning her around. He jerked her close, and Maude had to strain to hear his harsh whisper.

"You'll keep quiet, you old sot, or you'll be paid with nothing and you'll be out on the street again, like you were when I found you."

Filmont seemed to go limp in his grasp. He went on, "And if you show up for the next act with so much as a hint that you've had more to drink, I'll not only fire you but make sure the word is spread so you'll never work again for *anybody*. Do you understand that?" He released her.

She rubbed her wrists, whining, "You hurt me."

"Remember what I've just told you. Now start getting changed, but stay out of that bottle, damn you. Your next segment plays in less than an hour." Redwine turned and walked away.

Maude stayed right where she was, kneeling, and scribbled in her notebook.

NINE

FROM MAUDE THURINGER'S MYSTERY JOURNAL

1st Act. Millers hate Abercrombies. Abercrombie in control. Old man Miller likely killer, if Ab. is victim. Ab. could kill Miller. Maybe Brick Ab. kill father? Maybe Eliz. or even Martha. Plan: Wait to see who gets murdered. Then elim. him/her from suspect list, concentrate on others. Could be more than one, like in Orient Express. *Neat! Don't know if Red. & Fil. in hall part of show, maybe. Knees hurt.*

LAURA WAS IN her office about one thirty, trying to get through Pierre Motard's revised menu for the following week, when Colonel Roger Rodgers marched in. He faced her desk standing at attention. Splotches of facial color showed how angry he was. "Where is Mrs. Epperman?"

"I'm not sure. She said she had a surprise of some kind for us; then she seems to have disappeared."

"Drat the woman! She didn't say where she was going?"

"No," Laura admitted. "I'm sure she won't be gone long, Colonel, but I just have no idea what this surprise—"

"Here to lodge a formal complaint!"

"About?"

"It's bad enough that normal seating is rearranged in the chow hall. But *some* of us want no part of this stupid charade. I have discussed this with the Clines and the Kemmerers and they support my position. We protest the staging of mock incidents at times when we are compelled to watch, as if we approve—"

He got no further. George Vanlandingham, a sheet of paper

flapping in his hand, rushed in. "Laura, I can't find Mrs. Epperman. You need to duplicate this schedule and post copies all over the place right away. Can you make an announcement, too? You've got a PA system or something, haven't you?"

Colonel Rodgers whirled, offended. "I am conducting business here, sir!"

"What's the problem?" Laura asked Vanlandingham.

"Well, dammit, we didn't realize the old codgers would all just toot off to their rooms right after the first scene at lunch. The lobby is practically deserted, and the next scene plays there in just a few minutes."

"You mean—"

"The old coots will miss parts of the play. They aren't going to be downstairs at the right times." Vanlandingham thrust the paper at her. "This tells where, and about what time, all the rest of the scenes will play. You need to get this circulated so the folks will be at the right places to see stuff."

Another movement in the doorway, and J. Turner Redwine hove into view. "Laura! We need some additional furniture rearranged in the foyer. At once! Summon your handyman." He turned to Colonel Rodgers. "How about you, my good man? Be a good chap—lend us a hand."

The colonel's face twisted. "Never!"

Redwine eyed Laura, lowering his voice. "Is this a case of senile dementia? I apologize." He turned back to Colonel Rodgers. "Be of good cheer, old-timer. I meant no—"

With no warning, the colonel lunged at him, swinging a roundhouse right. Laura squeaked in warning, too late. Vanlandingham, closer, stepped between the men. Colonel Rodgers's wild swing caught him on the shoulder, knocking him back violently against the wall. Redwine backpedaled. The colonel started after him.

"Colonel!" Laura yelped. From somewhere came an inspiration. *"As you were!"*

Colonel Rodgers stopped in mid-swing, eyes glazing. "Say again?"

Laura pointed at the door. "Get out of here, Colonel. As you were. Go to your room. Dismissed."

His shoulders slumped. Breathing hard, he glowered at Redwine, wide-eyed against the wall. "You're right," he said finally. "Conduct unbecoming." He pointed a shaky finger at Redwine. "Stay out of my way. Don't ever address me again, or you'll be sorry." He rushed out of the office, making Vanlandingham scurry to the side to avoid him.

"Are you okay?" Laura asked him.

He rubbed his shoulder and looked palely at Redwine. "Me—taking a shot meant for you. Jesus, how ironic can it get?"

"Good man," Redwine rumbled. "Obviously a case of dementia. Sad case. Well done all around." He shook his head. "Thank you, George. I shan't forget your intervention, inept as it might have been. Well, let's get on with it. We need that furniture moved."

The expression that crossed Vanlandingham's face made Laura think for a second that he was going to be the next to attack Redwine. But then, as quickly as it came, the look was gone. He turned weakly to Laura. "That announcement has to be made right away."

Francie Blake rushed in. "Gee! What's going on? I heard yelling in here!"

"Francie," Laura said, smiling. "You're just in time to help."

Francie's eyes shot wide. "Oh! Golly, I wish I *could*. But I'm just up to *here* with my work on the plans for Thanksgiving, Laura. Maybe later?" She beamed an adorable smile. "'Bye!" Her legs twinkled as she fled.

Laura reached for the telephone. "I'll find Still Bill first. Then we'll copy this scene schedule and make an announcement on the public-address system."

Redwine, himself again, straightened the silk lapels of his old-fashioned suit. "Expeditiously, by all means."

A FEW MINUTES before two p.m., most residents had gotten the word and were either in the atrium or standing along the upstairs balcony railings. In the center of the atrium, some of the furniture had been pushed back against the west wall, leaving only one reading chair, an end table, and a floor lamp in the middle of a large carpeted space.

Residents on the balconies and surrounding the vacant area stirred and murmured as Redwine, dressed in his old-fashioned suit as before, tottered in from the front hallway, his exaggeratedly feeble movements threatening to break his cane. He shuffled over to the lone chair, sat down, pulled a small book from his inside coat pocket, and simulated reading.

A moment passed. Standing at the reception counter, Laura dug out her playbill and reminded herself who was playing whom.

Then Freddie Filmont—"Mary Miller"—appeared from the back, pushing past some of the startled residents there. Filmont had changed into another old-fashioned dress. She walked unsteadily up to confront Redwine.

MILLER: Harrington Abercrombie, we must talk.

ABERCROMBIE *(looking up from his book):* We have nothing to say to one another.

MILLER: You have no idea how angry you've made my husband, James. Or how much anquidge—anguish—you have caused everyone in two families.

ABERCROMBIE: It is your husband who has chosen to stir up old bitterness. I have taken up the challenge. My lawyer will be in court at this very hour, filing harassment charges against all of you.

MILLER *(hand on breast in shock):* But if this fight continuesh, the old secret will come to light!

ABERCROMBIE: The old secret? The old secret? Madam, that is the one promise we made to each other—that the old secret would never be revealed!

MILLER: But if this struggle continues—

ABERCROMBIE: The secret must be kept! Even if someone has to die, the story must never be told! All of us would be ruined! All!

MILLER (*stiffening and raising a hand to her lips*): Hush! Someone approaches!

Tad Raddell—"Brick Abercrombie," Laura reminded herself from the paper in her hand—walked in fast from the front foyer, waving his arms to show how excited he was.

BRICK: Father! Martha has broken up with me!

ABERCROMBIE: Thank your stars. She comes from a family of hyenas.

MILLER: Oh, you cruel man!

BRICK: You've caused this, Father. I never want to see you again.

ABERCROMBIE: Get out of my sight, you foul weakling. I am going to write you out of my will at once.

BRICK: What?

MILLER: You terrible man! You've lost your mind. Someone must stop you! (*She turns and hurries out, back atrium.*)

BRICK: She is right, Father. You have gone too far.

ABERCROMBIE: Is that a threat?

BRICK: Take it as you wish, you evil old man. (*exits, front foyer.*)

Left alone, Abercrombie picked his book up again from the end table where he had placed it when the scene opened. A general murmur rippled through the atrium as residents began to digest the scene. Laura started to turn away.

Then, however, a sharp cry of surprise from several female voices turned her around again. For an instant she didn't know if the scene was over, and reality was intruding, or what. Red-wine, playing the Abercrombie paterfamilias, continued to stare down at his little book. But a newcomer had appeared on the scene—none other than Mrs. Epperman.

She hustled in from the front hallway, the same route "Brick" had used moments before. With her reading glasses perched on the end of her nose and a large sheaf of papers in her arms, she clomped in faster and with more authority than Laura had ever seen in her. *What in the world—?*

Mrs. Epperman walked up to the reading actor.

MRS EPPERMAN: Mr. Abercrombie?

Good lord, she was *in the show*. That had been the surprise, dear girl.

ABERCROMBIE: Mrs. Epperman. Good day to you. It is a fine day here at Timberdale Retirement Center.

That brought a general loud ripple of whispered comments everywhere, and Mrs. Epperman paused to let it subside before delivering her next lines.

MRS. EPPERMAN: Mr. Abercrombie, Mr. and Mrs. Miller have not withdrawn their application for residency here at Timberdale Retirement Center.

ABERCROMBIE: What? I told you I do not want those people here!

MRS. EPPERMAN: Mr. Abercrombie, Timberdale's leasing policies are clearly stated. We cannot refuse a bona fide application.

ABERCROMBIE: What?

MRS. EPPERMAN: Mr. and Mrs. Miller will be moving in today.

ABERCROMBIE: Madam, this will mean trouble!

MRS EPPERMAN: Oh, I hope not. *(Pauses, looks around at sea of resident faces.)*

ABERCROMBIE: *(Waits, seems to think scene is over.)*

MRS. EPPERMAN: Because Timberdale is a unique facility for senior citizens, a place where independence and personal growth are nurtured and encouraged, and all the residents get along so well, the dears—

ABERCROMBIE: Yes, yes. Good-bye. *Leave*, now.

MRS. EPPERMAN:—because we have the finest possible facilities, from the gourmet dining room fare to the Nautilus exercise equipment and private sauna, featuring the Hudson 901 heating system for personal—

ABERCROMBIE: Yes, *yes!* Good-bye, Mrs. Epperman!

MRS. EPPERMAN *hurries off the way she came.*

ABERCROMBIE: *stands, puts book in pocket, and strides offstage, directly at the reception desk where Laura is standing.*

Behind him, George Vanlandingham hustled onto the vacant set and led the applause, signaling the end of the scene.

Redwine, shedding his "Abercrombie" gait, closed the gap between him and Laura. His face looked as if he had been in the sun all day. "Where is she?" he whispered, trembling violently. "God damn that woman! Did you hear her? Did you hear her, the way she ad-libbed out there? I'll wring her bloody neck!"

TEN

LAURA MANAGED to avert a catastrophe by hustling J. Turner Redwine to the rear of the atrium before Mrs. Epperman strolled in, beaming, for curtain calls. Residents surrounded Redwine back there, and their adulation quickly restored his good temper. Laura got Mrs. Epperman into her office with the door closed. Mrs. Epperman thought her performance had been the highlight of the show so far.

At 2:40, right on schedule, Janis Mahafey, playing Martha Miller, and Raddell, again playing Brick Abercrombie, staged a catfight in front of the dining room doors. Martha said she wished Brick's father were dead. Brick said maybe it was *her* father who should be dead. Then Deena Sweete, playing the elder Mrs. Abercrombie, tried to intervene and had an argument with Martha about Brick's character, or lack thereof. Then Freddie Filmont performed a soliloquy from the second-floor balcony, informing the world that she could not live if "the old secret" was revealed and that she had told her husband this fact.

Close on the heels of Filmont's soliloquy, a handful of residents reported to Laura that most people had missed a scene in the back hallway of One East, where Mahafey had screamed something at Redwine about "cheating us out of our money again," and had slapped his face. Shortly afterward, a scowling Redwine found Laura near the clinic office and asked for three dinner menus to use as additional clues. She got them for him and he strode off to the large activity room, where he used the master key to unlock the door and went inside, loudly slamming and locking it behind him.

Only minutes later, Laura was back in her office when Paula Burwell called from the front desk. "Laura, I've got a call holding for Mr. Redwine. She says it's important. Do you know where he might be?''

"Did you try his room?''

"Yes. No answer, and I don't see him out here anywhere.''

"Did he leave the big activity room?''

"I don't know.''

"Well, try Mr. Vanlandingham's room. They could be back there.''

Sometime past three-thirty, Vanlandingham showed up in the atrium. Laura spotted him and went out. His face streamed nervous sweat. Laura asked, "Did that call get to Mr. Redwine when we put it back to your room?''

"No,'' the small man snapped. "He's in the back, getting prepared for the four o'clock. I couldn't bother him now.''

Laura shrugged and forgot about it.

A few minutes before four, Aaron Lassiter appeared in the doorway of her office.

"Hey, somebody I want to see,'' she said gladly, going around the desk for a quick hug. "Are you here to rehearse?''

He removed his round-brimmed uniform hat and began mauling it around and around in his big, capable hands. "No, but has Mrs. Redwine showed up yet?''

"Mrs. Redwine? Here?''

"She's around. She was at the sheriff's office.''

"How did that happen?''

"She says they left her behind.''

"Great! If she comes out here, we'll have a scene that's not in the script.''

"You better believe it.''

"Did you tell her where he is?''

"No, but I didn't have to. All she has to do is look at yesterday's *Norman Transcript*. It had a little story on page four about this performance out here.''

"What do you mean, she says they left her?''

"She says she went to visit her kids somewhere and when she got back to Fort Worth last night they had bugged out, leaving no forwarding address, just a hefty motel bill for her to pay. She remembered they were coming to the Oklahoma City area, though.''

"Oh, lord, she'll be here, then.''

"When she finds out where Hubby is, she'll be here with bells on. Or maybe a hockey stick.''

Laura groaned and rubbed her temples, where a headache already lurked. "That ought to be wonderful.''

"I got off a little early. I was supposed to be here by six, to walk around in my uniform and ask folks who live here where they were at the time of the murder—do my part in the play. I thought I'd better come as soon as I could, though, with Mrs. Redwine likely to show up any minute and go bonkers on us.''

Mrs. Epperman appeared in the doorway. "Laura—hello, young man—isn't it almost time for the scene scheduled for the large activity room?''

"Fifteen minutes or so,'' Laura said. 'It's set for four-thirty.''

Mrs. Epperman scowled. "It's silent as a tomb in there. I can't get anyone to answer when I knock. That hateful man took my only key to that door, and I can't even get in. He's not in his room, either. No one seems to know where he's gotten to.''

Puzzled, Laura tried to read Mrs. Epperman's sweaty expression. "I'm sure everything must be all right. They're probably just waiting for the scheduled time for the next scene.'' She picked up the playbill. "See? It says right here, 'Scene in the large activity room, four-thirty.'''

Mrs. Epperman wrung her hands. "It would be just like him to run off and abscond with the money.''

"He wouldn't do that,'' Laura said with more conviction than she felt.

"He might—he might! He's acted like a beast ever since we played that little scene together. Did you think it was wrong for me to put in a few extra little promotional words about Timberdale? Isn't that my job? I thought it added realism to the script, didn't you? What a dreadful man.''

Laura looked at Lassiter and said nothing. She had an uneasy inkling of what was coming next.

It was. Mrs. Epperman cleared her throat. "Dear girl, I want you to run around the back way and look into the activity room. You can get in that way. Make sure everything is all right."

"Don't we have another master key?"

"Yes, of course we do," Mrs. Epperman snapped crossly. "But I have it at home. Just go make sure all is well. Is that asking too much?"

Laura hesitated, remembering the chill wind that had resumed outside. Without the key, she would have to go all the way outside the building and around to the back service door to reach the seldom-used rear corridor.

"That's a good girl," Mrs. Epperman said.

Lassiter's forehead wrinkled. "Want me to tag along? My instructions are to stay out of sight until after they stage the murder. But—"

"Sit tight," Laura said, heading for the door. "It won't take a sec."

Actually, she thought, hustling out of the office area, the journey would take considerably longer than a sec. She wondered what kind of set had been prepared that had to be kept so secret; the next time Mrs. Epperman left one of the submasters hanging from the hook behind her desk, Laura thought, she would sneak it out and have a copy duplicated for herself no matter what her boss thought about keeping masters to a minimum for security reasons.

She went out through the atrium to the dining room, down the kitchen pantry corridor, and out through the back food-service door. The cold wind tugged at her as she skirted the Dumpsters, cut across the back end of the kitchen employee's parking area, and cut through the south patio to the tunnellike back driveway used for ambulances or emergency units when the inevitable happened to some resident. It was really nasty and cold.

Maybe, she thought, Redwine had set up something fancy

in there. She remembered that Still Bill had had to drag an old desk out of the basement storage area and put it in there this morning, along with some extra chairs arranged theater-style. Someone had said something earlier about the four-thirty scene being "a biggie." Possibly—just possibly—Redwine's cloak-and-dagger stuff was justified, she tried to convince herself.

The wind sucked and pulled at her as she finally reached the emergency ramp and hurried down. Dried leaves whirled around her while she dug the back-door key out of her skirt pocket and inserted it into the lock of the metal security door.

As she inserted her key, however, she felt the door shift slightly. Looking down, she discovered that it was not closed all the way. Some of the dead leaves had blown out of the ramp area and into the crack, preventing the door from fully closing.

Mrs. Epperman would have cats if she heard about this breach of security. But she wouldn't hear about it from Laura. Nobody needed any more problems during this dumb mystery weekend.

Entering the dusty concrete tunnel of the lower building level, she walked past doors that led to heating and air-conditioning equipment, closets, and storage rooms. Forty-watt bulbs in bare sockets provided dim light. She hurried because it was always musty and spooky down here.

Reaching a paneled door at the far end of the tunnel, she saw the elevator was already up on One. She opened the door beside it and used the fire stairs to climb the single flight. Opening another door above, she stepped out into the seldom-used utility hallway of One South Rear.

On her left, a light shone out of a door leading into one of the rooms for storage of walkers, wheelchairs, and similar spare equipment. She poked her head inside. "Bill?" Getting no answer but a slight echo, she flipped off the lights, closed and locked the door, and hurried on. Turning another corner, she came to an intersection with a brighter, neater hallway, this one with Timberdale's familiar plum carpet. Almost there, thank goodness. She hurried.

One more turn in the hallway stood between her and the back door to the activity room. Just as she reached the turn, she heard odd sounds just ahead——grunting, and the squeaking of something metallic. Curious, she turned the corner to determine the source of the sounds.

What she saw made her stagger and moan with shock.

At the same instant, something moved behind her, muffled footsteps on the carpet. She started to turn. Something slammed into her skull. She was aware of a ringing sound and sharp pain and flashing yellow stars, and then blackness, and she fell off a cliff into oblivion.

BY 4:25, RESIDENTS milled around the atrium, their murmurs filling it. Judith Epperman peered out from the safety of her office. "It's almost time, and no sign of anybody! Why hasn't Laura come back? Where *is* that dreadful girl?" She glared at Lassiter as if it were his fault.

"I can go look," he suggested.

"No, I will," Mrs. Epperman fumed. "You had better stay here, as they ordered. Deviate one scintilla from their stupid little script, and they're all over you for it. I can attest to that from personal experience."

She hustled out into the atrium. Maude Thuringer was rushing around from resident to resident, clipboard and recorder at the ready, asking everybody questions. Mrs. Epperman did not ask why. She felt certain she did not want to know. Irked, she looked at her watch again, comparing it with the big clock on the far wall. Both showed 4:28.

George Vanlandingham rushed in from somewhere. His face was the color of fireplace ashes. His hands shook. "We're running late, Mrs. Epperman, but there's no problem." He held out something. "Here's your extra master key. Reddy said to return it to you."

"And where is he, if I may ask?"

Vanlandingham tilted his head toward the closed doors. "In

there. He went in quite some time ago to prepare himself for this scene."

Mrs. Epperman took the key and dropped it into the pocket of her dress. "Well? Let's open the doors and get going, then!"

The little man looked at his watch. "Two minutes. We try to start exactly on time. Why don't you unlock the doors now."

Mrs. Epperman did so and fidgeted. Vanlandingham stood guard by the doors as the crowd thickened. As the clock began tolling four, he pulled the doors open onto a pitch-black room.

People stopped milling, and the vast atrium hushed. Vanlandingham reached inside for a switch, and the lights came on. From the atrium nothing could be seen but rows of chairs arranged inside.

Vanlandingham gestured. "Everyone enter, please, and find a seat."

The crowd filed in. Mrs. Epperman joined them. What confronted her once she had taken up her station along the side wall was a small set at the far end of the room. It was clear at once why the company hadn't wanted anyone to view it ahead of time, because it gave away considerable plot.

It was arranged into two areas with a battered fiberboard partition in the middle, edgewise so the audience could see both sides at once. The partition had a flimsy door in it.

On the left side, on a gurney covered with white tissue paper, J. Turner Redwine lay face-up, half draped by a sheet, giving a good simulation of unconsciousness. A nearby table—Mrs. Epperman recognized it as junk from the storage room—had some bottles and pictures of medical equipment on it.

On the other side of the partition stood a desk out of the basement. It had papers and a stage telephone on it, and a chair nearby. A sign on the wall said EMERGENCY ROOM.

From the atrium doorway, Deena Sweete, wearing a white nurse's outfit, clattered in on four-inch spikes. She hurried to the desk and sat down behind it, starting to move papers around.

The telephone on her desk made an old-fashioned ringing noise. She snatched it up.

NURSE: Norman Hospital. Emergency room. Nurse Green speaking.... Yes, Mr. Abercrombie has just been admitted.... No, we do not yet know his condition.... Yes, that is correct.... He was stabbed at Timberdale Retirement Center less than one hour ago.

She hung up the phone. Enter from the atrium side James J. Miller, played by Franklin Pierce Lord, and his wife, Mary, played by Freddie Filmont. Right behind them, Tad Raddell and Janis Mahafey, gotten up in white smocks like a doctor and nurse, hurried in and went to the "treatment room" side of the set.

DOCTOR: Hurry, Nurse. Check his vital signs while I scrub.
NURSE: Yes, Doctor. I believe he is fading fast. *(Moves toward gurney where patient lies.)*
On the other side of the partition:

JAMES J. MILLER: Is it true? Who did this foul deed?

Sweete, playing the receptionist-nurse, opened her mouth to reply. But before she could do so, on the other side of the partition Janis Mahafey let out a shriek that made everybody in the room jump.

She staggered back from the gurney, almost knocking Raddell down.

"He's dead!" she cried. She held up one of her hands. Something bright red and glistening had gotten smeared all over it when she began her make-believe examination. "I mean," she yelled, "He's *really* dead!" And keeled over.

ELEVEN

SITTING IN LAURA'S office with his feet propped on the edge of her desk, Aaron Lassiter had just begun trying to figure out an article in *Family Therapy Networker* when the screaming started. Bowling into the atrium, he saw residents rushing out of the activity room as if monsters were after them.

A thin old woman in Indian buckskins spotted him. "He's dead! He's really been murdered! It's horrible!" She went running off, silver jewelry catching flashes of light.

Lassiter pushed through the crowd coming the other way and got inside the room. Everybody seemed to be talking and weeping at once. More residents pushed frantically past, jostling him in their hurry to get out. To his left, Mrs. Epperman and somebody else knelt beside an elderly woman who seemed to have fainted. To his right, on the far side of the makeshift stage, several of the acting company clustered around a gurney with white paper draped over what looked too much like a corpse. Somebody was out cold on the floor over there, too.

Lassiter pushed past the actors and got to the gurney. J. Turner Redwine lay on it, face-up, eyes closed in a good imitation of sleep. Red splatters covered the white sheeting tucked neatly up around his neck. Lassiter reached down and pulled the sheet down a few inches. Redwine's throat was covered with bright blood. He had a small round bullet hole in the center of his throat, just where it joined the chest. Ignoring the babble around him, Lassiter poked around for the carotid, not expecting to find a pulse, and didn't.

George Vanlandingham charged in, hair flying. "What's happened? What went wrong?"

"He's dead!" Deena Sweete wailed. "Poor Reddy has been

murdered!'' She turned and ran out of the room and into the atrium.

"Oh, no!" Vanlandingham clutched at his chest and went to one knee.

On the floor, Janis Mahafey groaned and tried to sit up.

Lassiter made a great number of decisions very fast. "Out of here," he snapped at the actors. "Now. All of you. But nobody leaves Timberdale." He turned. "Mrs. Epperman!"

The bulky administrator looked up from the resident on the floor. "This poor soul—"

"Get over here."

"But—"

His voice whiplashed. "Get over here!"

Wide-eyed with shock, she scrambled to her feet and hurried over. "Get everybody else out of here. Now. Get on the PA. Announce that nobody is to leave the premises. Nobody. For any reason. Put your people on all the outside doors and enforce it: Everybody stays. Find that handyman of yours and have him lock up both doors to this room. Nobody touches anything. Find Dr. Which. I want him pronto."

"But—"

"Don't 'but' me, lady. Do it!" Without waiting for another reply, he hurried out of the room, roughly pushing past gaping onlookers. Half-running to Laura's office across the way, he punched in 9 for an outside line, then jabbed the numbers for the sheriff's office in Norman.

The telephone at the other end rang...rang a second time. *Come on, come on!* With his free hand, he retrieved a bandana from his hip pocket and mopped his face.

At that moment his eyes fell on Laura's small purse on the corner of the desk. His blood felt like ice dashing through his veins. *Where's Laura?*

ORDINARILY THE DRIVE to Timberdale from the Cleveland County courthouse in downtown Norman took at least twenty minutes. Two sheriff's cruisers and a city police car hit the driveway, lights and sirens blaring, in fourteen. Three minutes later the Norman Emergency Medical Service ambulance wheeled in behind them.

Lassiter met them at the front door, explaining the situation as well as he knew it. With ashen-faced residents standing by mute, the medical team ran into the activity room, where Dr. Fred Which had already reported. Two city policemen went with them. Two deputies moved around the atrium, shepherding residents out of the immediate area. The sheriff drew Lassiter off to a vacant conversation room off the front hallway.

"Salt, what the hell else can you tell me about all this?"

Lassiter shook his head. "We've got a missing person, too."

The sheriff's grizzled head jerked back. "What?"

"Laura Michaels. The administrative assistant. She was at the office once. I introduced you."

"Sure, I remember. Cute brunette, mind like a bear trap. What do you mean, she's missing? Where? When? How?"

Lassiter rubbed aching eyes. He didn't know the answers to any of those questions. "She went out back to check on something before this latest act. Hasn't come back."

"Well, man, we'd better start searching for her!"

"I've already got Still Bill Mills on the hunt. If anybody knows every nook and cranny of this place, he's the man."

The sheriff stared. "Aren't you worried? Don't you want to hunt for her too?"

Lassiter's tattered nerves betrayed him. "Hell, yes, I'm worried! Do you think I'm an idiot? I'm worried out of my mind! I had all this other stuff to do—"

"You don't now. We're here. Look for her."

Lassiter gratefully hurried back into the main area of the first floor. He immediately spotted Judith Epperman standing with a small group of residents near the doors to the dining area at the back. He walked up and interrupted what seemed to be a speech about how no one should be concerned, the police had the situation in hand.

"Officer," she snapped, turning as he arrived. "Has Laura shown up yet?"

"No. That's what I want to ask you. How do I get to—"

Mrs. Epperman stamped her orthopedic shoe. "Isn't that just *like* the dreadful girl! Tooting off somewhere just when I need her the most!"

Lassiter spoke through set teeth. "She went to the back service area to check on what was happening there. How do I get to the back service area?"

Furrows made Mrs. Epperman's brow look ten inches high. "Well, of course she went around to the kitchen service door, I'm sure, because the entry to the activity room had been locked. But it's certainly open now. You can just go through the activity room and into the rear hallway through the far doorway."

"Thanks." He turned away.

"When you find her, I want to see her immediately!" Mrs. Epperman bawled after him "I intend to give her a piece of my mind."

Lassiter strode toward the open doors to the activity room. A little woman in a floral print silk dress, carrying a clipboard, intercepted him. She had eyes like warning lights. "Aaron! Aaron! Do you remember *me*? Maude! Maude Thuringer."

He started past. "Sorry, lady. I don't have time now."

"But I think I've cracked this case wide open!"

The Norman emergency paramedics blocked the activity room doorway for a few moments, pushing out a gurney. Sheeting completely covered the strapped-down body. Lassiter edged around them and went into the room. A burly Norman police detective named Hunzicker and two of Lassiter's fellow deputies had several members of the cast lined up for preliminary questioning.

The striking young actress named Janis Mahafey seemed to have the stage. "I don't know why I fainted," she declared. "It was just such a dreadful shock."

The older actress—Lassiter remembered her name was Freddie Something—sniffed in reply. "It shouldn't have been such a surprise to any of us."

Hunzicker picked up on that instantly. "Why do you say that?"

"Reddy was cheating all of us out of our pay. He was having terrible fights with Van, here, about the future of the company."

"That's not true!" Vanlandingham gasped indignantly.

Freddie Something sniffed again. "His affair with Deena was ending, and—"

"That's not true either!" the tall blond cried in outrage.

Mahafey's eyes sparkled with spite. "You had the best motive of all, Freddie. You're a has-been, and you can't stay off the booze. Reddy was going to let you go after this performance."

Freddie staggered back a step. "That's a lie. Just because you slept with him and then didn't get any better parts out of it, that doesn't mean—"

"You bitch!" Mahafey exclaimed.

"Now let's all hold it right there," Hunzicker snapped.

Lassiter walked on across the room and into the back hallway. It stood vacant, dusty. He looked right and left, trying to decide where to start. He decided to go to his left.

He had taken a dozen steps when someone yelled hoarsely behind him. Wheeling, he saw Still Bill Mills careen out of a doorway at the other end of the hall and come shambling in his direction at a high rate of speed.

Lassiter turned back and strode to meet the old man. Still Bill, out of breath and sickly pale, plucked at his jacket, tugging at him. "Come quick! Come quick! I found her, and she's been hurt real bad!"

Nausea rushed into Lassiter's throat. "Show me," he ordered.

Still Bill turned and hurried back the way he had come. Lassiter went as far as the rear door to the activity room. "Medic!" he shouted, and turned to run in pursuit of the custodian.

IF ANYONE HAD TOLD Lassiter that a man of Still Bill's age could rush down a flight of steps at such speed, he would never have believed them. By the time Lassiter reached the lower level and pushed through the back-swinging metal door to the concrete corridor beyond, the older man was almost out of sight again, ducking hurriedly through a doorway about ten feet to the right. Lassiter ran after him.

The door led into a storage area about twenty feet square— naked concrete walls, exposed piping and duct work overhead, cartons and crates of all sizes and descriptions stacked haphazardly everywhere. Bare light bulbs provided grayish overhead illumination. Still Bill Mills dodged around a stack of tattered cardboard cartons in the middle of the room and went out of sight. His voice echoed back: "Over here!" Lassiter followed, afraid of what he might find.

Beyond the boxes, in a clear spot on the dusty pavement, Laura lay sprawled on her back, a small smear of bright red blood on the side of her face. Still Bill Mills stood over her, wringing his hands.

Lassiter fell to his knees beside her. His hand shot out as he probed for the carotid. This time, thank the Good Lord, he felt the pulse instantly, strong and regular. Relief flooding hotly through him he gently felt her neck, looking for obvious damage to the spinal cord.

Laura's eyelids fluttered. She moaned and her eyes opened. They were dazed, unseeing for a moment. She gave a quick, frightened spasm and started to try to sit up.

"Hold on, hold on," Lassiter whispered urgently. He cradled her head on his thigh. "You're okay, babe. It's me. You're going to be fine."

Her lips opened and the words came out in a little croak. "Aaron?"

"Yeah, me. Lie still. Help is on the way."

She focused. "What happened?"

He touched gentle fingertips to the bloody spot on the side of her head, just at the hairline in front of her left ear. She winced but allowed it. He saw that the skin was broken, and like all scalp wounds it had bled profusely. But already purplish swelling had set in, shutting off the blood flow. Lassiter had had some paramedic training, in addition to checking more traffic accident victims than he liked to think about, and his experienced touch found no obvious sign of skull fracture.

"What happened?" Laura repeated hoarsely, dazed eyes watching him.

Two of the Norman paramedics hurried in, some of their equipment in hand. They took in the situation instantly and knelt on either side of Laura, nudging Lassiter out of the way. He stood, watching and feeling redundant, as one technician slapped a blood-pressure cuff on her while the other adjusted an inflatable collar around her neck and began the same kind of examination he had just done.

Still Bill Mills had tears in his eyes. "I don't think I would have ever found her so fast if she hadn't sorta moaned. I'd already been in here once, but I was hurrying—just gave it a quick look-see from the door, supercilious. So then I went down to the heater room and she wasn't there and I was on the way back to go outside but I decided to give this one an extraneous check. I don't know why. I guess it was an aspiration. Then she sorta moaned and I run in and there she was, like a chicken with her eyes plucked."

"Did you see any sign of anyone else?" Lassiter asked.

Still Bill shook his head. "No, and I was being obsequious, too. Fools rush in where they end up dead, I always say—"

Laura stirred and tried to sit up again. "Aaron? Aaron?"

Lassiter knelt again, taking her ice-cold hand. "Here."

One of the paramedics told him, "No sign of fracture, but we're transporting her to the ER in Norman."

"Right. I'm going with you."

"Aaron?" Laura murmured more urgently, sounding on the verge of panic.

Lassiter squeezed her hand. "It's all right, honey. You're safe. You're going to be just fine."

Her eyes stared, baffled and worried. "What happened?"

"It looks to me like somebody whacked you with something. Did you get a look at who did it?"

Her frown deepened. "Whacked? Me?"

"Tell me what you remember," Lassiter urged gently.

"Mrs. Epperman…"

"Yes?"

"Don't you remember?" she asked, sounding even more puzzled. "She told me to go out the back way—see if everything was all set for the next act."

"I remember, sure. What happened then?"

One of the paramedics, the red-haired one, hurried out of the room, evidently to get another gurney. Laura watched him go before turning back to stare again at Lassiter.

"Laura?" he said. "What happened then?"

She shook her head. "I don't remember."

Lassiter was thunderstruck. "You don't remember who hit you, you mean?"

"I don't remember anything."

TWELVE

A SECOND AMBULANCE was on the way. Leaving Laura in the hands of the medical emergency team, Lassiter bustled back upstairs to find the sheriff's crew and Detective Hunzicker closeted in the small activity room with a group that included members of the Redwine troupe. Mrs. Epperman had been brought in to join them. The doors to the atrium were closed.

Lassiter briefly reported what he had found.

Hunzicker scowled. "Have you interrogated her yet?"

Feeling all the eyes on him, Lassiter made the instant decision to broadcast as little information as possible. "No. She's still dazed."

The sheriff said, "You want to ride to the hospital, keep an eye on her?"

"Yes," Lassiter said gratefully.

"Call me here when you know more about her condition. I'll want you back here as soon as possible."

"Right."

Hunzicker turned back to the actors, who were standing wide-eyed. "Let's get back to what we were taking about."

George Vanlandingham patted at his face with a dark silk ascot. "It's just as I explained, Detective. We set up the stage and then locked the front doors because we didn't want anyone to look in and see the emergency room setup—it would simply have *destroyed* all the suspenseful illusion, don't you see? Reddy took his casual clothes for the scene in the hall behind the activity room—oh, dear, they may still be there, for all I know. The rest of us all left him back there...oh...it must have been three-ten or three-fifteen. He gave me the extra master key to lock the atrium doors on the outside in order that no one could peep in and see the set, or him, ahead of time.

I went back to my room and checked over my clue list to make sure all the necessary clues had been planted, and then at a little after three-thirty I came back to the atrium to make sure we had a nice crowd gathering, and to plant one more little clue. Then I went back to my room again briefly to change my shirt—I was simply drenched in perspiration after all the rushing about—and then I came back to the atrium again a bit before four-thirty.''

Hunzicker glowered at the circle of faces around him. ''Why were the lights turned out when the front doors were opened?''

''We didn't want anyone peeking in the moment we opened the doors, not until we were ready. Again, dramatic effect.''

''You finished the final setup on the stage a little before three-fifteen or so?''

''Yes,'' Deena Sweete said huskily, her eyes red from tears. ''All of us helped put the finishing touches on things—papers on the desk, and things like that—right after the scene that ended around three o'clock.''

''Of course,'' Franklin Pierce Lord intoned, ''most of the heavy setting up had been done earlier.''

''I'm not interested in that,'' Hunzicker snapped. ''What I want to know is what each of you was doing between the time you left Redwine alone back there about three-fifteen and when you discovered he was dead. About four-thirty.''

''I've told you my activities,'' Vanlandingham said, sighing.

''I,'' Lord said importantly, fitting a Chesterfield into the business end of his long holder, ''was in my room alone, rehearsing lines.''

''I took a walk out back,'' Deena Sweete said.

''I lay down for a while,'' Freddie Filmont said.

''I was in my room, talking long distance,'' Janis Mahafey said. She looked around defensively. ''All right, all of you might as well know it. I had a big argument with Reddy just before we came down here to give the final touches to the set.

He had had George cut my lines again. I was on the phone trying to get another gig."

Tad Raddell spoke last. "I was outside checking the van. We've had a slow leak on the right front, and I was trying to make sure the gas station in Ardmore fixed it the other day."

Hunzicker studied him. "I don't suppose anyone saw you out there."

Raddell's eyebrows rose. "Not that I know of."

"I don't suppose," Hunzicker said heavily, "any of you can prove what you were doing during the time when Redwine had to have been murdered, except for Ms. Mahafey."

No one spoke.

Hunzicker shot Lassiter and the sheriff a sour look. "So everybody leaves, the room lights are turned out, Redwine prepares to change clothes. That's about three-fifteen, three-twenty maybe. At a minute or two past four-thirty, the doors open and Redwine is dead. *Sometime* in there, Miss Michaels goes around the back way for a look-see and gets clobbered. And everybody is innocent. Does that about sum it up?"

One of the paramedics poked his head in the door and called to Lassiter, "We're rolling."

Lassiter went out and got to his cruiser as the big white-and-yellow Ford van rolled away. He followed closely. He noticed with some relief that they weren't using either siren or rack lights. She had to be okay, he told himself, or they would have run Code Three. He felt shaky and on the brink of tears.

At the hospital they took Laura directly into one of the examining alcoves off the main emergency-room entrance. As the officer on the scene, Lassiter found himself sitting at the desk used by the triage nurse. He had done this a thousand times before, for faceless victims. This time he heard a quake in his voice as he provided identification and the few details he felt he could give.

After that, he went to the front waiting room and paced back and forth, made a telephone call to the dispatcher to report his whereabouts and situation; had three cups of rancid coffee out of a machine, and waited some more.

Well over two hours later, a doctor finally came out. "Officer Lassiter?"

"Yes? Yes?"

"We're holding Ms. Michaels another couple of hours, just to be sure, but all the tests look fine. Concussion and mild shock, but no fractures or evidence of other internal injuries."

"Thank God for that," Lassiter said with feeling.

"She's a very lucky lady. She took a glancing blow, but the shape of the wound indicates a hard object swung with lethal intent. If it had hit an inch farther back on her skull, it might not have glanced off—could easily have driven bone fragments into the brain, killing her instantly."

"Can I see her?"

"Of course. Oh, by the way, she seems to be suffering from some temporary amnesia induced by the trauma to the head. Happens in cases of head injury sometimes. She seems very concerned about it."

"Is it something that will go away?" Lassiter asked quickly.

The doctor nodded. "Usually does."

"Usually?"

"Almost always."

"How soon?"

"No way to guess. Sometimes in a few hours, sometimes in days or even weeks...occasionally longer."

"Occasionally never?" Lassiter prodded, seeking the worst.

"Occasionally," the doctor conceded. "But certainly not often."

All the thoughts tumbled through Lassiter's brain at the same time. He was relieved, of course, she would be fine. He was taken aback that her amnesia seemed to have persisted past the first minutes of regained consciousness. Without her memory of what had happened, the entire mystery became infinitely more difficult.

And he could not see how the amnesia made Laura any more safe. The killer—whoever he was—wouldn't know she couldn't remember. That marked her.

THIRTEEN

FROM MAUDE THURINGER'S MYSTERY JOURNAL
They probably all did it. Just as I thought in the first place. Guess they won't finish the play now. Too bad. Had all clues listed, ready to nab killer, just as soon as I knew who victim was. Hope Laura M. OK.

AARON LASSITER WHEELED his sheriff's department cruiser into the curving front driveway at Timberdale. It was long after dark now, and only one other law-enforcement vehicle could be seen in the diagonal parking.

"You understand I don't approve of this," he muttered.

Seated beside him, Laura sucked the dregs out of her Braums milkshake container before replying. She still felt mildly woozy, and the headache was world-class. "I can't go home just yet, Aaron. I explained that—I've got to see what's happened out here. And for another thing, my car is here."

"We could have delivered your damned car." He wheeled the Ford into a parking place near the front canopy, jerked the radio microphone off its dashboard bracket, and held it close to his mouth. "County, this is unit three."

"County. Go ahead, three."

"Arrived at Timberdale."

"Ten-four."

He replaced the microphone and turned to Laura with perplexed concern. "You probably ought to have stayed in the hospital a day or two."

"Honey, I can't. Even if I didn't have obligations here, and school Monday, there's Trissie. Besides, I'm fine now."

"If you're fine, tell me what happened in that back hall—who hit you, and why."

Laura hesitated, looking into memory. Nothing. "I don't know yet."

Lassiter's voice grated with tension. "Then we've got a murderer running around in there, and he—or she—thinks you're a witness, and will be wanting to take you out permanently. So you just walk back in there."

"Aaron," Laura explained patiently, "you're right beside me. What can happen?"

"I can't always be with you!"

"Look at it this way. Pretend you're the killer. You conked me on the head but didn't manage to kill me. You must be waiting to see if I regain consciousness enough to identify you. But you hear I'm out of the hospital and back at Timberdale, yet nobody has come to take you into custody. *Then* you hear I can't remember a thing. So don't you just relax a little and stop worrying about me?"

She was so proud of her logic that she reached over and pinched his arm. "Don't you? Don't you?"

"Unless," Lassiter growled, "I figure amnesia can only be temporary, and I'd better kill you before your memory comes back."

"Pooh," Laura said, and climbed out of the car into the chill night. In truth, however, she hadn't thought of *that*. Suddenly she didn't feel nearly as secure.

She strode rapidly toward the Timberdale entrance, fighting the still-brisk wind. Lassiter hurried to catch up, then took her arm. "You won't listen to reason on this?"

"I'm not going to take any chances, Aaron. But I can't just go hide someplace, dammit. I've got a job here. I owe these people something—professional counseling, if they want it. They've had a terrible trauma here today."

He held the door for her. "What do you call what *you've* had?"

They blew into the atrium, which at this hour lay vast and deserted-looking and powered-down, with most of the lights dimmed. Laura waved to Stacy, the night receptionist, and started that way.

"There you are!" a female voice cried from the small front visiting alcove. High heels rattled on the tile of that area. "Your name is Lassiter, isn't it? Do you remember me? My God, this is all so horrible!"

Laura turned to see a tall, red-haired woman in a rainbow-colored nylon running suit rush out of the alcove to confront Lassiter. The woman seized his arm as if it were a life preserver. "Why did they tell me I had to sit right here until they came for me? Why can't I go to wherever they have poor Reddy's body? Who did this? What's going on?" She turned wide, hysterical eyes to Laura. "Who are you?"

Lassiter managed to extricate himself from the woman's grasp. "This is Mrs. Redwine," he said, and then asked her, "When did you arrive? How did you hear?"

Obviously frantic, Mrs. Redwine batted her eyelashes. "They found me at the Ramada Inn and notified me, of course. I came right out. Oh my God, I should have come out this afternoon when I learned where they were. But then I called and talked to George. He *promised* Reddy would return my call. How was I to know it was something bad when he didn't call me back? He never did what I asked him. I was just sitting there in that awful motel, watching educational TV and planning to come out tomorrow and have it out with him, and then they came for me."

Lassiter looked down at the tearful woman with genuine concern. "I'm real sorry, ma'am."

"I've been waiting here practically *forever*. Your sheriff, Mr. Davidson, said they wanted to interview me, and not to leave. But that was *hours* ago! Why am I being treated like a criminal?"

"I'm sure I don't have any answers right now," Lassiter said in a quiet, soothing tone. "Where is Bucky?"

"Who?"

"Sheriff Davidson, I mean."

She pointed, rattling several thin gold bracelets on her

skinny wrist. "Back there someplace. I don't know. I'm being treated terribly here, and I resent it. I want you to know that."

Lassiter glanced toward the back, where lights in the narrow doorway windows beside the dining hall entrance hinted at activity beyond. His chest heaved. "I'll tell you what, ma'am. This is Laura Michaels. She's a counselor here at Timberdale—Laura, why don't you take Mrs. Redwine back to your office and get her some coffee or something, and I'll track the sheriff down and try to get this thing sorted out a little."

Mrs. Redwine's bulging eyes swiveled to Laura. "Counselor? You work here? I suppose *you're* the reason he was so anxious to take this job in Oklahoma. Are you his latest little floozie? You're cute enough, I have to say that. Did he take this job so he could come up here and shack up with you over the weekend? Well, it wasn't the first time, honey. You're hardly special. I—"

"Let's go to my office," Laura suggested in her best therapist voice. "We can talk about it."

The woman stared back at Lassiter. "Must I?"

His forehead wrinkled. "It might be the fastest way to get this straightened out."

Mrs. Redwine scowled. "Oh, all right. Which way, Miss Whatever-Your-Name-Is?"

Laura led the way around the reception desk and Stacy Miller, who was so busy gaping that she had momentarily forgotten the white sack of Dunkin' Donuts in front of her. Lassiter bustled toward the dining area. Reaching her office, Laura turned on the lights and hurried to what felt like the relative safety of the far side of her desk.

"Sit down, Mrs. Redwine. Can I get you coffee or something?"

Mrs. Redwine flounced down in the chair that faced the desk, crossed long legs, and began tossing her foot with impatience. "What you can get me is a confession."

"Confession?"

"You *are* his latest little lover, aren't you!"

"I'm sorry, but you're way off base. I just met Mr. Redwine the other day, when he arrived here."

The accusing eyes widened. "You did?"

"Yes. And to tell you the truth, I thought he was a real jerk."

Mrs. Redwine's eyes flew open wide. "You can say that again! You're sure you weren't shacking up?"

"Very sure."

"Too bad more little cuties didn't feel that way. Don't ask *me* why, but a lot of women, especially younger women, seemed to really like him. He was a cheat and a liar and a damnable old fartface of a phony, but a lot of them just couldn't seem to wait to hop between the covers with him. Look at the people with him right now. He had an affair with that old drunk Freddie Filmont twenty or thirty years ago. He's been bedding Deena Sweete for months, and *now* I think he was starting in with the other girl, the new one, Janis Mahafey. My God, for all *I* know, he was even diddling George. Did you hear how they all just went off and left me in Forth Worth? Then he or somebody lists *me* as missing! I don't know what kind of nefarious scheme he had in the back of his mind. Maybe he thought he could lose me and then try to collect on my insurance. I wouldn't put it past him. He's been broke and we both have big insurance policies. Which makes me think of something. I guess I can collect on his policy now...unless he cashed it in sometime behind my back. I wouldn't put that past him, either. Cheat me just once more, from the grave. He was nothing but grief for me for ages. He lies, he cheats, he steals money, he never gave me anything, he had these constant shoddy little assignations with his corps of starstruck nymphets—we're all better off with him dead, if you want to know the truth."

Laura fell into her therapist mode without thought. "But you stayed with him."

"Of course I stayed with him!"

"If he was such a bad person—why?"

Mrs. Redwine looked stunned. "Why, because I loved him, of course!"

A movement in the office doorway interrupted. Laura looked up to see Maude Thuringer, wearing a long flannel robe and fuzzy bunny-rabbit slippers. Pink plastic curlers stuck out all over her head.

"Laura!" the old woman exclaimed. "You *are* back!"

"Not now, Maude," Laura said quickly.

Maude slipped in, producing her clipboard from behind her back. "What did you witness in the back hallway?"

"I have total amnesia," Laura told her. "Spread the word. Excuse us now, Maude."

"Total amnesia! Wow! Shades of Phyllis Whitney, that's her favorite plot. Let me ask—"

Laura cut in much more firmly. "*Excuse* us now, Maude."

Maude looked up sharply from her notes, read Laura's expression, glanced at Mrs. Redwine, and scurried out the door.

Mrs. Redwine asked, "Have you got any vodka?"

"I'm afraid not," Laura told her. "How about coffee? Or Coke?"

The older woman's expression softened with momentary optimism. "I don't suppose you mean nose candy."

"What?" It took Laura a second or two to get it. "Oh! No. Sorry."

"Coffee then," Mrs. Redwine said with resignation.

LAURA AND LASSITER had reached Timberdale at almost ten p.m., and Laura's watch showed almost eleven when Lassiter, with Sheriff Bucky Davidson along, appeared in her office. Davidson's round face was unreadable as usual, but he looked tired. Lassiter's scowl had deepened.

"It's about time!" Mrs. Redwine told them.

Davidson, a squat, plump man with a very big revolver strapped on his belt, ignored her. "Ms. Michaels, Deputy Lassiter tells me you can't remember a thing."

"I'm afraid that's right, Sheriff."

"Shit," he muttered almost under his breath.

Rebecca Redwine shrilled, "I demand satisfaction, Sheriff! Have you caught my poor husband's killer?"

"Not yet, ma'am," Davidson said heavily. "Now, if you'd accompany Deputy Lassiter, he wants to take you into the next office and ask you just a few questions."

"Questions? ask *me* questions? What about all the questions *I* want to ask?"

"He'll sure answer them, ma'am, to the best of his ability."

Mrs. Redwine, lips tight with anger, got to her feet and left the office behind Lassiter.

Davidson sank into the chair she had just vacated and began patting his forehead with a handkerchief. "What a day. You don't have any more coffee, do you?"

Laura pointed silently at the carafe she had brought in earlier from the coffee room down the hall. He grunted and poured himself a cup, then leaned back in the chair and studied her. "How do you feel?"

"A little confused still, but not bad."

"Close call."

"Yeah."

"Can't remember anything at all?"

"I'm afraid not. Believe me, Sheriff, I *wish* I could remember."

"Would make things a lot simpler."

"You've been interviewing people all these hours since it happened?"

"Yep, except for forty minutes off when all the TV stations in the world came roaring in on us to shoot tape for the ten o'clock news. I put a man on the job of watching the local channels later." Davidson clucked with disgust. "They went nuts over it. Lead story everywhere locally. 'Murder play gets real,' stuff like that." He looked thoughtful. "I wish there wasn't any TV."

"What have you learned so far?" Laura asked.

"Not a whole hell of a lot, if you want to know the truth. We've got the room where the body was found closed off with tape, and also the back halls and belowdecks. Our first search didn't reveal a whole lot—some bloodstains on the floor of that room down below where the cots and wheelchairs and that Timberdale gurney are stored; couple of drops on the carpet in the service elevator back there that might be blood—we won't be sure till we get a lab report—and a pair of broken reading glasses up against the hallway wall near the equipment storage room."

"Then the glasses might have belonged—" Laura began.

"Just what we were hoping, for ten or fifteen minutes there." Davidson made a face. "Then this George Vanlandingham character showed us where the broken glasses were a clue in the script for this thing. He says one of Redwine's last-minute jobs was to go down and break 'em and plant 'em before the four o'clock scene."

"They were planting clues all over the place," Laura confirmed, disappointed.

"Well, we're going to be going over everything with a really fine-tooth comb starting in the morning. I hope we find some real stuff along with whatever other crap they had planted."

Laura studied his pudgy, cynical face. "You haven't found anything else?"

"The door to Redwine's room back here on One East was standing wide open when somebody went back there after his body was found. Inside, the bedroom is a mess—stuff was pulled out of drawers, filing boxes, and a big steamer trunk, and thrown all over the place. It looks like somebody got in there either right before the murder or right after, looking for something."

"But no one saw anybody?"

"Nope."

"The door was broken in, you say?"

"Nope, I didn't say that. Somebody used a key."

"Redwine's key?"

The sheriff's burly shoulders rose and fell in a shrug. "Dunno. He had two keys on his room key ring, your boss says. The ring was in his pants pocket, but there was only one key on it. Somebody must have removed the other one and used that to get into his room.''

''The killer?'' Laura surmised.

''We'd settle for that theory,'' the sheriff agreed, and thoughtfully sipped his coffee. ''Man, I'm tired. Well. This ain't going to be an easy one. It's practically your classic locked-room case, and it seems like practically everybody around here had a fairly decent motive for killing that so-and-so.''

''I was afraid of that.''

The sheriff looked off into a corner of the ceiling and ticked points off on his blunt fingers. He seemed to be talking to himself. ''He's been holding back money on members of the cast. Some of them think he got a check from your boss yesterday, or earlier, and went to Norman and cashed it. That looks like a good theory; we found a big wad of money hidden in the bottom of his desk drawer.''

Davidson heaved a sigh and went on. ''He had been sleeping with this Sweete lady. They'd had some heavy-duty fights lately, but she says she spent the night with him here Wednesday night, just after they got here. The Mahafey woman went nuts when she heard that—says Redwine was in love with *her*, and was planning to disband the company in order to take her to Hollywood and set up her career as a big star. The older gal, Freddie, says Redwine was going to fire her for no good reason. Even Raddell, the younger guy, was hacked because he had the hots for Mahafey and knew Redwine was beating his time. And that big Dodge van belongs to him, and Redwine had been promising forever to compensate him for the company using it all the time. But all Raddell was getting was his van worn out.

''I had about started to cross Franklin Lord off my suspect list, but then I learned he had been complaining about not getting any decent parts, and sometime during the drive up here from Dallas earlier in the week, he actually told Redwine he'd better pay up and be more fair with the good male parts or Redwine would be, quote, permanently sorry, unquote.

"Even this guy Vanlandingham has a possible motive. He thought he owned half the company with Redwine. Very funny. Redwine took all his money to invest in it, right? But the partnership papers were never finalized. Vanlandingham ends up with nothing."

The sheriff sipped his coffee and made a face. "Your Mrs. Epperman has a motive. He jacked the price up on her so late in the game she had no choice but to pay. Your handyman, Mills, got yelled at and insulted, I understand. Mrs. Epperman says one of your residents got bilked out of a large sum of money by Redwine many years ago, and is still bitter about it. Good God, Redwine had a genius for hacking people off. He insulted people all over this place, even your cook. And he *sure* made his wife mad enough, dumping her in Fort Worth and then listing her missing, to make her look like some kind of nut case that maybe he could more easily divorce."

Laura nodded. "Complicated."

"'Complicated' ain't the word for it," Davidson grunted. Then he stopped abruptly and looked hard at her.

"What?" Laura said.

"You're good," he told her.

"What?"

His grin looked rueful. "How do you do that—just sit there and nod and look interested, and get somebody to spill everything to you? Some kind of therapist's trick, right?"

Inwardly Laura checked her memory and found that baffling vacancy still there. She did not try to explain the lurking fear that she would not be wholly safe again until Redwine's killer had been arrested.

Feeling a chill, she hugged herself. "I just like to listen, Sheriff. That's all."

Sheriff Davidson's crooked smile broadened. "Right. And Michael Jordan just likes to shoot buckets, that's all. Right."

"What will happen to Mrs. Redwine?" Laura asked.

"Good question. Salt will get a pretty good preliminary statement in there tonight, that's for sure. Tomorrow, we go over everything with everybody again down at the courthouse, with the DA running the interrogations and recording it all, and so forth. If Mrs. Redwine looks like a suspect at that point, she stays around while we poke some more. If not, I suppose she would be free to go.''

"She says she didn't know anything until your officer contacted her.''

"That's what she says.''

"You believe her?''

Davidson gave an elaborate shrug. "I've had somebody go ahead and check out a couple of things right away. She was in our office early in the afternoon. She'd driven up in a car she rented in Fort Worth, so she had transportation to go anywhere and do anything. She says she drove around town a while and then took a nap at the motel. We got no verification of any of that. It's possible she learned where he was, drove out here, found him, shot him, somehow got him up on that table, hit you on the head when you walked in on her, and then drove back to Norman and waited to come out later and be real shocked, and so forth.''

"It doesn't sound very plausible,' Laura said gently.

"No, it sure doesn't.''

"Where was the gun he was shot with?''

Davidson glared. "You tell me.''

"I beg your pardon?''

"We haven't found it yet.''

Laura must have registered surprise because the sheriff glowered and added instantly, "It's not like this place is small and easy to search.''

"I know that. I'm just startled.''

"If you want to be 'startled,' think about somebody being shot with a small-caliber weapon, probably a .22, maybe a .25, and people all over the area, and nobody hearing the shot.''

"Maybe the killer used a silencer.''

"Silencers on small-bore weapons ain't your everyday thing.''

"Then what—''

"I'm not saying it wasn't a silencer. Could have been.

Makes sense. But if it was, then we're putting the crime on the shoulders of somebody with some savvy and professional equipment. And none of these suspects we've got fit that category, that I can see.''

Laura studied the sheriff's beefy face. ''Then you've already made a list of possible suspects?''

''Yes,'' he replied bitterly. ''I told you that. Everybody in the acting company. Your boss, Mrs. Epperman. Your handyman, Mills. Your chef. Mrs. Redwine.''

''Colonel Rodgers,'' Laura blurted before thinking about it.

Davidson jerked. ''Who?''

Damn. There was nothing to do but explain now. ''A resident you've heard about, Colonel Rodgers.''

''The old military nut. Right.''

''He says Redwine bilked him out of a large investment several years ago. They had words about it right here in this office.''

Out came a battered leather notebook and a ballpoint. ''So he's the one. Thank you very much. I need more suspects.''

Laura refreshed her coffee. ''Sheriff, am I going to be able to go home?''

His eyebrows arched. ''Matter of being in danger?''

''Might I be?''

He leaned over in the chair, elbows on knees, and locked large hands. ''Everybody knows you survived. We made it a point to let the word spread about how you couldn't remember anything—I thought it would keep the killer from running, in any case, and you would come back and finger him for us. Now it's harder. Shit, maybe you'll never remember. But the killer—whoever he is—has been sitting tight so far. Now you're out of the hospital and we still ain't coming for him. Therefore, best thing for him to do is keep on sitting tight and bluff it through if he can. Of course, he might be thinking, 'Take her out for good and remove the chance she'll remember later.' On the other hand, he takes a big risk by striking again.'' He sighed and sat up straight. ''I'm assigning Lassiter to you. He's going to stick to you like glue until something breaks. Of course nobody can guarantee your safety every minute of the day and night. But I don't see what more I can do." He paused again and studied her face. "If you're scared, I can recommend leave for you."

"Leave?"

"Take your daughter and bug out for a couple of weeks."

"I can't do that. She's in school. I'm in school. I've got this job."

The sheriff spread his hands.

"I'll hang in," Laura decided. "I have to."

He nodded, then glanced toward the door. "Salt ought to be getting back."

"I'm going to call my daughter. I talked with her from the hospital and made sure she knows I'm okay, but she's with a neighbor. She might be getting worried again."

"Good idea."

By the time Laura had talked to Trissie, Aaron Lassiter had come back, scowling with worry. "I'll be there soon to pick you up, honey," Laura assured her daughter. "I'm just fine." She hung up and looked up at Lassiter, standing mute until she finished.

"I didn't get anything much out of the lady," he said.

"Why ain't I surprised?" Davidson muttered.

"What now?"

The sheriff got ponderously to his feet. "Nothing to do but let her loose, make sure she understands she isn't to leave the area. You can go with Ms. Michaels." He glanced at Laura again. "You don't have to stay any more tonight on my account."

Laura stood too. "Then we'll go."

"Your boss is back in the clinic with your doctor. Seems she got a humdinger of a migraine and had to go lie down. You want to talk to her before you go?"

Laura thought about it for approximately five seconds. "I'll just go."

Davidson turned back to Lassiter. "Salt, until further notice, you're full-time on this case, and your primary responsibility is her safety. Oh, hell, wait a minute, you're on your days off.''

"I'll do it anyway," Lassiter said quickly.

"I got no money for this kind of overtime, Salt."

"I'll do it anyway."

The sheriff glanced from Lassiter to Laura and back again. Laura saw him drawing all the right conclusions. "Fine," he said at last. "I got Regan on guard in back. He'll be here all night. We got the Norman PD and the state crime lab coming in the morning. Maybe we'll turn up something good then. See you here at that time."

Lassiter helped Laura into her lightweight coat. They walked out past the reception desk, toward the front doors.

Lassiter put a protective arm through hers. "I'll stay there with you."

"All right," she said instantly.

"I can sleep on the couch."

She moved closer to his side. "You don't have to sleep on the couch, Aaron."

He colored slightly. "Maybe under the circumstances I ought to be...kind of official."

"Oh. Right."

Nearing the doors, she glanced back and was struck by how normal everything appeared. Only the easel hinted there had been the start of a mystery melodrama. A visitor certainly would never have guessed that anything bad had happened. *Then why do I have this quivery fear inside me right now?*

Lassiter held the door for her. They went outside. The north wind hit them hard. Tonight it would freeze. Winter had come.

FOURTEEN

"COWABUNGA!" Trissie murmured, coming to the breakfast table and holding up the front page of the morning's *Daily Oklahoman.* The Redwine murder had made the top left of the front page—the number two position; a large headline read "Pretend Murder/Becomes Real/in Norman Play."

"Sit down and eat your cereal," Laura said, trying to take the paper from her.

Trissie, bright-eyed and ready for school, took the chair next to Aaron Lassiter's, but hunched over the paper as she read avidly. "Hey! You both made it here! Listen: 'Laura Michaels, assistant manager, was struck on the head by an assailant she did not see. Michaels was treated at Norman Regional Hospital and later released. Deputy sheriff Aaron Lassiter was the first law-enforcement officer on the scene.'"

Laura smiled at Lassiter, morning-pale and handsome in his uniform. In the daylight things didn't seem quite so spooky. "We're famous."

"It says here," Trissie persisted, "'Sheriff Davidson said the investigation is ongoing.' What does that mean?"

"It means we don't have a thing," Lassiter told her.

"Oh."

"Come on, guys," Laura prodded. "Tris, you've got five minutes to get next door for your ride. We've got ten before we have to head for Timberdale."

Trissie put the paper down and looked up at Laura with suddenly clear worry. She stared at the bandage on the side of Laura's head. "You're really okay?"

"Yes, honey, I am."

"You're really really *really* okay?"

Laura bent and gave her a quick hug, managing finally to

extract the newspaper from her grasp. "Eat, or *you* won't be okay!"

Trissie gulped a few bites and was gone. When Laura and Lassiter left a few minutes later, the wind had subsided and the sun was trying to get through low, turgid, gray clouds. It was comforting to look in the rearview mirror of her Toyota and see the nose of the sheriff's cruiser close behind.

At Timberdale, despite the early hour, the TV mobile unit trucks were all over the entrance driveway. Parked at odd angles among the hulking news trucks with their pop-up antenna towers, Laura saw two other sheriff's cruisers and one black-and-white Norman police car. There seemed to be a mob of reporters and cameramen packed in around someone under the front canopy.

Laura wheeled around to the side parking lot. Lassiter pulled in right beside her. Taking another look at the mess out front, Laura pointed to the side service door, half-concealed by a Dumpster and nearby shrubs. "My key will let me in that way."

Lassiter's protective hand closed on her arm. "Go."

Hurrying, they entered Timberdale by the side door. It took them into the west hallway behind the clinic area. Laura led the way around a corner and started past the clinic. Through the open door she caught a glimpse of three residents in the waiting room chairs, and Nurse Kay Svendsen standing behind the desk. As soon as Svendsen saw her, she got up and hurried toward the door. "Laura!"

Laura stopped in her tracks, Lassiter beside her. Svendsen bustled out, eyes darting with worry. "I guess you saw all the TV people out front?"

"Yes," Laura began, "but—"

"Then I guess you know?"

"Know? Know what?"

"They've arrested Colonel Rodgers."

JUDITH EPPERMAN strode furiously back and forth in her office, heavy black shoes clumping on the carpet, reading glasses bouncing around on her chest. "It's outrageous! It's unforgivable! How could anyone think that poor old dear would commit a murder?"

Lassiter, still close by Laura's side, looked solemn. "You heard what the sheriff said. They found a .22 pistol hidden in some trash behind the furnace. It had been fired recently. It's the same caliber as the one that killed Redwine. The colonel admits it's his gun."

"But he says it must have been stolen!"

"He had a motive. He admits he threatened Redwine. He hadn't reported the weapon missing."

"But that's all circumstantial!" Mrs. Epperman stamped a heavy foot. "You can't just arrest an old man on circumstantial evidence alone. Even I know that. Just last week, on the Sunday night movie, Perry Mason—"

"He hasn't been charged yet," Lassiter explained patiently. "He'll be held and questioned—"

"But he's not a young man! He's had an honorable military career. It isn't fair to him."

Laura could not remember seeing Timberdale's manager this deeply concerned about a resident. She was touched. "I know how you feel, Mrs. Epperman. I really do. But he's strong. He'll get through this. We both know he couldn't have done it. He'll be proven innocent. It may take a little time, but—"

"We don't have any time!" Mrs. Epperman shot back. "The publicity will be ruinous. I can see it now: 'Timberdale Retirement Center houses a murderer.' We'll *never* lease those vacant units."

Laura finally got it. She didn't say anything.

Lassiter fidgeted. "I've got to go talk to the sheriff. I guess that was him out there in front with the TV people. Maybe I can pry him loose...get updated on what's going on here."

"Ask him when all of you will be getting out of here so we can try to return to normal," Mrs. Epperman said. "This commotion is terrible. If it keeps up much longer, we'll have residents wanting to cancel their contracts and move out; we promised them peace and quiet, not this kind of furor. Laura, maybe you can help, use some of your little psychobabble.''

Laura caught Lassiter's quick glance, but showed nothing. ''What do you suggest, Mrs. Epperman?''

''Everyone is out in the atrium, walking around and whispering rumors and just *hysterical.* That horrible old Maude Thuringer is running all over the place, spreading the most incredible stories. Go out there. Try to calm them down. Make sure to remind them that Pierre promised eggs Benedict for breakfast this morning. Get them talking about that.'' She dropped into her desk chair and began rummaging furiously through the top drawer. ''I knew it, I knew it. I can feel another migraine coming on.''

Frowning blackly, Lassiter went away. Laura gladly escaped the Epperman office and headed for the atrium.

Mrs. Epperman's description had not been far off. Usually at this early hour only a handful of residents were near the dining room doors, jockeying for position. This morning everyone seemed to be down early and all over the place. Laura had no sooner walked out from behind the reception desk when Ellen Smith detached herself from a nearby group and came over to her. ''Laura, it's *terrible!*''

''I know,'' Laura said sympathetically, patting Ellen's leather-fringed shoulder. ''We just have to hope other evidence is found soon—something to clear poor Colonel Rodgers.''

''More important,'' Smith snapped, ''how much longer are they going to keep the large activity room sealed off the way it is? When are they going to be *out* of here?''

''Well, I suppose they might be clearing out later today. Why?''

Smith put a silver-encrusted hand on her hip. ''Have you forgotten? Doesn't anyone around here care about the serious arts anymore? I'm supposed to have a showing starting Monday. I have to get in there sometime today at the latest if I'm to have all my paintings hung in time.''

Old Judge Emil Young drifted over, wobbly on his cane,

along with Mr. and Mrs. Stoney Castle. The judge nodded
solemnly at Smith's last pronouncement. "I feel reasonably
confident, Ellen, that I can assure you the law-enforcement
officers will indeed vacate said domain with efficacious celerity now that a suspect has been identified."

"Yeah," Stoney Castle said, glum. "Pin it on an innocent
man and bug out. That's what Maude Thuringer said a few
minutes ago. She said she's got clues that point—"

"Contentiousness and idle speculation," the judge told him,
"will in no way vitiate the preponderance of evidentiary certitude pointing to Colonel Rodgers at the present juncture."

"You think the colonel killed that blubbery jerk?"

"Sir, my opinion is of no consequence. But I do have some
insight into the workings of the constabulary. Having identified a suspect, they will complete their investigation with no-
table celerity, lest further inquiry might result in uncovering
additional facts which might paradoxically weaken, rather than
bolster, the theoretical edifice already constructed. They will
do everything in their power now to close the probe quickly
and—to employ the vernacular—pin it on him."

Maude Thuringer rushed into view from a larger group beginning to sift closer to the closed dining room doors. She
stopped halfway across the atrium and frantically waggled a
handful of papers at Laura, signaling her to hurry.

Laura sighed. "Will you excuse me?" She walked over.
Maude ducked into the small room where resident mailboxes
filled one wall. Laura followed. If she could quiet Maude
down, she thought, maybe things would get calmer.

"I've got something neat!" Maude told her, closing the
door for privacy.

"Maude, you've got to try to calm down. Everyone is already upset. We have to pull together on this. We don't
need—"

"It's a copy of the script!" Maude flapped a sheaf of dog-
eared pages.

"Where did you get that?" Laura demanded. "Did you

steal it? Maude, what are we going to *do* with you? That was a bad thing.''

"Ends justify the means! Ends justify the means! Hercule Poirot. Look! According to this, old man Abercrombie was supposed to be in the ER—that's what us insiders call the emergency room—with a stab wound. He—''

"Maude, my God—''

"Listen. This is *good*. He was supposed to be in the ER with a stab wound. *Then* the kid playing the doctor was supposed to go out into the back hall, saying he was going to get additional medical help, and *then* he was supposed to rush back in and say *another* victim was being rushed in from Timberdale, and *then* George Vanlandingham, in a cop suit, was supposed to come in and announce Brick Abercrombie was dead, maybe from poison!''

Laura fought to maintain her sanity. "That's impossible. Tad Raddell played Brick and he was already onstage, playing the doctor.''

"We're not talking about the real people, Laura. We're talking about the characters.''

That was true. But Laura couldn't see what any of it meant anyway. "I don't see—''

"Of course you don't, but I do!'' Maude waved the papers again. "Think about it! The script called for Vanlandingham to come in wearing a cop suit. So he should have been there in the back hall, in his outfit. But he wasn't. He was still out in the atrium. How come he wasn't following the script, unless he knew Redwine was going to be really dead and the script didn't matter?''

"JESUS CHRIST,'' Aaron Lassiter said, holding the script. "Does this really say that?''

"Yes!'' Maude chirped, triumphant. "Page seven.''

Lassiter glanced at Laura. "We'd better get this cleared up right away. Have you seen Vanlandingham?''

Maude volunteered, "He was in his room less than fifteen minutes ago.''

Lassiter, eyebrows tight, started to turn away.

"I'll go with you," Laura said.

"Okay. I might want a witness. Come on."

"Me, too," Maude said.

"No."

"But I'm the one who—"

"No, dammit. Come on, Laura."

They left the mail room and walked down the back hallway, leaving Maude behind.

"She might really be on to something," Lassiter told Laura. "Stranger things have happened. I just hope the sucker is still in his room. We need to get this ironed out before the sheriff heads back to town in a few minutes."

The corridor was empty and quiet. Reaching the room assigned to Vanlandingham, Lassiter rapped on the door. Laura stood by, her nerves jumpy. If Maude Thuringer had actually come up with a meaningful clue, she thought, her whole opinion of the old lady had to be reevaluated.

The door opened and Tad Raddell, barefoot, in corduroy pants and a light sweater, peered out. Behind him, the apartment living room seemed to be aswirl in smoke. He looked startled to see Lassiter in uniform.

"What are you doing here?" Lassiter demanded. "Isn't this Vanlandingham's room?"

Raddell's eyes went wide with worry. "Yes, it is! I'm just visiting. We were talking about what happens to the company now—"

"Is Vanlandingham here?"

"Yes." Raddell's eyes darted guiltily. "I'll—send him out."

"We'll come in," Lassiter said, and pushed past him into the smoky room. "Mr. Vanlandingham?"

Laura followed, leaving the stunned Raddell in the doorway. Once inside, she instantly understood one reason he looked so nervous. The smoke carried the unmistakable odor of marijuana.

Vanlandingham, fully dressed in Levi's, sweatshirt and sandals, was just getting up hurriedly from the corner desk, which was covered with what looked like legal documents and correspondence. A small metal file box stood on the corner of the desk.

Lassiter told him, "We have some questions."

"I wasn't doing it," Vanlandingham said. "I don't use it. It's Tad. Dammit, Tad, I told you—"

Lassiter waved the pages. "According to this script, you were supposed to be in the hallway behind the activity room, wearing a police officer's uniform."

Vanlandingham stared. "What?"

Raddell hurried into the other room. A toilet flushed.

Lassiter ignored it. Holding the script pages up, he said, "Why weren't you in the back hall, in an officer's uniform, the way the script says you should have been?"

Vanlandingham looked dazed. "What are you *talking* about?"

"This script," Lassiter replied patiently. "It says—"

Vanlandingham grabbed the pages out of his hand and glanced at them. "Where did you get this?"

"That doesn't matter."

"*This* isn't the script we were using," Vanlandingham said, aggrieved. "Who stole this? The last time I saw it, I think I forgot and left it on the table in the dining room."

"Once more," Lassiter said. "Why—"

"I wasn't supposed to be in a cop outfit," Vanlandingham cut in.

"It says—"

"Sure, it says that. But this isn't the script we were using. We had an almost total revision." The little man turned and shuffled madly through some of the stacks on the desk, knocking pages of letters to the carpet. He retrieved what he wanted—a thicker sheaf of pages, much fresher, in gray paper covers that Laura recognized from seeing them in his hand during preparations yesterday. "*This* is the script we were playing for Timberdale," he said, agitated and beginning to sound resentful. "What in the hell do you mean, bursting in this way and asking these questions? Where did you get this old script? What's going on here, anyway?"

FIFTEEN

LOCKED IN the manager's office, with a deputy standing by in the hall to prevent interruptions, Sheriff Bucky Davidson angrily flipped through pages of his battered old leather notebook. Mrs. Epperman sat glumly behind her desk and Laura and Lassiter sat in chairs at the side.

The sheriff's voice dripped disgust. "Just so nobody else gallops off on some other stupid side trip, I want to review for you exactly where we stand on this investigation, and where we go from here." He looked at Lassiter. "So we don't have any more Lone Ranger crap."

Lassiter went dark red and looked down at his knuckles.

The sheriff looked down at his notebook. "We seem to have the murder weapon. Ballistics tests won't be available from the state until late Monday, but the caliber checks out. The gun was found near the murder scene, and it belongs to Colonel Rodgers, known to have an old, serious gripe with the victim. We have testimony that Rodgers went after Redwine right in one of these offices not long after the actors got here. Rodgers wasn't in the audience. He hadn't been around all day. He alleges he was in his room, not wanting to take any part in the mystery-weekend stuff. He's got no witnesses for that alibi. He's been taken into custody. He'll be arraigned Monday morning."

A page or two flipped over. "The medical examiner says Redwine had been dead an hour or two—no more, and maybe less—when they found him in the activity room. There was little blood on that gurney he was laid out on. We found some more blood downstairs, where the gurney was usually stored. Also some drops that are probably blood in the elevator. So we think he was shot downstairs, put on the gurney, brought up in the elevator, and rolled into the activity room. We theorize that somebody lured him down to the storage room, closed the door, and shot him in there—the concrete walls and ceiling would swallow up a little twink from a .22. Then the perpetrator hauled him upstairs to the activity room because it was the one place that was locked, with the lights out, and scheduled to stay that way a while.''

Flip.

"The only person who might shed additional light on this thing is you, Ms. Michaels. But I guess you still can't remember who hit you, or anything else?"

Laura looked into her mind for an instant and found nothing there but the baffling haze. "No. I'm sorry."

"Well, I am too, and that's the truth. But what we figure happened is, the colonel was about to roll the gurney into the activity room when you walked up the hall to check on things. You saw the whole deal. The colonel hammered you with something, deposited Redwine, looked you over and decided you were dead, and dragged you downstairs to put you out of sight as long as possible."

"Why would he do all that?" Laura asked. "Why not just put me in the activity room too?"

The sheriff frowned. "Maybe because there was a script reason for one body to be in the activity room, but anyone of the cast who went in would immediately know something was wrong if they saw two. Maybe the old codger figured you were better hid downstairs. Or maybe he just panicked, who knows?"

"But I couldn't have walked up and surprised him the way you described," Laura protested.

"Why?"

"Because the person who hit me came up from behind me."

"How do you know that? You don't remember anything!"

Laura met the sheriff's keen eyes and felt a deep chill. For an instant—and only for that long—something had been in her mind: a fragmentary picture. Someone. The gurney. Someone bending over it. Someone...something...on the gurney. A sound. Starting to turn. Pain.

Nothing more.

The bit of memory had occurred out of nowhere. Now as she tried to examine it, it vanished. That part of her mind was blank again. She had nothing. Only a quick, deep terror that made her shiver with cold.

Lassiter said worriedly, "Laura?"

She turned to him. "I don't know. I guess I didn't have any reason to say that. I thought—I remembered something."

"What?" the sheriff snapped.

"I'm sorry. It's gone again."

Davidson studied her for an uncomfortably long time. "Well, all right. It would sure make things simpler if you remembered. We'll just have to keep on keeping on with what we've got."

Flip, flip.

"We're continuing a search for additional evidence with the help of the Norman police and a couple of guys from the state. They're going over the colonel's rooms now. Then they'll go back over the activity room, the back hall, elevator and stairs, and the rooms below. We're ordering members of the acting company to stay here through the rest of the weekend. I've told Mrs. Redwine not to leave the area. Aaron, I'm putting you in charge out here. I can't spend the rest of my life on this case; I've got a lot of other things to do too."

Mrs. Epperman stirred. "And we need to start trying to get back to normal. This has been terrible for our morale, not to mention our public relations."

The notebook snapped closed. "Anything else? No? Good. Aaron, take over. I'm outta here. Oh. And try not to take too many more clues from that old hag with the Sherlock Holmes complex, okay? This is really a stupid, messed-up case, but I think maybe we can hang it on the old guy all right if nobody messes up."

THE SHERIFF departed and the last of the TV crewmen vanished, perhaps in pursuit to the courthouse. Lassiter grimly said he had to check with the search technicians still working on the building's lower level. Mrs. Epperman said she felt a migraine coming on. "Laura, it's imperative for someone to stay on duty right through the weekend. Can you arrange something for your daughter so you can do that?"

Dismayed, Laura thought about it. "Trissie went in today for a special field trip to the Omniplex. But—"

"You can arrange something, dear. I know you can. We owe it to the poor old dears to provide leadership and advice at this time, isn't that so? And you're so wonderfully qualified, with your psychological things. That's a dear. We can't afford any overtime; I'm sure you understand how that is. But we'll arrange compensatory time off sometime, right? It's your willingness to take on extra responsibility like this that makes me keep you on the payroll, dear, even though our last quarterly earnings statements gave me *every* justification for eliminating your position. You're a dear. Thank you."

Laura made arrangements for her daughter. She felt bad about it. Next weekend her ex-husband had privileges, and she wouldn't see Trissie for almost three days. She swallowed her disappointment and tried to get with the program.

Within thirty minutes Lassiter was back in her office with two plastic bags in hand. "They found some additional stuff." He carefully put the bags on the corner of her desk. "Do they mean anything to you?"

In one of the bags Laura saw a small, vicious-looking silver dagger with colored glass stones embedded in the ornate handle. The other bag contained a small, vicious-looking black revolver.

"What's commonly called a Saturday night special," Lassiter told her. "El cheapo. Holds five .22 shots. Wasn't loaded. They found it in the boxes of junk in the room where you were discovered. They're going through all the rest of the stuff now in case there's something else, or maybe the rounds were tossed in separately. Doesn't smell like it's been fired in a long time, though."

"Then it couldn't be the murder weapon?"

"No, but what was it doing down there?"

"What was the dagger doing down there?"

"That's something I'd like to know too. Maybe they're more of those damned script clues. We'll go ask Vanlandingham in a minute. I want to go back and ask the cast a few more things anyway."

Laura studied his face. "Then you don't buy the theory that the colonel did it, either."

He shook his head. "I don't know what the hell I believe on this one. He just doesn't seem like the type to me. And the sheriff is whistling in the dark, too, and he knows it. We don't have enough to convict a known felon, much less an old war hero with a record as spotless as a saint's."

"Oh, good," Laura said, intensely relieved. "Then he'll get out of jail soon."

"Huh! Maybe, if he can afford it." Lassiter saw her questioning look. "If we don't come up with anything better, the DA will want to hold him."

"But you said—"

"I know what I said. But you don't just admit you have no bloody idea who did the deed. If you've got even a half-assed case on somebody, you go for it. Any suspect to charge is better than no suspect at all, and who knows? You can always get lucky with a stupid jury on something like this."

Laura didn't say anything. She wondered if there was any practical purpose to her ability to be dismayed.

Lassiter patted his tunic pockets for his notebook and pen. "I'm going to go around the cast and ask a few more questions. I'd like you to go with me, if you can."

She smiled without humor. "To keep me safe?"

An eyebrow tilted. "That. But also because of your training. You can read people sometimes. If somebody is lying, or sweating me out, maybe you can pick up on it."

GEORGE VANLANDINGHAM was first. Laura and Lassiter didn't even have to go to his room. When they walked out of the office area, they found the slender little man busily folding up the easel and poster in the front of the atrium. Lassiter led the way over to talk to him.

Vanlandingham looked up nervously at his approach. "Now look, officer. I am *deeply* chagrined about that scene in the room. I have told Tad a hundred times—"

"I have just a couple of additional questions to ask you," Lassiter broke in, "and it doesn't have anything to do with that incense burning in your room."

Vanlandingham's lower lip trembled. "Incense? Oh! Yes. Terrible stuff. The room hasn't been occupied for a while, and there was this musty odor, you see—"

"What are the plans for the Redwine company once everything is squared away here?"

The small man frowned and tugged at his ear. "We have to meet about that. We have a contract to play in a town called Guthrie. Is that far?"

"Just north of Oklahoma City," Lassiter told him. "Then you think you can carry on without Redwine?"

"Carry on without him? We'll probably be far better off!"

Laura had intended to keep quiet, but the intensity of Vanlandingham's reply set off alert signals in her mind. Seeing Lassiter pause, she decided to satisfy her curiosity. "But wasn't Mr. Redwine the guiding genius behind the troupe?"

Vanlandingham's eyes flared with resentment. "If the company had worked as we originally dreamed, perhaps yes. As things turned out, *I* was the one who had to hold everything together. All Reddy seemed interested in doing was strutting about. Oh, and devising fiendish ways to hold back the money all of us had coming, of course."

"It was that bad?"

Vanlandingham heaved a theatrical sigh. "To tell you the truth, Miss Michaels, I really don't believe we could have gone on much longer."

Lassiter said, "Tell me about that."

"There isn't really a lot to tell that you don't already know, I suspect."

"Humor me."

"Well! In the first place, when Reddy approached me about forming the company, it was supposed to be a partnership. Everything fifty-fifty. He provided the artistic direction and recruitment of players, while I provided business management and of course creative input in terms of appropriate scripts. But I discovered only recently—after another of our endless arguments over money—that the partnership papers had never been properly filed in California. *I* thought we were a legal partnership, with binding agreements. In fact, the papers didn't mean a thing—didn't mean a *thing!* Without a legal partnership, I, like everyone else, served at his pleasure, without a leg to stand on."

Laura said, "That must have made you furious."

"Well! 'Furious' hardly describes it!"

"Why," Lassiter asked, "did you stay on?"

The small man flushed and looked down at the pieces of easel on the carpet. "It was a job. I planned to remain only until something more challenging came along." He looked up, defensive. "I have feelers out. Negotiations are under way with several major companies. It was only a matter of time until I could walk out on my own terms."

"Did you invest money in the original setup?"

"Certainly."

"May I ask—"

"All I had—ten thousand dollars then, and more later."

Lassiter's forehead wrinkled the way it did when he was thinking his hardest. "And now you finally get to have some control, possibly recoup your investment."

"It's possible. That will depend on how the cast members vote today. But I expect a favorable outcome on that. They all know I've been the real force behind the company from its inception. With me in charge, we'll secure more bookings, have fairer scripts—Reddy always had to have the lead when he was around, of course—and maybe we can even have an honest, regular accounting of where the money is going."

Lassiter spoke with a slow and watchful intonation: "You had a lot to gain from his death, then, actually."

"I don't deny that! Not for a second. All of us did. I can't imagine any of us wasting much time mourning his passing, unless that poor Deena still believed he was going to make her a movie star. Honestly, she is *so* naïve. There he was, almost certainly already diddling Janis on the side, and Deena still believed she was special to him...that he had great plans for her career."

Lassiter paused and Laura waited to see how he might pursue those angles. Instead, he fooled her: "Mr. Vanlandingham, we found a dagger."

"A—oh! The *dagger!* I'm sorry, Deputy, that's another script clue."

"How about a small revolver?"

"Yes. That too. Oh, dear." Vanlandingham put his chin in a cupped hand. "We've all been so upset...I wonder if there are any more planted clues around. I'll have to check the script very carefully."

"I'd like to have a copy of that final script," Lassiter growled.

"Well, you shall have it. Of course I can only let it out of my hands for a short time, and you understand that it is fully protected by copyright."

Lassiter looked decidedly unhappy. "I just want to look. I won't even take it out of your sight."

"Of course!" Vanlandingham knelt to pick up the parts of the easel. "Give me two minutes and come to my room. You shall have it at once."

Lassiter nodded at Laura and they walked to the far side of the atrium. He looked not only unhappy but furious. "Weirdo," he muttered under his breath.

"You can't tell the real clues from the script ones without a program," Laura said, sympathizing.

Out of the blue, Lassiter asked, "Is Colonel Rodgers right-handed or left-handed?"

"What?" She was so surprised she had to stop a minute and think. "He's left-handed."

"Are you sure?"

"Sure, I'm sure. I did a little survey a couple of months ago on handedness and tendency toward chronic depression. He—"

"You mean there's a connection?" Lassiter looked astonished.

Laura smiled. "Not that my survey showed. I thought it was nonsense, anyway. But you do all kinds of dumb stuff like that as a graduate student. A paper is a paper."

He nodded. "And the colonel is left-handed for sure?"

"He and Ellen Smith were the only left-handed ones in my group. I remember her saying that proved how creative she was, and Stoney Castle jumping right in and saying it more likely proved how authoritarian she was, given the fact that the colonel was left-handed too. Why, Aaron? Where did *that* question come from?"

His frown deepened. "Vanlandingham and everybody else in the company had a better motive for killing Redwine than the colonel did."

"Well, I agree with that for sure. But—"

He interrupted by reaching up and gently touching the bandage on her temple. "Wound on the left side of your head. Doctor said you were hit from the front. You're facing me right now. Which hand do I use to touch the side of your head like this?"

"Your right, of course." She felt a small pulse of excitement. "Then you think this proves the colonel couldn't have—"

"No, no." He shook his head impatiently. "The only time this kind of theory changed the outcome of a case was probably back in some story by Edgar Allan Poe. But it's a straw in the wind. You don't think the old colonel was capable of murder; you've said that. Every time I talk to someone like Vanlandingham, the way we just did, I get a stronger feeling that somebody in that cast—or Mrs. Redwine—must have done the deed. This handedness thing just bolsters all that.''

"So what do we do next?" Laura demanded.

"Well, unless your memory has come back—''

"It hasn't.''

"Then I think since I'm ordered to be out here anyway, we dig a little more.'' Lassiter's brow furrowed again. "Can't hurt. Oops, there goes Tootsie, headed for his room. Let's go look at that script.''

SIXTEEN

FROM MAUDE THURINGER'S MYSTERY JOURNAL

Should have known col. did it. Was the one I least suspected. Brick was killer in play?? Will try steal script—right one this time—& verify. Will be real hard with cops all over place, everybody edgy. Go slow.

IN THE GLASSED-IN interrogation room in the new annex to the Cleveland County courthouse, Sheriff Bucky Davidson and Norman detective Fred Hunzicker faced Colonel Roger Rodgers across a barren metal table.

The colonel, wearing shapeless gray jail coveralls, had not shaved or combed his usually perfect steel-gray hair. Unkempt, with eyes bloodshot from lack of sleep, he looked twenty years older than the man they had taken into custody yesterday. Jail was hard on anyone. For a man with his obvious pride, one night there had caused havoc. Under any other circumstances the sheriff would have felt sorry for him.

But you learned in this job not to feel a lot of normal feelings.

"You say the pistol must have been stolen," he repeated.

The old colonel set his jaw and glared back. "No other explanation. Military leadership requires logical analysis."

"When did you first notice it was missing?"

"Thursday night. But it must have been taken earlier."

"But you admit it is your weapon."

Old eyes narrowed with impatience. "Hardly could deny that, could I? Name and social security number engraved right on the barrel."

"When did you see it last?"

Colonel Rodgers shook his head. It was a weary gesture. He looked like a man who had suddenly lost all faith in himself and all will to live. "Why ask? Just the muttering of a senile old man, can't even keep his weapons in order."

The sheriff repeated patiently, "When did you see it last?"

"You know the gun range south of Norman, off the interstate? I'm a member. Went there last weekend. Fired fifty rounds with that, twenty with my Luger. Brought both pieces home...I *thought*—cleaned them...put them both back in the glass-topped display table...I *thought*."

"You don't remember for sure?"

The colonel's eyes flared with impotent anger. "The memory is crystal clear. But it must be wrong. That's the way it is when you start into Alzheimer's, isn't it? You don't *know* your mind is gone until they're having to feed you with a bib around your damned neck. Then it's too late...you don't have enough brainpower left to go jump off the nearest tall building."

It gave Sheriff Bucky Davidson genuine pain to be going through this. Colonel Rodgers was the kind of man he had always wanted to be. "Goddammit, sir," he said gruffly, "I'm just trying to get the facts here."

Colonel Rodgers sat up straighter and squared his shoulders. "Proceed."

"Why didn't you report it missing Thursday night?"

"And admit I probably lost it, like a pimply-faced youth dropping his slingshot at the river bottom?"

"You say you always keep your handguns in that glass-topped table."

"Affirmative. You saw it in my room: solid cherry, first-class work, heavy plate-glass top that lets you look right down through to the weapons arranged on the dark felt backing. Fine, solid lock. Take a hell of a hammering to break that glass and get inside."

"And you always kept it locked."

"Affirmative."

Hunzicker stirred. "Who could have stolen your key?"

"Nobody! Only one key, and it's on my key ring, which I have with me at all times."

"How about Timberdale help? Cleaning people, a repair-man?"

The colonel colored. "We don't have thieves at Timberdale. Only people ever in the apartment besides friends are the household staff. They know if they so much as go near my gun table, I'll have their heads."

"Did you have many visitors in the past few days?" Davidson asked.

"Two."

"Who?"

"Don't know if a man ought to…compromise a lady."

"Colonel, you'd damned well better be willing to compromise anybody, if it might help you."

The colonel sat up ramrod proud. "Lady named Smith out there. Ellen Smith. Artist. I've been posing for sketches for her."

"For a portrait?"

The colonel blushed slightly. "Don't know. Thought so. Last time, she acted quite…flighty."

"Flighty?"

"You know," the old man growled. "Eyelashes going up and down like a drum major's baton. Wiggling around. Talking about how two can live as cheaply as one, and she always admired me. *You* know."

The sheriff fought back his smile. "You don't think she might have stolen the pistol?"

"Impossible! The crazy woman won't even sit on the end of the couch where the table is. Says guns make her feel faint."

Davidson drew a thin line under the name "Ellen Smith" on his notepad. Out of the corner of his eye he saw Hunzicker make a note, too. A tape recorder's cassette spool turned on the corner of the table, but old note-taking habits died hard. "You said there were two visitors."

"Yes. Other one was just Thursday night. Lady in the cast. An old friend of mine. Freddie Filmont."

This was more interesting. "Old friends, you say?"

"Well, we met years ago. She did a USO-type show in 'Nam. Gave her a drink afterward. Woman can really drink."

"So you renewed old acquaintances Thursday night."

"Affirmative. Interesting woman. We discovered a mutual antipathy toward that bounder Redwine. She was fatigued from the long drive up from Dallas. She was distraught because her liquor supply had run out. I invited her to my billet for a drink, and she accepted."

Davidson watched and waited. Time ticked off. The colonel colored again. "Nothing happened! Just a friendly drink, a bit of conversation. I pointed out the weapons table to her, and when we looked in together, that's when I saw the Targetsman was missing. I was very upset. She left right after that. I gave her a fifth of Smirnoff's to take along."

"And you don't think she might have—"

"Impossible. I wasn't out of the room more than thirty seconds all the time she was there."

The sheriff breathed deeply. "You really think you could have lost the weapon and not remember it?"

The colonel grimaced. "It's a bastard, sir, getting old. You feel the same inside, but nothing works the same anymore." The colonel pointed to himself. "Eyeglasses for reading, see? Hearing aid. Bridge with four false teeth in it. Nothing standard-issue anymore. Especially the mind. First you forget names sometimes, then you can't think of the right word. Then it all goes."

The sheriff chose to ignore this. "You feel sure that neither Ellen Smith nor Freddie Filmont was the thief?"

"Positive. No opportunity, either of them."

"You indicated you were out of the room when Filmont was there, maybe thirty seconds or so. Why? Where did you go? Was that unusual?"

The colonel showed embarrassment again. "When you get to be my age, Sheriff, you'll know about prostate trouble. No one visits me more than ten minutes without having to wait while I go to the head.''

"We'll talk to both ladies," Davidson promised. "Is there anything else you might like to tell us, Colonel?"

"I've told you everything. What more could there be?"

The sheriff closed his notebook. "Anything from your end, Fred?"

"Can't think of it," Hunzicker grunted.

"Will I be granted bail?" the colonel asked. His voice faltered slightly, and the words came out sounding like a small, bewildered child: "I want to go home."

The sheriff got to his feet. "I'm sorry, Colonel. I don't think that's in the cards."

The jailer was summoned and the old man was taken away, feet shuffling in the loose jail clogs. Davidson and Hunzicker looked at each other.

"Pitiful case," Hunzicker said.

"Yes, he is," Davidson replied.

"I meant the case against him."

"What case against him? We've got shit, and you know it."

"We need more, that's for sure."

"Maybe something more will turn up."

Hunzicker reached for a cigar. "It better."

SEVENTEEN

By the time Laura returned from accompanying Lassiter on his expedition to look at the murder-mystery script, residents were filing out from Saturday morning breakfast. Most were unusually subdued. The weekend was often a time of quiet excitement due to family visits. But the continuing foul weather had caused cancellations by some out-of-town relatives, while others had elected to stay away because they thought loved ones would be wrapped up in the mystery weekend. Those that did come would be asking questions about safety—the calls were already coming in.

Laura saw worry and sadness on some faces. The shock of J. Turner Redwine's death had put an ugly ending to what many had anticipated as a fun weekend. Under any circumstances, too, a murder left shock waves that reverberated: *The victim's life appeared as secure as mine. It can happen to anyone.* In addition, the Timberdale residents were old; it did not take a murderer somewhere nearby to remind them that time was short.

There might be still another factor behind the unusually quiet, sober mood Laura detected throughout the atrium crowd, she thought. Not everyone had liked the stiffly military, bossy demeanor of Colonel Roger Rodgers, but most residents had been more amused than irritated by his speeches demanding "discipline in the chow hall" and "mandatory morning calisthenics for all hands." He was a longtime fixture here, as comfortable and comforting as the familiar grandfather clock or Mrs. Epperman's periodic eccentric bulletins over the PA system. Now he was gone—shockingly arrested—and there was a sense of loss, almost of bereavement. The shock waves were stronger because the police had taken away one of Timberdale's own.

Troubled, Laura postponed returning to her office and circulated through the atrium.

She found Judge Emil Young and Ellen Smith in deep conversation, and put on her cheeriest face. "Hi! Good morning! My, do we look glum."

Ellen Smith frowned. "He hasn't been released."

Laura did not pretend ignorance. "No, I'm afraid not yet."

"But he didn't do it," Smith said.

"I agree, but—"

"If something like this can happen to the colonel, it could happen to *any* of us."

"Oh, I hardly think—"

"In addition," the old judge rumbled, "an incontrovertible conclusion to be drawn as a result of our certitude concerning his innocence must be that the culprit in the Redwine slaying remains at large, and indisputably that perpetrator must remain in close proximity to these environs."

Ellen Smith shivered. "I don't like it."

Laura tried to reassure them without much obvious effect and moved on to another clot of people that included lecherous Ken Keen, birdlike Davilla Rose, and one of Timberdale's stellar couples, Julius and Dot Pfeister.

"Good morning!"

Julius Pfeister, a handsome barrel of a man in a lemon-colored sportcoat and lime ascot, rolled bulbous eyes her way. "We have been discussing the possibility of raising a fund for the colonel's bail."

"I'm not sure bail will be granted," Laura replied.

Ken Keen frowned. "It's not fair." He didn't even leer or make a suggestive remark.

"Laura," Davilla Rose piped up, "everyone is upset. Everyone! I intend to write a tragic poem about this terrible thing at once. What can we do? Must we just sit by and watch the mills of the gods grind poor Roger into oblivion?"

Laura got an idea. "Maybe we ought to have a special group session later today and talk some of this out."

Rose narrowed her eyes. "The Wednesday Breakfast Club or the Friday Lone Rangers?"

"Maybe we should all meet," Laura suggested. "How about eleven o'clock?"

Some of them seemed to brighten a tiny bit. Ken Keen waggled his eyebrows and moved his hand behind Davilla Rose. She let out a sharp *"Eek!"* and turned furiously to slap at him.

"Aw, you love it," he chuckled.

That settled it. If even the mention of a session restored Ken Keen to his lecherous normalcy, the meetings must be therapeutic. "Eleven it will be," Laura said. "In the small activity room. Will you guys pass the word? Thanks."

She hurried on toward her office, wondering if Mrs. Epperman would show up at all today. She knew Francie Blake wouldn't; Francie would be off with her wealthy young surgeon, Dirk somebodyorother, hoping today would be the day he planned to announce his big surprise trip south of the border—the one Francie had seen airline tickets for, somehow or other.

The visit to look at the mystery script had confirmed that the broken reading glasses, the Saturday night special, and the dagger found in the basement had been part of the mystery weekend scenario. Lassiter had looked exceedingly disappointed about that, and had left with the announced intention of asking a few questions of chef Pierre Motard. Going toward her office, Laura thought she might actually get through some of the mountain of paperwork on her desk.

She was not quite at the reception desk, however, when the front doors opened with a loud rush of wind and Rebecca Redwine, bundled up in a fur-collared coat, blew in. She spied Laura at once and hurried over, high heels hammering.

"I spoke with the sheriff," she announced breathlessly. "He said the search of Reddy's room here was completed last night. He said it would be perfectly proper for me to go in and look for some things I need.''

"In your husband's room?'' Laura said. "I'll have to check with Deputy Lassiter—''

"A checkbook,'' Mrs. Redwine snapped. "Not that there's likely to be any money in the account. The damned stupid sheriff says he's holding as evidence that huge wad of cash they found in the drawer. I suppose I'll get it eventually. He said so. But when I think that someone got into that room after the murder—well, the money was obviously what they were searching for. I can only thank my lucky stars they didn't find it in the time they had. Reddy was so stupid.''

She paused and gasped for air. "Also, there's a key to a deposit box in our bank in Los Angeles. Also, if he happened to have them with him, some insurance papers and a copy of his will. Not that he had anything to leave, that I know about. It's just like I told George on the telephone yesterday: any joint property Reddy and I had was sent down the toilet in his pursuit of young female flesh long ago.''

With some relief, Laura spotted Lassiter hurrying across the back of the atrium, intent on going somewhere else. She waved, caught his attention, and gestured him over.

Mrs. Redwine repeated her request.

"I guess it's okay,'' Lassiter said. "Let me make a quick call to verify it with the sheriff.'' He hustled into Laura's office.

Mrs. Redwine tapped her foot. As weathered as she was, she still had a nice body and beautiful legs, Laura noticed. Once she must have been a perfect watch fob for someone like J. Turner Redwine.

Lassiter came back. "Bucky says okay.'' He blinked at Laura. "Will you accompany Mrs. Redwine up there?''

"Sure,'' Laura said, surprised.

"Mrs. Redwine, you're authorized only to remove personal papers from the apartment. You understand that?''

She drew herself up imperiously. "What else would I take? His traveling porno collection?''

"I have a couple of things to talk to Dr. Which about, Laura. Meet you down here in a bit?" He steamed away.

Giving up all thought of her paperwork, Laura got the room submaster key from the office security cabinet and walked Rebecca Redwine to the back hall leading to One East. She wondered who had run this way after the murder, gotten into Redwine's room with one of his own keys, and frantically searched...for *what?*

Eyelids fluttering nervously, Rebecca Redwine talked all the way.

"Oh, he had his good points, you know. I've seen some of his early films. He had gotten copies of all of them, and then he spent an ungodly amount of money getting those old ace-tates copied onto videotape a few years ago. He was a wonderful actor in the early days. So young and handsome. So sincere. He would have been as famous as Barrymore or Brando if he had just gotten a few breaks. But he was always so headstrong. That was one of the things that I loved him for and hated him for at the same time. He simply had to have his way. A lot of people thought he was selfish. It wasn't that he was selfish. He was a genius. You have to take that into consideration. Here he was, a great talent neglected and rejected, and finally doomed to these horrible little weekend melodramas with no-talent twits like Deena Sweete. How he suffered! Can you blame him?

"Of course I'm not forgiving him, exactly. He was a liar. He cheated everybody. The concept of honesty simply never entered his mind. We lived in Kansas City for two years back in the sixties—he bought into a dinner theater there—and our house was lovely. Darling, it was *huge.* It had a swimming pool the size of this building, I swear. In the winter we swam every evening, no matter how cold it was. People wondered how he paid for all the gas to run the heater when it was ten degrees outside. I wondered, too. Then the gas company came one day and said he had piped around the meter out back and used gas for two winters without paying a thing for it. They gave us a bill for nine thousand dollars. He refused to pay.

They shut off our gas, so for four months we tried to heat that monstrously large house with the four fireplaces and a Kero-Sun heater or two, and went down to the gas station on the corner to take sponge-baths in the public restrooms. Then the gas company finally sued us and we went to Oregon and some-how they got the house and everything in it. I guess he hadn't made the payments on the mortgage or anything, either.

"I know he cheated a lot of people out of money. He always had a scheme. People hated him. I fought with him about it all the time. But every time I was about to walk out for good, he would do something just so tremendously sweet, like once he took me to Cancún, and then on the *QE2*. Later they sued us for not paying, of course.

"Artists have insatiable appetites. He was such a lover! My God, darling, he could take your breath away. He was good for all night, every night, when he was in the mood. It was *nothing* for him to give me six, eight, even ten huge orgasms in a single night. Of course, I was always multi-orgasmic. I guess all our troubles over money and everything—and his sadness about his mistreatment by Hollywood—were what made him a womanizer. I always hated that. I hated him for it. I could always tell when he had a new floozy. He had a lot of them. I was trying to ignore it, about that slut Deena. I think maybe we were headed for an ultimate showdown over her.

"What did he have in mind, ditching me and then listing me as a missing person? My God, I don't know, I really have no idea. I think he was setting up something to divorce me. He was such a bastard, so selfish. I hated him. Sometimes I feel so sad and alone. Other times I'm almost glad the bastard is dead. He deserved to be killed. Everybody in the company hated him. He cheated them just like everyone else. It's strange, isn't it, that that old colonel who lived here was finally the one to do what a hundred other enemies dreamed about doing?

"Is this the door to his room? Good. This won't take long. Look, if I cry, please try not to be too disturbed by it. I'm an artist too, you know. We're all very emotional. We must be. All of us live on the edge. It's what you have to sacrifice in terms of personal pain in order to be able to project strong feelings for your audience.''

Laura unlocked the door and swung it open. The apartment that had been used by J. Turner Redwine was dim, slatted curtains drawn tight on the far windows. She turned on the overhead lights and crossed the small living room to open the slats, letting the light of the windy gray day flood in.

Except for a box of cigars, a couple of magazines, and several partly consumed bottles of alcohol, the living room looked as if no one had ever lived there. Mrs. Redwine strode into the kitchen, heels clacking on the tile, and turned on the light to inspect a sinkful of glasses and coffee cups. Pressing a dainty toe on the floor button on the trash can, she made the lid flip up to reveal a thick mound of crumpled wrappers from candy bars, crackers, cheese, and Ding Dongs.

The lid slammed sharply. ''I told him all the time about eating junk food. His cholesterol was over three hundred. But would he listen? No.'' She turned and headed through the door to the bedroom.

Laura followed, switching on the overhead light here, too. The unmade bed was piled high with rumpled covers and newspapers. More drinking glasses and cigarette-packed ashtrays stood on the night table and the dresser, which also held Redwine's enormous collection of after-shaves, powders, hair-coloring solutions, and various ointments and unguents scattered all about. Mixed in with them Laura noticed a woman's lipstick and hairbrush. She picked up the lipstick and opened it, noting the bright red color, and then put it back down before Mrs. Redwine noticed.

In a corner stood two suitcases, a steamer trunk with its lid open, and two battered brown cardboard cartons. Mrs. Redwine started for the steamer trunk and paused to glance down at the ashtray on the table beside the bed. ''The bastard! The miserable, no-good, filthy, obscene, two-timing lowlife liar!''

Almost all the butts in the ashtray were heavily stained with deep red lipstick.

Mrs. Redwine went to her knees and dove up to her elbows into the steamer trunk's jumbled papers and costumes. Things flew over her shoulder as she muttered and sifted. "Maybe that was all there was to it.... Now where the hell would he have the checkbook, anyway?... Just wanted to get me out of the way a few days so he could lollop around all night with that chippie. Maybe I wouldn't mind *quite* so much if she were even halfway attractive, but she's so damned coarse and obvious—I mean, those vulgar short skirts, and breasts hanging halfway out, how could anyone look at them and not think of Elsie the Cow? Hello. What's this?"

Laura looked and saw she was holding up a stapled sheaf of legal-size documents, frowning at the first page, flipping others.

"This is a contract," she told Laura. "I didn't know anything about this. You know who Mavis Murnam is, don't you?"

Laura searched her memory. "I'm afraid I don't."

"Well, obviously you don't keep up, darling. She was a great star back in Reddy's heyday. They played in some movies together. *Texas Baling Wire Strangler,* I recall, and I think *The Mystery of the Missing Head.* Lately she's been on one of the soaps. Somebody's mother, I think." She flipped more pages. "My God, she was joining this troupe. Let's see...let's see... Why, she was supposed to start November thirteenth. That's next week!"

"I wonder who knew about this," Laura said.

"I don't know, but it doesn't sound good for poor Freddie Filmont. Reddy certainly couldn't afford to stable two old hags for motherly and grandmotherly parts. Very interesting. Let's see...."

More papers and costumes flew. Then Mrs. Redwine stopped again, this time holding up a pack of snapshots. "I wonder what *this* is." She opened the envelope flap and slid the pictures out into her hand, looked, and fell backward with a shriek. "I can't believe it! Oh, this is the worst yet! I could just vomit!"

Laura leaned closer. Mrs. Redwine flung out her arm in a despairing theatrical gesture, offering the pack of pictures. Laura took them and glanced at the top two. Mrs. Redwine, on her feet again, rammed around the room, knocking cologne bottles off the dresser and kicking furniture while she raved.

Apparently Janis Mahafey had been enjoying herself when she posed for the color snapshots. Laura wondered where Mahafey—or Redwine—had found a commercial lab willing to develop them. Many, at least in this part of the country, were very sensitive about nudes this explicit, especially when they involved apparatus.

"What do you think of *that?*" Mrs. Redwine cried. "Is it any wonder I'm half-glad the beast is dead?"

Laura extended the photos to her. She shied away, eyes widening. "I don't want the horrible things! Put them away! Burn them! Do whatever you want with them! My God, the *police* saw those! They have to know Reddy was probably the photographer. More disgrace."

Laura put the pack on the remaining pile in the trunk. "You said you were looking for a checkbook," she said, pointing. "Is that a checkbook on the dresser there?"

Mrs. Redwine snatched it up. "Yes!" She looked at the register pages. "No current total, of course. The boob never kept track of anything but his obscene amorous conquests." She stared at Laura with ravaged eyes. "I didn't really think he was diddling Janis too. I had my suspicions, but I didn't really think so." She shoved the checkbook into her purse. "I suppose there are other things—insurance—but I just can't go on right now. I can't! Get me out of this sordid place. I'll come back later. I have the checkbook. That's the main thing he stole from me in Fort Worth. At least this gives me the account number. I can call down there and see if he left me a farthing."

Maintaining a discreet silence, Laura followed her out

through the living room and into the hall. She locked up. They started back toward the atrium.

"Secrets," Rebecca Redwine said. "Nothing but secrets. He was *such* a foul man!"

Laura heard a slight sound behind them as they approached the last turn in the hallway. Looking back, she caught only the briefest glimpse of an old-fashioned dark floral silk dress flipping out of sight down the side hall. Maude Thuringer.

EIGHTEEN

Must use code to prevent detection. Saw L and Mrs. R in room R used. Searching. For what? Anybody know? In cahoots? R made pass at L once in act. rm. She mad. Mrs. R. scorned. Both have motive. Got together and killed R? Maybe L's amnesia big fake. Imp. not tell anybody theory yet. Could L do it? Ha. How much wood would a wood-chuck chuck if a woodchuck could chuck wood?

REBECCA REDWINE scooted out the first-floor side door closest to where she had parked her rental car. Laura hurried on into the atrium, where she found Aaron Lassiter waiting impatiently at the front desk. Day receptionist Paula Burwell seemed thrilled out of her mind by his proximity, and seemed to be doing a lot of touching up of her makeup.

"You got her taken care of?" Lassiter asked.

"Sure," Laura said, feeling unaccountably cranky. She glanced from him to Burwell's pretty, hectic face. "And I guess you've got everything in hand here?"

His forehead corrugated. "Please?"

"Never mind." She started toward her office.

"Can I talk to you?" he called after her.

She looked back. Her voice dripped acid. "If you're not too busy, darling."

Why am I being a bitch? she wondered, preceding him into the office.

Lassiter sat down in the chair facing her desk. He continued to look troubled. "This whole thing still doesn't feel right to me. You still can't remember who hit you?"

"No." She shuffled some papers around.

"Is there something wrong?" he asked.

"No. Of course not. Why should something be wrong? I just spend all my time doing stuff the darned sheriff's department should be doing, like taking Mrs. Redwine up to her husband's former apartment, and I've got a screeching headache, Mrs. Epperman is gone as usual, Francie is off living her latest romance novel, I've got a month's paperwork piled up here, I'm supposed to attend a weekend seminar tonight that I won't make, and you—" She stopped abruptly, realizing what she had been about to say.

Lassiter, mightily troubled, studied her expression. "I what?"

"Nothing. Really." She had been about to say, "and you lollygag around with Paula, and I know she has beautiful eyes and a cute body…if you like the *Penthouse* type…but I'm so mad I'd like to beat you up and scratch her eyes out." She was stunned. The jealousy had jumped up like a Notre Dame alum at the mention of Lou Holtz.

She had to get hold of herself. "I'm sorry, Aaron. I'm just out of sorts. You were saying…?"

"You're sure you're okay? The headache—is it really bad?"

"No, I've just got a bad case of being a witch. You were saying?"

"I've been talking to your doctor and nurse, and a couple of other staff people. *Nobody* thinks Colonel Rodgers was the type who would commit murder, even as mad as he was. It doesn't ring true to me, anyway. Why would the colonel kill Redwine downstairs someplace and then move the body into the activity room? How could the colonel even have known there was a gurney downstairs? Or that Redwine would be there, for that matter?"

Laura forgot to be crabby. "You make it sound like you suspect a member of the cast."

"Well, that would make more sense than suspecting the colonel."

"So would suspecting Mrs. Redwine."

Lassiter's antennae went up. "Yeah? She say something while you were upstairs?"

Laura gave him a condensed version, including the Janis Mahafey porno.

"I heard about that," Lassiter told her.

"You didn't look at them?"

His forehead wrinkled again. "No. Why should I?"

You have got to stop this. "No reason, honey. Sorry I asked."

He nodded and locked his hands over his knee the way he often did when puzzled or worried. "I suppose Mrs. Redwine could have come out here, parked in an out-of-the-way spot, gotten in, and knocked him off. But how the hell did she get the colonel's gun? How could she have lifted Redwine's body onto that gurney?"

"She couldn't," Laura replied.

"Unless she had help."

"Oh, hell, I hadn't thought of that."

"I talked to Deena Sweete," Lassiter told her. "She says the cast had a brief meeting not long after the lunchtime scene, and before Redwine showed up for a scene in the lobby that Mrs. Epperman had something to do with. After that, people split up to do their individual parts to get ready for later segments of the show, she says, That dovetails with what the sheriff says he was told yesterday."

"Aaron," Laura said slowly, "why are you going back over this?"

"Dammit, it's all I know to do. I'm trying to construct a timetable—get a clearer picture of where everybody was and when. There's something we're missing here. This crime is so bizarre, there's got to be something we're missing."

Laura sighed. "There aren't many clues, really."

He snorted. "To the contrary. I never saw so many clues in my life. We've got the gun, we've got *another* gun, we've got broken reading glasses, we've got the gurney with blood on it, we've got blood other places, we've got the time of the murder narrowed down to less than an hour, we've got threats made by the victim's wife, we've got motives for several other people.''

"So where do we go from here—if anywhere?"

"Well, I'm going to go talk to everybody in the troupe again, one more time. I'd like you to come with me—see if you pick up on any body language or anything." He looked hesitant, worried. "Would you do that?"

A wave of remorse about her unaccountable bitchiness swept over Laura. "Sure."

DEENA SWEETE grimaced in the doorway of her room. "You again?"

"Just a couple of quick additional questions," Lassiter said apologetically. "I would really appreciate it."

When he got that bashful little smile, he could melt the Arctic ice cap, Laura thought, and Sweete was by no means impervious. Spots of color appeared on her cheeks and she ran long fingers through tangled hair as she stepped back to let them in.

Her room had clothes strewn everywhere, and her capri pants and sweater looked as if they had been on the floor earlier, too.

"Sorry," she muttered, dropping onto one end of the couch. "So what now?"

"Getting ready to go somewhere?" Lassiter asked, eyeing the mess.

Her eyes brimmed resentment. "We'll all have to go after we're cleared tomorrow. Did you think we would just stay here forever?"

"Let's talk about your relationship with Mr. Redwine."

"That was private. It's nobody's business. If you think I'm going to tell anyone anything that that horrid Rebecca could use in a lawsuit or something, you're crazy."

Lassiter looked puzzled. "What kind of lawsuit could she file against you?"

"How do I know? I just know she hates me, just like she hated Reddy."

"Why did she hate you?"

"Because he—because we—" She stopped. Big tears appeared in her eyes.

Lassiter handed her the box of Kleenex from the coffee table. "You liked him a lot."

Sweete dabbed at her eyes and blew her nose. "Yes, and I think it's horrible for you to come back and poke around at me again. I'm the *last* person who had any reason to want him dead. He loved me. He was going to make me a star. He was going to get a divorce and marry me."

"I WAS UP HERE in the room getting ready for the four o'clock," Tad Raddell told Lassiter and Laura. He gestured at the costumes tossed over the back of the studio couch. "One of our rules is, you try to stay out of sight in the little while before a scene. If you're out there chatting with the patrons one minute, and then show up in a scene, it's hard for them to identify you as the character you're playing."

"So," Lassiter said, "you were here around three-thirty."

"I certainly was."

"George Vanlandingham went off to look for Redwine about that time."

"I understand that's right."

"But you didn't help him."

"No. Why should I? I had to prepare myself emotionally for the next scene."

Lassiter spoke slowly, with care. "Sounds like you were annoyed about something."

Raddell's handsome face went slack, and for a moment he looked about sixteen years old—very young and very scared. "I had no quarrel with Reddy. He was giving me my big chance."

"Big chance, playing in this little company?"

"Don't knock it! It's work. Somebody might discover you at any stop on the tour."

"You weren't upset about not getting paid properly?"

"Not really."

"How about the big Dodge van? It's registered in your name, but it has Redwine Players signs all over it. I heard from someone you were angry because Redwine had promised to buy it from you, but you were just putting the miles on, wearing it out, acting like a chauffeur, getting nothing."

"He would have paid me...eventually."

"Would he?"

"What are you implying here?" Raddell demanded hotly.

"Nothing," Lassiter replied.

"You have the killer, don't you?"

"Sure. I'm just trying to get a clearer picture of how things went."

"Well, if you want a clearer picture, I suggest you talk to some of the people who had problems with Reddy. *I* certainly had no such problems. I thought he was a great man—difficult sometimes, surely. But we got along beautifully, everything considered." Raddell glanced at Laura. "Unlike some people I could mention."

"Who?" Lassiter asked quickly.

"I hesitate to name names."

"Name names." Lassiter's smile had a chill in it. "Please."

"Well. George, for one. He and Reddy were constantly sniping at each other about all Reddy's demands for script changes, not to mention whatever arguments they were having about control of the company, wages, splits, things like that. And my goodness, what about Deena?"

"I thought Deena and Redwine were an item."

Raddell snorted amusement. "Once they might have been. But, my goodness, I thought *everybody* knew he had dumped her for Janis. Oh, he might have still been somewhat involved with Deena, but she was irate—positively seething—about half the time, seeing she was slipping out of favor with him."

FRANKLIN PIERCE LORD placed a cigarette in his long holder and lit it with a flourish of his gold Colibri lighter. Leaning back in the overstuffed chair in a corner of the atrium, he puffed and then watched smoke drift upward. "I was getting costumed and prepared," he said, voice low to prevent being overheard by the handful of residents scattered around the area. "I know nothing of Reddy's possible whereabouts. Or anyone else's, for that matter."

"What do you think will happen now, with Redwine gone?" Lassiter asked.

Lord adjusted the collar of his lavender shirt, open at the throat to accommodate his black ascot. "I suspect George will want us to go on under his management."

"What do you think about that?"

"I am ambivalent. Certainly, if we are to go on, some changes will have to be made, unfortunately for some of us."

"Like who?"

The old actor's face tightened. "I shouldn't gossip, but it is common knowledge, after all. Poor Freddie was on the brink of being dismissed. Her drinking has simply gotten out of control. Reddy was preparing to release her quite soon, I believe. That must be followed through. The woman simply has to go."

Lassiter frowned and made a quick note. "Will Vanlandingham follow through on that, do you think?"

"Oh, I suspect he might. George may be able to do an adequate job. As for myself, I shall continue, if asked, while investigating other artistic possibilities. But I must say it does trouble me, the idea of George taking command, as it were."

Lassiter frowned. "Why would it trouble you?"

"Because George and Reddy were so on the outs for such a long time. Because George so obviously *wanted* Reddy out and himself in. I suspect all of us would welcome being paid honestly and on time, for a change. But of all of us, George is the one with the most to gain from Reddy's demise, and I hate to see such an opportunistic son of a bitch get his way as a result of a tragedy. For all his faults, Reddy was a genius.

That was why I had no problem with him personally—one should overlook a lot, where a genius is concerned. But George was a constant schemer and thorn in his side. I should think George has more reason than anyone to be happy Reddy is dead.'' Lord removed the long holder from his mouth. "With the obvious exception of Janis, of course."

"Why would Janis be glad he's gone? I heard she was his favorite."

Lord chuckled with patronizing amusement. "The poor child was, for a brief period of time. But everyone knew he had returned his affections to Deena. Janis was insanely jealous about that. I myself overheard an argument between them only last week in which she threatened in so many words to kill him."

FREDDIE FILMONT staggered as she escorted them into her room. A half-consumed water glass of what looked like straight bourbon on the rocks sat in a small puddle on the coffee table. The actress's eyes seemed slightly unfocused.

"I prepared in coshtume a bit early," she said, her voice thick. "Then I shtayed here alone, awaiting the time for my appearance."

"You don't know where Redwine was, or who might have been with him?" Lassiter said.

"I don't have the slightest."

"Hadn't you had some trouble with Redwine about your drinking?"

Filmont jerked violently. "Drinking? Drinking? Why should we have had trouble about drinking?" She put her glass down with a rattle. "If you're referring to thish, I am having a sip because of allergies."

Lassiter paused. Laura spoke up for the first time. "Miss Filmont, do you know an actress named Mavis Murnan?"

"That old bimbo? Yes, we've met, unfortunately."

"Did you know she was scheduled to join the company next week?"

Filmont's eyes shot wide in a fine impression of disbelief.

"That's ridiculous! Where did you ever get sush an idea? Why would we need her? *I* am the senior actress in the Redwine troupe, and intend to remain so!"

JANIS MAHAFEY dabbed a tear from her eye.

"He loved me. He was going to divorce that terrible woman and marry me. We were going to return to Hollywood and he was going to make me a star."

"But people heard you having a fight with him in the hallway," Lassiter said.

"That was nothing—a lover's quarrel! We made up right away. He could never stay mad at me. He adored me. That's why Deena was so hateful to me—she knew she had lost him, and Reddy and I were going to be happy together forever."

Lassiter closed the interview and took Laura back into the hall.

"What now?" she asked.

"I guess," he said disgustedly, "it's time to talk to our friend George again."

THIRTY MINUTES later, they walked back into Laura's office.

"Okay," Lassiter grunted, reaching for the coffee urn. "Vanlandingham says that after he found Redwine out behind the activity room and got the script change approved, he left him there. The time he says he did that checks out. He says nobody else was back there with him; he left Redwine alone and came back out, locking up, and quickly ran off the new pages on the copy machine in time to be ready for his intro work on the scene in the activity room. He admits he was furious with Redwine, but says everybody else was, too. He says everybody was so busy, none of them could have done it."

He poured coffee and looked at Laura. "So, counselor: Who's lying?"

"If I knew that," Laura told him, "I'd be ready for my

Ph.D., not fighting to keep my head above water trying to get an M.S.W.''

Lassiter sipped from the Styrofoam cup. "Shit."

Laura got up from her desk—she couldn't look at all the undone paperwork another moment—and started around the desk, intent on giving him a consoling hug.

Staring bleakly into space, he said, "Somebody went around the building just like you did. Got in the back way. No telling how many hours that door had been stuck ajar by the blowing leaves. They got in, found Redwine, shot him with the colonel's pistol. *Who*, goddammit?''

Laura reached out toward him. As she did, a funny feeling of disorientation made her mind wobble.

It was almost painful. A psychic door swung open for an instant onto a blurry, smoke-filled moment—and then it banged closed again:

The gurney. Someone on it. Shock of recognition because it was Redwine, his head lolling grotesquely to one side. Someone beside him, bent over him, turning at her approach. A sound. Someone else—a second person—*making a slight sound behind her. Turning. A sharp blow. A sound like a gong ringing in her head. Nothingness.*

The picture was almost complete. The memory was *right there*, on the brink of consciousness. Her nervous system shot a spurt of adrenaline into her bloodstream, making her hot and jumpy for a split second.

Then the picture was gone. She gasped for air. Dizziness made her stumble and grab for the edge of the desk to keep from falling.

Lassiter jumped to his feet, knocking his chair over backward, and grabbed her by both arms. "Hey! What is it? You look like a ghost!"

She shook her aching head. "I'm okay. I'm okay."

"What happened? You stumbled, and then I thought you were going down."

"I had a— I almost remembered it all."

His eyes bored into her with the keenest concern. "What? What?"

"I'm sorry, Aaron." She could have wept—with disappointment over her own inability to dredge up the memory, and with regret that she couldn't help him. "It's gone again."

"What? What?"

"I saw him."

"Who?"

"Redwine. On the gurney. I think he was already dead."

"Christ. Anything else?"

"Someone bent over him."

"You don't know who?"

"It was blurry, like I didn't *want* to know, or something— just...someone." She met his gaze. "But there was something else. For sure. Aaron, there was a second person. I know it."

He held her. "Take your time. Take your time, babe."

She pulled away. "There was somebody else. A second person. They came up behind me. I started to turn. That was when I got hit."

"You're sure? Are you sure about that?" He was very excited. "I mean—could your memory be all mixed up?"

"How do I know?" she asked, and wanted to weep with frustration. Then she looked again at what had blipped into consciousness. "No. I'm not mixed up about that. I saw two people. Two figures. No faces. Just—two *somebodies*."

Lassiter pulled her close again. "Fantastic. Then we know one thing for sure."

"What?"

"Either for sure the colonel didn't do it, or at least he didn't do it alone."

NINETEEN

SHERIFF BUCKY DAVIDSON rolled into the Timberdale parking lot at mid-morning, and went first to confer with the crime lab boys still poking around in the activity room and back hallways. The technician in charge, a lanky, lantern-jawed man named Slade, admitted they hadn't found anything promising.

"Vacuumed up some dirt off somebody's shoes down below, but that could've been off anybody's shoes. Dusted for prints in the elevator and found about sixteen sets. The bloodstains will be analyzed. The boys who went over the colonel's room upstairs didn't find anything helpful."

The sheriff told Slade to keep after it, and trudged back into the main part of the building. After asking around, he found his first subject in the crafts room off One West.

The stringy old woman jumped violently when his shoe scraped on the tile entry of the long, narrow room. She was working near the back, at the spot closest to the room's lone window. Seeing him, she rushed around her easel and frantically pulled a plastic cover over from the back, covering the canvas she had been working on.

"What do you want?" she shrilled angrily. "Didn't your mother ever teach you to knock?"

The sheriff went in slowly, picking his way between a towering metal sculpture and a gigantic paper-and-plastic rabbit, or maybe a cow. There were arts-and-crafts projects everywhere, making him feel as uneasy as he did when wending his way through a glass shop or antique store. Some of the projects, to his unschooled eye at least, looked very good. "Miz Smith?" he asked deferentially.

"What if I am? What do you want? Can't a body have any privacy for her art?"

"Ma'am, Colonel Rodgers says you visited him in his apartment recently."

Ellen Smith's eyes went narrow with suspicion. "He said that? What else did he say? I deny it, whatever it was."

"He didn't allege anything," the sheriff told her. "I just need to see if, when you were in his apartment the last time, you noticed whether his Colt .22 Targetsman pistol was in the display table. I've got a Polaroid of the weapon here—"

"No!" Ellen Smith shrank back from the proffered photo. "Guns make me ill! It's my artistic temperament."

"You can't say whether it was there when you last visited him?"

"No! I don't know anything about anything. Get out of here!"

FREDDIE FILMONT stood out on one of the sheltered patios, her coat collar turned up against the wind that managed to swoop over the high walls of the building. She had a cigarette in her lips, which she dropped when the sheriff approached her.

"Wash this?" she mumbled, staring at the Polaroid print.

"The alleged murder weapon. Have you ever seen it before?"

"Of course not! How could I?"

The sheriff tried an old trick: "Colonel Rodgers told us he showed it to you the other night."

"No! Wrong. Quite to the contrary. He said he would show it to me, along with his other weapons. He seems terribly proud of all of them."

The sheriff continued to play dumb. "So why didn't he?"

"Show me?"

"Yes."

"Because it was already missing. He pointed to its place in the case and there was nothing there. He got terribly upset, poor man. It must have meant a lot to him. Little did we know then that it would figure in a ghastly murder."

The sheriff inwardly wrote off his minuscule suspicions

about the old actress. He felt sure she was telling the truth. Even an actress like her could not appear this truthful if she was lying, he told himself. His hopes of learning anything useful from either her or Ellen Smith were gone.

JUDGE EMIL YOUNG approached Maude Thuringer and told her about the special group-therapy session scheduled for eleven.

"I don't have time to go to a group meeting today," Maude protested. "I've got a murder to solve here!"

"Madam," Judge Young ponderously replied, "I am only spreading the word, as Laura asked that we do. But if I may volunteer an observation, it would appear to me, as an unbiased observer, that participation in a therapeutic experience at this juncture might be an eminently desirable step for you. You appear, in a word, unsound."

"I'm as sane as you are!" Maude shot back.

The judge's liver-colored lips twitched "I should aspire to better, if I were you. My latest blood test clearly corroborated an imbalance in my electrolytes, induced no doubt by some misreckoning of pharmaceutical interactions somewhere in my recently reconstituted medicational arsenal."

"Well, pardon me," Maude grated, "if I didn't understand a word of that."

"Further proof in the pudding, I should speculate."

Maude stamped her foot. "Listen, did you ever read any Donald Hamilton? *Death of a Citizen?* The first Matt Helm book? He would have never solved that caper if he hadn't stayed with it through thick or thin. He had lots of reasons to chicken out, but he didn't. Or look at Mrs. Fletcher on TV; she doesn't traipse off to some shrink-twink session when things get difficult. Listen, when the going gets tough, the people who are going keep on doing it."

The judge sighed. "Case closed. Good day, Maude." He turned and hobbled off, relying heavily on his cane.

Standing defiantly near the closed doors to the dining room, Maude glared after him. What kind of an old cuckoo did he think she was? He didn't even realize Laura had become a suspect. Where did he get off, anyway, telling her she needed therapy, especially from a suspect? Just because he had been a district judge, and later on a magistrate at the Court of Criminal Appeals, he thought he knew everything. He reminded her of that Major Minden, in *Stranger at the Gates*. Maybe Evelyn Anthony had patterned that mean old Nazi after the judge, always making his nasty little condescending speeches. Well, Major Minden had gotten *his*. One day maybe the judge would, too. Serve him right, the old fart.

Maude walked slowly into the main part of the atrium, noticing the residents sitting around in some of the easy chairs, doing nothing, and Mr. Costello up at the card table near the front, still working on his ten-thousand-piece jigsaw puzzle, the one of green weeds growing in green shrubbery on a green lawn beside a green pond with green scum all over it. Didn't any of them have better things to do? Old farts.

Maude made it a point to miss nothing. She was watching everyone. She was looking everywhere for additional clues, too. She was going to crack this case, save the colonel in the process, and bring the real perpetrator to justice. They would probably want her on *60 Minutes* after that. She hoped it would be Ed Bradley who interviewed her. She liked him the best.

Maude knew the police forensics people were just about done with their search. She didn't think they had found much. She had overheard them saying they hadn't gotten any good prints off Redwine's door, the one that had been mysteriously opened by someone right after the murder.

None of that discouraged Maude. She knew there had to be clues around that they had missed. There was no such thing as a perfect crime; Jim Chee had proved that in every one of Tony Hillerman's Indian books, and so had a lot of other people. She also knew that Colonel Rodgers could not be the murderer. He had a motive and the murder weapon might belong to him, but he did not fit the classic profile of a homicidal maniac. For one thing, he wouldn't have sneaked around back

someplace to do the deed; he would have stood everybody at
Timberdale up at attention, given J. Turner Redwine a blind-
fold, and brought in some boys from the ROTC down at Norman to shoot him right, standing against the wall outside the
mail room.

No, the colonel was innocent and there had to be more clues
around here to prove it. Maude did not intend to give up. She
walked along the west wall, looking carefully in the sphagnum
moss around each potted plant. Skirting a sofa and easy chair,
she glanced with elaborate casualness into the small brass
wastebasket between them, making sure no one had dumped
something incriminating since her last inspection. She went
into the mail room and hurriedly, with constant glances back
over her shoulder, took out every piece of mail she could
reach, checking for something suspicious. Looking around
sharply, she noticed that the picture of Abraham Lincoln on
the north wall was a little crooked. Her disappointment, when
she felt behind it and found nothing stuck on the back, was
intense.

Going back out into the atrium, she noticed Laura Michaels
leaving the office area and heading for the activity room,
where several residents had already drifted in for the extra
psychobabble. Maude considered going in after all, just to ob-
serve for signs of guilt and to rest. Her knees were killing her
again.

Partway across the atrium, Laura encountered one of the
troupe, that awful little writer man named Vanlandingham,
coming out of the hall from the direction of the photocopy
room with some papers in his hand. Maude saw Laura speak
to him, and then he frowned and pointed back toward the copy
room corridor, and she said something in response.

Obviously a conspiracy. Maude hustled over as close to
them as she dared, and dropped into the nearest leather re-
cliner. The cushions made a ghastly air-squishing noise, but
Laura and Vanlandingham didn't seem to notice. Gripping the
slick edges of the seat cushion in an attempt to prevent future

squishes, Maude wriggled on the chair, trying to get her good ear downwind.

As she moved her hand, it encountered something crinkly and sharp in the crack between the cushions and the chair arm. She went tingly all over. *The good detective is always alert.* She forgot Laura and Vanlandingham and probed with achy fingertips in the crack. Her fingers closed around whatever her hand had encountered. She pulled it out and examined it.

It was a small piece of paper, white, wadded up into a tight little ball. She carefully pried it open and spread it on her lap.

A short message, printed in pen, stared up at her:

he lied again. No prop. must talk immed.

There was no signature.

She read it three times and had a hot flash each time.

Forgetting her list of suspects, she bounded out of the chair and ran over to where Laura was just turning away from Vanlandingham. "Look at this!" Maude yelped, waving the scrap of paper.

Vanlandingham stared. Laura seemed to hold her notebooks closer to her bosom. "What is it, Maude? Are you all right? You look—"

"Dang betcha I'm all right! I am more than all right! I am super! You all thought I was some kind of nut, but I've read all those mysteries. I'm nobody's fool! I knew if I just kept looking—"

"Maude, what is it?" Laura repeated, concern etched on her face.

Maude waved the paper again. "A clue! Probably a significant clue! Look at this—it's a note somebody wrote somebody, and then tried to hide it down in that chair over there, and I'd bet dollars to doughnuts it's a note from one of the killers to another one!"

Laura held out her hand. "Can I see?"

"Hold it by the edges. There may be fingerprints."

Laura frowned over the message.

Vanlandingham looked over her shoulder. "Oh, no!" he groaned.

"What?" Maude chirped.

"It's another one," Vanlandingham said, and began to giggle. "Oh, this is ridiculous. This is priceless! Ho ho ho."

"What?" Maude repeated in dismay.

Laura said, "Another script clue, George?"

"Yes. Brick Abercrombie was supposed to find this note in the chair in scene six. I guess we all forgot about it, with all the excitement."

Maude began to feel nauseated. "You mean—"

Laura handed the scrap back to her. "It's a clue that was planted for the play, Maude. We found some broken glasses and a little gun earlier, too. Same stuff. Oh, don't look so sad. Really, it's awfully easy to be fooled at a time like this. We've had script clues misidentified as real ones before."

Maude studied Vanlandingham's horrid, chuckling face. "Are you sure about this?"

"Of course! My dear woman, I am so sorry! What a disappointment this must be for you."

Maude stood there, all her pep draining down through her throbbing knees and pooling somewhere at the bottom of her shoes. This was really pretty hard to take.

Wearily she told Laura, "Maybe I'd better come to this session after all."

FEELING REALLY SORRY for her, Laura patted Maude's shoulder. The little woman suddenly looked a hundred years old, and very close to tears. "Why don't you go on in, then, Maude? I've got to run down and put some paper in the duplicating machine, and run a couple of copies of things. Then I'll be right in." She turned to Vanlandingham, who was by now wiping tears of laughter out of his eyes. "You can come along and copy that notice for the company just as soon as I run these three pages."

Vanlandingham replaced his handkerchief. "No, that's fine.

I'll do it a little later. I just remembered one more thing I really ought to include in this notice.'' He turned and hurried away.

Maude Thuringer, shoulders slumped, walked toward the activity room doorway, meeting the Castles there. They went in together.

Poor Maude, Laura thought, hurrying to the copy room.

As Vanlandingham had reported, the machine had run out of paper. Laura grabbed a stack out of the metal supply cabinet and pulled out the machine's drawer. Reloading it was simplicity itself, but Mrs. Epperman had put a sign on the wall implying the death penalty for any non-staff member ''attempting maintenance of any kind.''

Mrs. Epperman was very efficient in such areas, Laura reflected, patting down the stack of pink copier paper she had installed. The Timberdale manager had gotten a wonderful deal on paper the last time she ordered: she'd paid less than half price. The only problem was that it turned out to be paper no one else would buy—some red, some green, some yellow, some blue, some pink, all of it making copies that were hard to read because the colors were quite dark.

Maybe, Laura thought, the pink wouldn't be quite as bad as the green supply they had just finally depleted. She wondered if any members of the acting company would have to get new eyeglasses as a result of trying to make out all the script changes Vanlandingham had printed out on the green stuff.

She ran her copies of the three pages about dealing with stress and grief. The pink paper was just as bad—and even uglier—than the green had been. Abandoning *that* little hope, she left the machine running for Vanlandingham's imminent return and headed for the activity room.

So here I go to try to help them, she thought despairingly, *and I can't even help myself.*

I can't even remember something that just happened to me, and might change everything.

The memory was *right there*, just beyond a gauzy curtain in her mind. She could not reach it. But she had to reach it. How?

TWENTY

THE SIZE of the crowd in the activity room instantly told Laura more about resident turmoil than anything she might have intuited earlier. She had never had this many in any single session before today.

Most of the members of the Breakfast Club already had taken the chairs she had had Still Bill Mills arrange in a large semicircle, and the Friday Lone Rangers were well represented too. As she walked to the front and put down her notebooks as casually as possible, she counted them: fifteen in all, familiar faces including Ellen Smith, Maude Thuringer, the Castles, Judge Young, Davilla Rose, Ken Keen, the Pfeisters, Sada Hoff, the Buckinghams and the Clovers, all looking solemn and worried.

The fifteenth person in the room, however, surprised Laura most of all. Seated on the end of the second row nearest the wall, the lanky figure in bib overalls looked more uncomfortable than all the others put together. He had never come to a session before.

Laura smiled in his direction. "Bill, you did a great job arranging the chairs for all of us. We thank you for that. But my goodness, I know you don't even ordinarily come in on the weekends. You certainly don't have to stick around. I don't think we need any more help right now, if you have other stuff to do."

Several of the members turned to look at Still Bill Mills, whose face worked as he formulated a reply. "I've got a lot of cleaning to do downstairs, Laura, but if it's okay with everybody, I'd sort of like to stay."

"Why, sure, Bill." Laura glanced around. "I'm sure that's fine with everybody, isn't it, guys?"

A few heads nodded agreement. Still Bill's big Adam's apple went up and down. He added, "It ain't like I'm mourning Redwine or anything. You all know I had a serious distruption with him over the easel when he first destinated. He wanted me to be a subservant to him, and I don't like that. Like they always say, 'Never a beggar or a bender be.' But maybe I ought to have been back there making sure I couldn't help more. Maybe if I had, this wouldn't have happened. The colonel might still be with us."

"You're upset because you're blaming yourself," Laura interpreted.

Still Bill's eyes became wetter and brighter than normal. "I feel," he said in a choking voice, "like I have almost totally evaptuated as a person."

Maude Thuringer flipped pages of her notebook. "Relax! You're not even on my list of suspects anymore."

Ellen Smith's Indian jewelry rattled. "And my goodness, Bill, it wasn't your fault!"

"Right," Stoney Castle chimed in, turning in his chair. "I mean, glory be, you can't be everyplace at once. Get aholt of yourself, man."

Laura smiled sympathetically. "I know what you're trying to say, Stoney, but I'm sure all of us remember one of the key things we've learned in earlier sessions. When someone is upset, it doesn't help to tell them to 'get a hold of themselves' or 'straighten up,' or something like that. They're *upset;* they have a right to whatever feelings they're feeling. What they need is help working through the feelings, not advice to stop feeling that way." She swung her gaze back to Still Bill Mills. "If you could just stop feeling that way, you already would have, right, Bill?"

Still Bill nodded so hard his baseball cap fell off. "I can subside my own emotions, usually. I mean, I'm selfcontainered and stabled. But this thing has shocked me down to my gallbladder."

Laura hesitated. She loved this old man. He had been her

best ally during all her time at Timberdale. "What would you have to do, Bill, to feel better?"

"I guess get the colonel out of the clink!"

"I mean, is there something you can think of that you might do for yourself right now to try to ease some of these bad feelings? Something you've done before when you were having a bad time?"

He thought about it. "Might go fishing."

"Fishing sometimes cheers you up?"

"Uh-huh."

Laura addressed the group. "What do you think, guys? Do you think he might feel a little better if he took the afternoon off and just went fishing?"

Again heads nodded.

Sada Hoff said dubiously, "It's cold out there again today."

Laura turned back. "Is it too cold, Bill?"

"Heck no," he said instantly. He seemed to look more cheerful.

"Maybe you ought to think about that a few minutes, then. Let us hear from some of the others, and then we'll get back to you. Okay?"

The Adam's apple took several more trips. He *did* look more upbeat. "Good idea."

Laura scanned again. "Who else needs something today from the group?" Hands went up. Laura pretended not to see Maude Thuringer's frantic waving. "Dot?"

Mrs. Pfeister's small bosom rose and fell with emotion. All in pink today, a tiny woman who walked in a regular cloud of sachet, she looked like a florist's summer concoction. "We thought we would have a lot of fun. Mrs. Epperman *told us* we were going to have a lot of fun."

"I know." Laura murmured sympathetically.

The old woman's jaw hardened. "*You* told us it would be fun."

"I know. I thought it would be."

"Now we've had violence—murder—right here in Timberdale. This is our *home*. We're supposed to feel secure. Last year, when those residents died, it was horrible. But we got over all that. Now something terrible has happened *again*.''

Laura nodded and tried to restate: ''It's like a big rubber band snapped, and we're all back in those bad feelings we had a year ago.''

''Yes! And the colonel didn't do it, either!''

The murmur of approval was louder this time.

Ken Keen piped up from the second row, ''Laura, how come you can't remember who conked you?''

''I don't know, Ken. I just can't. I guess I will.''

''Dr. Which says amnesia is temporary.''

''I understand it usually is. There are cases, though—''

''He said that's only a small percentage. So when are you going to remember?''

''I don't know.''

Keen shook his head. ''That's *terrible*. You ought to be able to remember something that happened like that.''

Ellen Smith interrupted testily, ''She would if she could, Ken. We all know that.''

''Well,'' Keen whined, ''I know, I know. But maybe she just ought to try harder.''

''Perhaps,'' Judge Young rumbled, ''she is among those in that lilliputian percentage.''

Keen frowned. ''*What* kind of percentage?''

''The small percentage you mentioned who never regain it.''

''Regain what?''

''I believe, sir, you were speaking of short-term memory.''

Keen's face twisted, puzzled. ''I never said anything about memory.''

Laura stepped in to break the impasse. ''Actually, I haven't remembered much yet. But I really think I'm going to...any minute.''

''What makes you think so?'' Stoney Castle demanded suspiciously.

''Well, because there have been a few times when ...*almost*...remembered. I mean, it was right there at the brink. I felt as if it were ready to pop out, and all I had to do was sort of…look at it. Then it blipped away again.'' She gave them all a reassuring smile that had more certainty in it than she truly felt. ''I'm going to remember any time now. I know it.''

They all stared at her for a moment, and the silence became deep. She saw she had made a point of some kind, one she hoped made them feel better.

''Wow,'' Maude Thuringer said. ''Do you know what you just did, Laura? Assuming it isn't a trick to take yourself off the suspect list, I mean?''

Laura almost showed her irritation. ''I didn't know I was a suspect, Maude.''

''Of course you're a suspect! Almost everybody is a suspect.''

''I—''

''You dangled!'' Maude went right on. She looked frenetic with excitement. ''You dangled yourself.''

Stoney Castle turned violently in his chair. ''What the hell are you talking about now, woman?''

''Stoney,'' his wife warned, mortified.

''Well, dammit, she isn't making sense!''

''Of course I am,'' Maude shot back. ''When the FBI wants to trap somebody, one of the ways they do it, sometimes, is to let the word leak out that so-and-so is another criminal, maybe, or that so-and-so has info that the bad guys have to shut up. They call that 'dangling' somebody—they put the person out there in plain view, and watch them like a hawk, and then when the bad guys approach the dangle, the FBI can arrest them.'' Her bright eyes swung back to Laura. ''You just made yourself a dangle. If the colonel didn't do it, the minute word spreads that you're almost remembering, the real killer is going to have to take you out.'' Maude paused again before loftily explaining, ''That's the term we insiders use for murder. Sometimes we call it elimination, too. The CIA calls it termination with—''

"Could we get on with something worthwhile?" Castle asked.

Laura hesitated. She hadn't intended to make herself a "dangle," and her first impulse was to think Maude had just had another of her delusions. But a small voice inside started whispering alarm. *What if I did just dangle myself?* She felt a gust of fear, which she quickly tried to extinguish.

"Let's go on," she told the group. "There must be other things we need to talk about."

Davilla Rose waved her hand.

"Yes, Davilla?"

The tiny woman held up her notebook, which had purple paper flowers glued to the cover. "I've written a poem about the poor colonel," she announced.

Several people groaned.

"It expresses our sadness!" Davilla protested, hurt.

"I think we should let Davilla read her poem," Laura said.

"Couldn't stop her anyway," Ellen Smith snapped.

"Nobody appreciates me," Davilla said in a tiny voice.

"Please share your poem with us, Davilla," Laura urged.

The little woman opened the notebook and cleared her throat as she peered down her nose through her reading glasses. "It's called 'The Colonel Is in Jail.'"

"Hear, hear," Stoney Castle muttered sarcastically.

Davilla began to read:

"Sunset and evening star!
And the colonel is in jail,
Far away from all his friends,
And they even read his mail.

"Sunset and evening bell!
And you may write it in your journal:
We loved him all, and now he's gone,
Alas! We miss the colonel.

"Sunset and evening tide!
And though he sometimes irked us,
Life is sad without the colonel,

With his love he never shirked us.
"Sunset, and the day is gone,
And how can we retrieve it?
The colonel's gone—we may be next.
The end is near; believe it."

Davilla stopped, blinking. The room had gone totally silent. Laura held her breath. She could hear someone's stomach growling.

"Madam," Judge Young said at last, "you have outdone yourself." Pulling out a large linen handkerchief, he dabbed at his eyes.

"Beautiful," Ellen Smith whispered.

Davilla looked stunned. "You *liked* it?"

Ken Keen said, "Could you read it again?"

"Good heavens, Ken!" Ellen Smith snarled. "Give us a break!"

Laura intervened. "I think we're just a little bit on edge, after what's happened. Would you all agree with that?"

Someone else began speaking. The group was unusually polite today. First one, then another member talked about his or her shock. An outsider might have thought some of the descriptions were melodramatic. But Laura had started to understand the oldsters at least a little bit, and the dynamic at work. When you were old, your health went up and down, and so did your emotions. Every illness, every scare, every night alone thinking you would soon die, stripped away a little more of your emotional resources. Some of them had very few emotional tools left. Their upsets were not a laughing matter.

The session lasted an hour. No one left early. Wishing she were smarter and could feel she had done a lot more for them, Laura finally had to close things off for the moment. "We can have another special session on Monday, if you like."

Several voices called out yeses. She closed her notebook with what she hoped was a cheerful smile and waited while they shuffled to the door. She heard Still Bill Mills telling the Buckinghams, "She's great, that's all, just *great*. I never realized how great. She's car-asthmatic, is what she is. I tell you, I hold her in the highest self-exteem.''

"And," Mrs. Buckingham said, nodding agreement, "she's still just a student. Can you imagine that? She's still learning.''

Hearing that, Laura thought of some of her teachers at OU, and especially of her faculty adviser. Dr. Barnett Hodges was one of the smartest men she had ever met. She wondered what he would think about her amnesia.

Then it occurred to her that there might be something she could do about that question. Feeble hope stirred. She hurried outside and across the atrium.

In her office, some additional mail and paperwork had piled up. On top of the pile was a single sheet of pink duplicating machine paper with a jotted Post-It note stuck on it. In George Vanlandingham's huge scrawl, it said: *Just FYI.—George.* The sheet seemed to be a page out of the script. In it, the Brick Abercrombie character was finding the note that Maude Thuringer had just discovered in the atrium chair.

She stuck the page back on the top of the paper pile and reached for the telephone. Dr. Barnett Hodges had often made it clear that he liked being called at home on the weekend about like getting a bad head cold. But she just had to risk it.

Besides, she told herself, remembering the crazy things Maude Thuringer had said, if she really had dangled herself, she would be safer on the Oklahoma campus than here.

She would be safer anywhere than here.

TWENTY-ONE

COLD, BRISK WIND tattered the sound of the student union carillons chiming five o'clock as Laura got out of her Toyota just west of the main campus in Norman. Fighting her skirt and hair at the same time, she ran across the lawn of the old brick residence that the university had taken over to use as headquarters for the school of social work.

Ducking inside with relief, she climbed the rickety wood stairs to the second floor, where faculty offices were located. It felt odd not to have Aaron Lassiter at her side, but she had insisted and he had reluctantly agreed: She could talk to her faculty adviser about this alone as long as she agreed to wait in the safety of the school building afterward until Lassiter came to escort her home.

This being Saturday, the secretaries' desks in the cramped reception area were vacant, the computer terminals dim, the ceiling lights out. Laura felt a stab of anxiety, based on nothing, as she crossed the dimly lit area and entered the hallway that led to Dr. Barnett Hodges's office. She tried to put the sudden, irrational fear out of her mind and went on to find his door open, the lights ablaze, the good professor himself slouched behind an old wood desk piled high with papers and books of all descriptions, a haze of his pipe smoke in the air.

Spying her, he removed the big Oom Paul pipe from the thicket of beard around his mouth and gave a wave. "Laura. Get in here."

She entered and sat down in the familiar chair facing his mountain of disorganized work. "I thought you had quit smoking that thing," she told him with a smile.

Hodges, a gorillalike man with fierce dark eyebrows and a disposition that swung between Godzilla and Snow White, replaced the pipestem between his teeth and puffed. "I did. But then our nonsmoking president came out with his latest plan to ban smoking everywhere on campus, and I thought I needed to strike a small blow for freedom. The goddam fascist, I don't know how we can ever get rid of him. Give him another two years and there won't be any students left, or classes, just wall-to-wall administrators writing more of these goddam regulations."

"Maybe," Laura suggested, "he'll go away."

Hodges snorted. "Who would have him?" He put the pipe down in the mess on his desk. "But that isn't what you came to talk about. You want coffee?"

"No thanks."

He got up and ponderously moved the two steps from overloaded desk to incredibly messed-up bookshelf, where a coffee maker lurked among the textbooks. Pouring some vile-looking black brew into a red OU Sooners cup, he said, "You mentioned amnesia?"

"Yes."

"You've got it?"

"Yes."

He came back and sat down, peering over the desk mountains with genuine concern. "You said you got hit on the head. I see the little bandage. Do you want to tell me about that?"

"I'll tell you what I know about it," Laura said ruefully, and she did.

When she finished, Hodges sipped his coffee and scowled into space a long moment. Then he asked, "Any severe headaches since then? Maybe migraines?"

"No. I don't do migraines. I've had some little headaches, but nothing too bad."

Hodges's eyes narrowed. "What's your home telephone number?"

Surprised, Laura said, "Five five five, two two nine oh."

"Our departmental number?"

"Five five five, two seven two one. What is this?"

"How many hours did you take last semester?"

"Ten. What's this all about?"

"Humor me. Where did you go to high school?"

"Tulsa Rogers. What *is* this?"

"You don't seem to have any impairment of general background memory. Try this one: What was the first thing you said when you walked in here a minute ago?"

"Something about that stinky pipe, and you quitting smoking."

"Good. Have you been having any nightmares? Flashbacks?"

"Well, I've had a couple of occasions when I almost remembered what I've forgotten, but then it goes away again."

"Any restricted range of affect that you've noticed?"

"Not really." Laura felt her face warm. "Actually, I had a really dumb burst of jealousy a while ago that isn't like me at all."

Hodges leaned back and fiddled with his pipe again. "I think we can rule out post-traumatic stress disorder, at least as it's defined in the DSM-IIIR. You show no signs of anterograde amnesia, either. No fugue states? No hysteria?"

"Well," Laura admitted reluctantly, "I do get these brief moments of panic, like when I walked in here just now and everything was quiet and dark up front."

Hodges's keen eyes seemed to bore into her. "But you didn't run, did you? Or scream?"

"No. I was just—uneasy for a few seconds."

"After what happened to you the other day, I'd say a certain amount of fear is a healthy reaction. Any dizziness? Nausea?"

"Not really."

"Well, Laura, it sounds to me like a fairly straightforward case of what we would characterize under the generalization 'retrograde amnesia.' It doesn't sound like there was serious trauma to the cortex or the limbic area. I think you're going to be fine."

"I do too," Laura said. "But when am I going to remember? Dammit, I might know who the killer is!"

Hodges locked beefy hands over his chest. "In a case like

yours, as I understand it, there might be a problem because you suffered slight bleeding somewhere in the brain, and there was actually some small minor cellular damage—a problem with the hardware, as it were—which will heal up in maybe a day, maybe a week, maybe a month.''

"A month!"

"That's all possible. On the other hand, there could have been virtually no physical damage, but what you've got is some kind of trick of the unconscious mind, protecting your consciousness from an ugly, shocking memory by keeping it repressed for right now—more of a software problem, to maintain the silly computer metaphor."

"What can I do?" Laura asked, already feeling a touch of despondency because she thought she saw the obvious answer.

"Cool it," Hodges told her bluntly. "It will come back when it comes back. I don't think there's a damned thing in the world you can do to hurry matters along, and you might even bury the memory deeper by obsessing about it. I'm guessing, but your best bet might be to stop looking for it, and try to think about other stuff entirely. Lost memories sometimes are a little like insights in therapy: They jump out at you when you're least expecting them."

Laura studied his gruff, kindly expression and then got slowly to her feet. "So maybe I should just try *not* to search for the memory?"

"Maybe. It's a shadow area nobody can advise you about with any authority, I think. Least of all me."

She clutched her purse. "I want to thank you for seeing me like this."

He shrugged massive sloped shoulders. "I had to come in anyway. To smoke. Laura…"

"Yes?"

"Take it easy on yourself. Be careful. A lot of people around here think very highly of you for more reasons than one." He paused, seemed to think about it, and then grimaced. "Including me, actually, if you must know. Some of your classwork has been outstanding. The geriatric counseling you're doing out there is excellent. We would like to see you both safe and happy for a while.'' His keen eyes studied her. "Okay?''

"Okay,'' she replied, flushed with good feelings. "Thanks, Dr. Hodges.''

"Get outta here,'' he growled. "I've got work to do.''

She went back down the dim, dusty hall with a feeling of disappointment and a new flickering of that nameless fear. She had hoped Hodges could give her more hope, possibly even suggest a line of thought that might flush memory out of hiding. Instead, he had told her that all she could do was be patient and wait.

If she waited, she thought, and memory did not return, it seemed crystal clear that the sheriff could not detain cast members or Rebecca Redwine beyond the first of the week. They would leave, perhaps scatter; and her instincts told her that the last chance of finding the real murderer would be gone with them. That would leave thin circumstantial evidence, and the colonel.

Colonel Roger Rodgers was no more a murderer than she was, she thought. She somehow felt that this certainty was based on more than her acquaintance with him for over a year at Timberdale. Was she also so certain because of what was in her memory, even though it remained maddeningly out of consciousness? Like so many other questions, this one seemed to have no answer.

Peering out through the front door of the building, she saw no sign yet of Lassiter's sheriff's cruiser. She leaned against the wall and waited, watching the seemingly ceaseless wind hurl dried leaves and dirt across Jenkins Avenue. She felt depressed.

Whatever had happened to her in that back hallway of Timberdale had changed something about her, and she was beginning to become increasingly—dismayingly—aware of that. She had a scare inside her that would not go away. She felt as if somebody were watching her. She felt as if something bad were about to happen. The pervasive, unfocused feeling of dread resembled descriptions she had read about chronic depression. But she had been deeply depressed three years ago when her marriage was crumbling, and for some time afterward; this black sensation was not quite the same.

Standing in the dim hallway, she shook her head and tried again, for what seemed the thousandth time, to remember. There wasn't any more. She thought about what Dr. Hodges had just told her: Perhaps striving to dredge up those lost moments was the worst possible thing she could be doing.

Maybe, then she needed to try to forget about forgetting—just think of other things entirely. But that idea sounded nutty as well as paradoxical. It made additional depression stir inside her. How, after all, *could* she stop thinking about it? What in the hell was she supposed to think about instead? About when she might get back the grade on that test she had taken what now seemed like a hundred years ago? About Pierre Motard's menu for next week? About whether Mrs. Epperman would get through to Cleopatra over the weekend?

A car turned the corner outside, headlights shining through the gathering cloudy gloom of the afternoon. She saw the star emblem on the passenger-side door and went out to meet Lassiter.

TWENTY-TWO

WITH A GLOOMY sandwich supper out of the way, members of the Redwine Players filed into the meeting called by George Vanlandingham in his third-floor apartment at Timberdale Retirement Center. No one seemed happy, but four low-key conversations started going at once.

Vanlandingham, wearing charcoal sweats with a red bandanna knotted around his neck, hopped up on one of the dining room chairs and issued a piercing whistle that stopped all those present dead in their tracks. "Okay, people, let's have your attention, please. We've got several important topics to discuss here. Sit down someplace. If you want a Coke or something, go out to the vending machine now and get it—we don't want people wandering in and out, and I sure don't have anything in the fridge."

For a few seconds everyone stood still, startled expressions on their faces. Then Franklin Pierce Lord, standing at the end of the sofa, drew himself up dramatically. "Since when, Van, have you assumed proprietorship of the Redwine Players?"

Vanlandingham's jaw worked. "I haven't 'assumed' anything, F.P. I just want to get this show on the road."

Lord, wearing pin-striped suit trousers and a white dress shirt open at the throat, stared back with obvious hostility. "This company was a dictatorship far too long. I, for one, am not about to stand idly by and allow you to take control by default."

Tad Raddell came back in from the kitchen alcove with a box of Triscuits in hand. "I agree with that. We *all* get a say now."

"I'm not trying to take control of anything. Tomorrow or the next day the goddamned police will tell us we're free to leave, and I just think *somebody* has to take the bull by the horns and see that we know what the hell we're going to do at that time."

Lord continued to stare. "And you automatically become the person who runs the show?"

"I'm not trying to run anything!"

Janis Mahafey, in shorts and a lightweight sweater, draped a long, bare leg over one arm of the easy chair she had appropriated. "If we're to go on at all, the rule has to be one member, one vote."

Deena Sweete, standing near the draped windows, impatiently tapped a high-heeled shoe. The movement made reflections scintillate on the length of her skin-tight metallic pants. "No one said *you* had to go on with the troupe, Janis."

"Fuck you, Deena."

"In your ear."

"You—!"

"Ladies!"

Freddie Filmont, wearing a one-piece corduroy jumpsuit that had never seen an iron, made an impatient gesture that rattled the ice cubes in her tall highball glass. Her uneven lipstick and smeared mascara made her look like a picture taken out of focus. "This ish no time for dishager—dishgree—fighting."

"I certainly subscribe to that," Vanlandingham exclaimed gratefully.

"Madam," Lord told Filmont with heavy dignity, "disagreement—which is the word I believe you found it impossible to articulate in your present condition—is to be expected here. The question is, whether the Redwine Players will, at long last, function in a fair manner with everyone's voice being heard."

Vanlandingham protested, "I was only trying to get a meeting started."

Mahafey waved a taloned hand. "Then go ahead, Van, for God's sake!"

"Maybe somebody else would rather run the meeting."

"You may *chair* the meeting," Lord told him. "Just understand that you are not de facto dictator of our little organization."

"God," Vanlandingham murmured.

Sweete said, "Reddy's funeral will be Monday."

"Where?" Mahafey asked.

"Here. I mean in Norman."

"Who told you that?"

"Rebecca."

"But they're from—"

"I know. But she said there's not enough money to ship his body halfway across the country. She said she's already bought a plot in the Norman cemetery, and he's to be buried there."

Vanlandingham added, "I was on the other phone here when Rebecca called to inform us. There's to be no wake or anything like that. The funeral director will say a few words at the graveside."

"Well," Mahafey said, "we certainly all have to stay around for *that*."

"To the contrary," Vanlandingham told her.

Mahafey's big green eyes widened. "What?"

"The reason Rebecca called to inform us of the plans was to tell me she wants none of us there. She said she plans to have two off-duty policemen on hand, and if any of us try to show up at the graveside, we'll be arrested."

Mahafey made a small moue of outrage.

"That's nutty!" Raddell exclaimed.

"It's what she wants," Vanlandingham said.

"But *why?*" Mahafey cried.

"Because," Sweete said, "she's a bitch."

"Or perhaps," Lord said, "she wants to put him in the ground, at least, without any of his girlfriends present."

"What do you mean by that?" Sweete shrilled.

"Yes, what do you mean by that?" Mahafey added.

Filmont drained her glass and plunked it down on the end

table. "Thish ish a waste of time. I'm going to my own
room."

"Freddie, please don't go. We have important issues to decide," said Vanlandingham.

Lord said, "Then by all means let us get on with it."

"May I raise some of the questions?" Vanlandingham's
voice dripped sarcasm.

"Get on with it, get on with it," Raddell muttered.

Vanlandingham glanced at a scrap of paper in his hand.
"We have a contract to put on a mystery weekend in a town
up north of Oklahoma City next weekend. It isn't far. We
could all go up there Monday or Tuesday, look the site over,
make sure payment is in order, and then take two days off.
Of course I'll be working on the script during that time—"

"Retreading the same old pages, you mean," Sweete put
in.

"—but all of you can get some rest," Vanlandingham went
on as if she hadn't spoken. "We now have five actors—Deena,
Janis, Freddie, F.P., and Tad. I can rewrite scripts to use no
more actors than that. I am also willing to take over duties as
tour business manager. The five of you, plus me, six persons
in all. I propose that we continue to call ourselves the Redwine
Players for the time being. Maybe we can even get some publicity mileage out of Reddy's death. You know: 'Acting troupe
carries on mystery scene after real-life murder takes leader.'
That kind of crap. We—"

"How is the money divided?" Lord cut in rudely.

"A weekly budget is drawn," Vanlandingham replied.

"One of Reddy's secret budgets?"

Vanlandingham's face had gotten dark and sweaty. "No.
Everyone gets a copy every Monday morning. It shows what
we took in, what our expenses were, including gasoline, food,
equipment—everything—and what our net was after all those
deductions. The five actors receive equal payment—fifteen
percent each—because you'll all be speaking more lines, pulling together in this thing. I—"

"That's seventy-five percent," Sweete said.

"Right, right. You see—"

"Where does the other twenty-five percent go?"

"Well, I should receive an equal share for handling arrangements, doing advance work, constantly revising and updating scripts, and so on. I *certainly* don't think it's unfair that I should also be paid another ten percent for all the bookkeeping, planning, public relations, and other work I'll be doing to keep the company intact."

"Is that equality?" Lord demanded.

"Yeah!" Raddell put in. "There's got to be equity, man."

"Precisely," Lord said. "As the senior actor who will be called upon to carry a grave additional burden of dramatic contribution, I believe it would only be fair if *I* were the one to receive additional remuneration, if any were to be voted."

"My ass," Sweete said acidly. "You couldn't act your way out of a paper hat. I'm the one people pay money to see."

"My dear girl—"

"Whersh *this* money?" Filmont broke in.

Lord swung around to face her. "What?"

She waved, rattling jewelry. "Whersh the money we're s'posed to get for thish gig here?"

All eyes turned to Vanlandingham. Looking more nervous, he said, "I talked to Mrs. Epperman at home a while ago. She had already called the bank yesterday. She wrote a check to Reddy, and do you remember the other day when he was gone somewhere for a couple of hours? He must have driven into Norman and cashed the check at the bank, because it had already been paid when Mrs. Epperman looked into it. That has to be the large amount of cash that I understand the police found in his room."

"Then whersh it now?" Filmont asked.

"Held as evidence."

"Lodda good that does us!"

"It will be released to Rebecca at some point, I am told. I've called her motel and left a message. I'm sure she will want to be fair with the distribution when it comes into her possession."

"Right," Raddell said acidly. "I'm sure she'll bust her butt, getting us our fair share."

"Right," Sweete said. "And maybe she'll become an astronaut, too."

"Damnation," Lord fumed. "Perhaps if Miss Michaels continues to regain her memory, she will be able to shed light on some of this."

Vanlandingham squinted. "*Continue* to regain her memory?"

Lord nodded. "Some of the oldsters are quite agog. Talking and speculating about little else. It seems Miss Michaels told some of them in a meeting earlier today that bits and pieces of memory are coming back, and she expects to remember everything at any minute."

"She might remember something about the money," Mahafey exclaimed.

"Or the murderer," Lord added. "Which could lead to a solution and result in the release of the money sooner."

"We can't hope for that, though," Raddell said. "I just hope to hell Rebecca will listen to reason. I don't think she will, but I can hope."

"Has she ever?" Sweete asked.

Vanlandingham fidgeted. "We can't do anything about that for the moment. But maybe we can reach some of these other decisions. Do we want to honor the contract next weekend?"

"Yes," Lord said at once. "Assuming an equitable, guaranteed distribution of payment."

"I'll photocopy the check," Vanlandingham said. "Then I'll cash it. I'll withhold past expenses and enough to get us through to the next date, which I think I can set up for Wichita, from what I know about arrangements pending. Whatever is left, we'll divide: cash payments."

"Evenly," Lord said.

"We'll argue that later," Vanlandingham said.

Mahafey uncoiled her legs. "What I want to know is—"

An insistent rapping on the door interrupted her. Raddell,

closest to it, stepped over and opened it. Rebecca Redwine strode into the room, tail of her mink coat flaring.

The lady looked furious. She stopped in the kitchen doorway and canted her hands on her hips. "What's going on here?"

"Rebecca," Vanlandingham said nervously. "I'm so glad you came. We're trying to decide the future of the Redwine Players, you see, and—"

"Well, you can just forget anything you've decided!"

"What?"

Rebecca Redwine pointed a thumb at her own chest. "This company isn't just a hobby organization, kids. It *is* a company. And as Reddy's widow, I inherit sole and total ownership. *I* make the decisions from now on—if this wacko organization is even to continue to exist."

"But we are the players!" Lord protested.

"And I am the owner. So shut up. I've made some decisions, and here they are."

TWENTY-THREE

Squatting behind a five-foot plastic schefflera plant in the alcove just outside George Vanlandingham's room, Maude Thuringer could hear all the shouting and some of the words.

Maude's knees were killing her, but this was really good stuff.

She had known it would be when she saw Rebecca Redwine steam in from the parking lot and head for the back elevators like the 82nd Airborne going to Iraq. Maude had been on her way up to see if she could sneak around and get any information out of the actors' meeting anyway, but Mrs. Redwine's expression and pace made her hurry into a riskier hiding place than she might otherwise have taken, getting there just in time to see the lady rush up the corridor, bang on the door, and go in with verbal guns blazing.

They were all yelling in there now, but Maude could get just enough to understand what was going on. Mrs. Redwine was asserting her ownership of the company. Nobody appreciated that. One of the younger actresses—Maude thought it sounded like Deena Sweete—called Mrs Redwine an old bag. Mrs. Redwine called Sweete an opportunistic chippie. Somebody—maybe Franklin Pierce Lord—tried to calm things down. Someone else—Freddie Filmont, Maude thought—told Lord to shut his fat mouth. Then everybody yelled at once for a while.

It had been going on like that for a long time.

Now Maude heard Mrs. Redwine's voice more clearly, evidently nearer the closed door: "*You've heard the facts, and you can take it or leave it.*"

The door banged open and Mrs. Redwine came out into the hall, making Maude shrink back in terror of being spotted.

Mrs. Redwine stabbed a finger back at the people in the room. "I'll expect an answer by noon tomorrow. That's my last word on it."

Franklin Pierce Lord came halfway out of the room. "My dear lady—"

"Don't 'my dear lady' me, you windbag! My husband is dead and none of you give a hoot. But you're not going to start making a profit from his dear reputation. *I'm* the Redwine Players now, and don't you forget it."

Lord stood transfixed as Mrs. Redwine turned her back on him and rushed down the hall, around the corner, and out of sight. Some of the others who had been in the room spilled out into the hallway.

"My God, what do we do now?" George Vanlandingham moaned, wringing his hands.

"I won't work for her!" Janis Mahafey cried.

"She said you were fired anyway," Deena Sweete said. "What did she mean about having some awful pictures?"

Tad Raddell glowered. "The old biddy. Somebody should kill her, too."

Freddie Filmont staggered out, bumping into Lord and almost falling. "Thish terrible. Thish worsh thing worl'. Oh, Vanny, whadda we do now?"

"Be quiet, be quiet," Vanlandingham said nervously. "Look, everybody. I'll let her cool down an hour or two and then try to call her. Maybe I can talk some sense into her."

Deena Sweete wailed, "But what do we do right now?"

"Just... let me try to think.... Oh, dear.... Just go to your rooms. Try to relax. Oh, I know that's impossible, but just— take it easy. Maybe I can talk sense to her. We'll all get together here in my room again at seven in the morning, all right?"

Lord said heavily. "If she makes this stick, Van, all of us are doomed. We can't work for her. She would be worse than Reddy was. You must find a way to change her mind."

Vanlandingham looked at the older man, and his voice went

flat with bitterness. "It's all up for grabs, and suddenly I can be in charge again?"

"Oh, I say, old man. This is no time for resentment."

The clot of people started to break up, making Maude shrink even deeper in the corner.

"I'm going out to the parking lot for a sec," Raddell said. "I think there's still some beer in the chest out there."

"I shall accompany you," Lord said.

Sweete and Mahafey exchanged a glare and then walked away, each pretending the other didn't exist.

Vanlandingham stood dejected in his doorway. Filmont, bleary-eyed, hung back until the others had gone around the corner.

"What do we do?" she asked in a thick whisper.

"I don't know," Vanlandingham said in a tone that made Maude chill. "Go to your room and stay there."

"But—"

"Go to your room and stay there, goddammit. I'll be in touch."

Filmont stared at him for a long moment. "We're in thish together."

"*Go*, will you?"

She turned and staggered up the hall and out of sight. Vanlandingham went back into his room. The door closed.

Maude tried to get up. Her knees screamed at her. Moaning through gritted teeth, she rolled over onto her back, managed to sit up, and then turned over on hands and knees, and narrowly managed to get upright. Clutching her notebook close to her breast, she limped away in the direction opposite that taken by the others, heading for the back fire stairs.

Safely back in her own room ten minutes later, she went immediately to the telephone. Her desk directory had Laura Michaels's home number in it. She dialed it. The telephone at the other end rang four times, and then Laura's familiar voice came on, a recorded message on an answering machine.

Maude waited anxiously for the beep. It came. "Laura, Maude here. When you get in, call me. I've got some really neat info this time. Mrs. Redwine is taking over the company, and everybody is mad as the dickens about it. George Van-What's-His-Name is in cahoots with Freddie Filmont, about what I don't know yet. I'm going to watch them like a hawk, kiddo. I've got more other good stuff to tell you too, so call me when you get in. 'Bye.''

That vital thing done, Maude sat down at her mahogany secretary and started writing up her notes just as fast as she could make her trembly hand form the letters.

TWENTY-FOUR

TRISSIE LOOKED UP at her mother as Red Riding Hood must have looked at the Big Bad Wolf. "Who *said* I'd have a nicer night over at Jill's house?"

Laura knelt and gave her daughter a hug. "Honey, I explained all that to you. There's all kinds of stuff going on with my job, and you've had a nice time with Jill and her mom so far this weekend."

Trissie's pout went ballistic. "You said I could come home as soon as you got back tonight after that dumb old weekend seminar thing. You *said.*"

Laura looked up despairingly at Aaron Lassiter, standing by with a glum washboard forehead, and her usual babysitter, Jill, whose pretty teenage face had the hot pink flush of excitement she always seemed to get when Lassiter was around. "Trissie, I just explained to you, honey. There's so much going on with my job and everything, I'm not even getting to attend the seminar session tonight."

"Then you oughta let me stay home."

Lassiter squatted beside Laura and patted Trissie's arm. "This will all get squared away, Tris, and next weekend we'll do something special. Okay?"

Trissie glared. "Next weekend is Dad's weekend, and I'll have to sit around and work puzzles and stuff while he and Heather make out."

"Oh, God," Laura breathed.

Jill's blond hair fluffed in her own breeze as she pounced on Trissie. "Come on, honey. We'll have lots of fun. Mom's making oatmeal cookies."

"Oatmeal. Yuk!"

"Trissie," Laura said firmly, "this is not negotiable."

"I didn't think it was," Trissie shot back. "Nothing ever is, with you. What we're seeing here is the Balkanization of our whole relationship. I'm getting real sick of it, Mom."

"Honey, do this for me without any more argument, okay? We'll talk about Balkanization tomorrow night when you come home."

"The DSM-IIIR would say you've got some kind of an authority problem," Trissie told her.

"Have you been reading the DSM-IIIR again? Dammit, Trissie—"

"All right, all right!" Trissie exhaled a sigh that would have blown out a candle at fifty paces. "I'll go." She turned to Jill. "Can we stay up late and watch Showtime?"

"We'll negotiate on that," Jill said cautiously.

"Negotiate," Trissie muttered. "That means we talk about it and then you say no. Okay. I give. I'll get my coat."

"And your school stuff so you can do some homework," Laura added.

"*Maw*-um!"

Laura walked her daughter to the door, promised to call in the morning, and stood on the front porch until she had seen the two of them—the pretty tall teenager and the willowy little girl who meant everything to her—cross the quad to her neighbor's doorway and go inside with the brief flash of interior light caused by the door opening and closing again.

She went back inside, closed her own door, and turned to Lassiter. She felt unaccountably close to tears. "Dammit—"

He came and took her in his arms. "You'll remember, babe, and then we'll know what really happened out there at Timberdale, and you won't have to have twenty-four-hour protection anymore."

"Or I won't remember a thing," she whispered against the stiff wool of his jacket, "and we'll never know anything."

"Hey, it's better to have Tris safe and sound over there, regardless, you know that."

"Yes, but what kind of a mother am I, when I've got to send off my own daughter like this?"

"It's for her own good. You—"

"My dad used to say that to me when he made me sit at the table until I ate all my damned cold spinach."

"Speaking of eating, you haven't."

"I'm not hungry."

"You're always hungry, and always dieting."

"Hey, are you looking for a fight?"

He grinned at her. "No. I'm looking to take you out for a sandwich or something. We can talk about everything while we eat."

She thought about it. "I don't know," she admitted. "It makes me feel like we dumped Trissie so we could have some fun. That's the kind of thing her dumb father does all the time. Let me check the recorder for messages and I'll think about it."

He nodded. "Good. I want to call headquarters and verify where I am, too."

She walked into the kitchen, where the telephone sat beside her small black Phonemate machine. It showed two messages. Taking a pencil from the soup can Trissie had pasted floral wallpaper on to make it a holder (*How can I be such a crummy mom?*), she punched the playback button.

"*Laura?*" the voice blatted. "*Judith Epperman here. My migraine is much improved. I intend to be in the office tomorrow—Sunday—between ten and noon. We need to discuss ways to minimize the public relations damage suffered because of the death of that dreadful man. Please plan to meet me there, dear. Thank you.*"

Beep.

"*Laura. Maude here. When you get in, call me. I've got some really neat info this time. Mrs. Redwine is taking over the company, and everybody is mad as the dickens about it. George Van-What's-His-Name is in cahoots with Freddie Filmont, about what I don't know yet. I'm going to watch them like a hawk, kiddo. I've got more other good stuff to tell you too, so call me when you get in. 'Bye.*"

Lassiter, hovering at her shoulder, frowned. "What's that all about, do you suppose?"

"Let me call her and get it over with," Laura sighed, flipping through her small Rolodex. "Here it is." She tapped in Maude Thuringer's number.

The telephone rang a dozen times with no answer.

"Where do you suppose she is?" Lassiter asked as Laura finally hung up.

"Oh God, probably out trying to install a one-way mirror in somebody's living room wall." Suddenly she felt disgusted with the whole thing. "Hey. Does that meal offer still go?"

"Durn betcha."

"Give me a sec to brush my hair, and we'll go."

They took Laura's car, Lassiter leaving the cruiser in the parking lot "to show the flag, just in case," and hauling along his handi-talkie to maintain communications. The small gray Motorola unit remained on his belt during supper, and did not bleep at him. Laura tried her best to relax and have fun, but she kept thinking about Trissie at Jill's house and the colonel in the county jail. She kept feeling they had both been put away on her account.

She tried not to talk about it or even think about it. Remembering what Dr. Hodges had advised, she wanted to leave her mind relaxed as much as possible on the off chance that memory would sneak up the moment she stopped beating on its door.

That didn't work either, and she was feeling low when they parked again outside her apartment complex on Norman's west side, beyond the Sooner Fashion Mall.

Lassiter unbelted his radio and thumbed the transmit button. "Lassiter to headquarters."

"Go ahead."

"I'll be ten-eight previous location."

"Ten-four."

They went inside and Laura started to brew some coffee. The telephone rang. She picked it up, half-expecting Maude.

A male voice asked for Lassiter. She handed him the phone. He listened.

"What?"

He listened again.

"Yeah," he said finally, grim. "Right. Understood. I'm on the way."

He hung up, his forehead more corrugated than Laura had ever seen it. "I want you to lock yourself in," he told her. "Open up for nobody. I'll talk to the Norman PD and make sure they keep a car cruising the neighborhood as often as possible."

"Where are you going?" Laura asked, fright gusting.

"To the Ramada Inn."

"Why?"

"Rebecca Redwine just tried to kill herself."

TWENTY-FIVE

Dec Laura is clear, so called her on clues. She not home, left msg. Mrs. Redwine had plot all along to take over co???? May be sig. Think she did it.

MAKING THE BRAKES of his cruiser squeal, Aaron Lassiter wheeled sharply into the parking lot of Norman's Ramada Inn. Flashing red-and-blue strobe lights on the roof of a city police car scintillated under the front entrance roof. Lassiter parked nearby and hurried in.

He found two city officers at the counter in the lobby and Sheriff Bucky Davidson nearby.

"You made good time, Salt. I wanted you in on this. It's a city deal, but there's a tie-in to the business out at Timberdale."

"What did she do? When? How?"

"Pills of some kind."

"How was she discovered?"

"Phone calls. No answer. The caller—a man who didn't identify himself—complained, got abusive. The desk clerk got concerned, sent somebody back there. When they couldn't get a response, they called the police."

"How is she?"

"Not good. Coma. Look, I want you over at the hospital. This might mean she did her husband in, and tried to kill herself in remorse. If she regains consciousness and has anything to say, I want you there to hear it."

TWO EMPTY AMBULANCES and three police cars clogged the lower level emergency ramp at Norman Regional. Lassiter parked behind one of the city units and hot-footed it inside, where he found the waiting rooms packed. It seemed there had been several auto accidents, a teenagers' knife fight, two heart attacks, a dog bite, and a nasty brawl at a local beer joint all within a few minutes. It was quite enough to tax the weekend ER staff and turn the waiting areas into zoos.

Lassiter checked with the harried triage nurse, spoke briefly to one of the Norman cops at the doorway to the back, and went on into the business end of the unit. He found two more policemen standing near a curtained-off section where, judging by the number of pants legs seen below the draperies, it was a busy scene indeed.

"'lo, Salt," one of the cops, whose name was McKenzie, said.

"She making it?" Lassiter asked.

"Well, she's not dead yet, put it that way."

"She said anything?"

"Out cold."

Lassiter studied his city colleague's bleak expression. "You saw her?"

"I did."

"Did it look to you like she's going to make it?"

"Nope."

One of the LPNs from the admitting desk hurried in, white shoes squeaking on the tile. She was new. "Deputy Lassiter?"

"That's me," Lassiter told her.

"They want you on the telephone up front."

Lassiter raised an eyebrow at McKenzie and hurried out after the nurse. He filtered his way through the waiting room and identified himself to the woman at the admitting area.

"You can take it right there," she said, sliding a white telephone across the counter one chair away. He moved and picked it up.

"Lassiter speaking."

Bucky Davidson's bubbly growl came back: "Your Handi is turned off."

"I know."

"Change of plans. You'd better get back out there where your Michaels lady lives."

Lassiter's heart dropped like a boulder. "What's happened?"

"City says somebody tried to break in, maybe kill her."

AFTER AARON LASSITER left her apartment, Laura locked and bolted the front door, then went immediately to the other door, the one out of the kitchen into the carport, and made sure both of its locks were secure too. She felt a sharp panic that made her ashamed of herself. But it was night now, and darkness—the time for spooks and goblins, not to mention regrets about personal failures and the slightly bitter knowledge that she still couldn't remember—always made things seem worse. Her most pressing problem was inside her own dumb, dim, recalcitrant brain, not out there someplace with imagined werewolves and vampires.

She wished Trissie were here after all. But as she went back into the living room she realized how selfish that was. Tris was far better off across the quad with Jill and her mother. If anything happened here, she would be safe.

Not that anything was likely to happen, of course. She was just imagining things when she got that crawly sensation up her back and arms, right? If the real murderer had intended to try to remove the threat of her recollection once and for all, he would have done it long before now, right? So she had little to worry about, right? Right? Right? Right?

Nerves jumping, she decided to try Maude Thuringer's number again. Going into the kitchen, she redialed.

Maude's voice came on the line: "Hi. This is Maude. I can't answer right now, but you can leave a message—"

"Maude," Laura cut in impatiently, "cut that out. I know you don't have an answering machine."

"Oh! Laura? Hi. I was just going out the door."

"Where, at this hour? It's almost your bedtime, Maude, and—"

"Pooh. I've got some neat stuff to check out. I think I'm about to crack this thing wide open."

Laura mentally counted to ten. "You said you had some new clues?"

"Yeah. First of all, the actors all got together and had a meeting, and Rebecca Redwine came in and told them she's in charge now, and they'll do what she says or get out. Well, they were hacked about that. I can tell you for sure. Second, I overheard Van-What's-It and Freddie Filmont talking about what they had to do about it, like they're conspirators. A while ago, he went down and ran off a bunch more stuff on the copier. What's he duplicating stuff for now? I'm just on the way down to his room to check it out."

Laura's internal alarm started clamoring. "What do you mean, you're going down to his room to check it out? You just stay—"

"It's no problem. I stole the extra key off his key ring this morning."

"Maude, my God!"

"And he's off somewhere in that company Cadillac they've got, so as long as I hurry and get done before he returns, I'm in like a porch climber. 'Bye."

"Maude! Wait! Don't you dare hang up on me."

"I've gotta hurry, Laura. It's like that nasty reporter, Tyrone, says in *Forfeit*. Sometimes you just know you have to do something."

"Maude, don't quote Dick Francis to me."

"You recognized the title. Wow! Maybe there's hope for you yet, kiddo. 'Bye."

"Maude, you just stay in your room. Something else has happened—"

But the line had already gone dead. Maude had hung up.

Damn! Going back into the living room, Laura dropped onto her sofa with a feeling of total helplessness. One of these days Maude Thuringer was going to get herself into truly serious trouble with all her meddling. This might be the time. Unless

Rebecca Redwine had committed the murder and had done so single-handedly, someone in the acting company was involved.

How did Rebecca Redwine's ultimatum to the actors, as just reported by Maude, link with her attempted suicide? It didn't make sense.

Considering the bad feeling Laura had right now about Maude, the whys and hows didn't seem to matter much. The facts were uncomplicated: There was almost certainly a killer loose at Timberdale; Maude was roaming the halls, even entering guest rooms, in search of her beloved clues; the killer had already proven that he was willing to strike more than once to protect himself.

Minutes passed. The more Laura thought about it, the worse she felt.

She went back to the kitchen telephone.

"Timberdale Retirement Center. This is Stacy, can I help you?"

Laura imagined Stacy, sitting there in a rubbish heap of pizza. "Stacy, this is Laura. I—"

"Hi!"

"Hi. Listen, Stacy. Maude Thuringer is not feeling well. She may be out roaming the halls. Is there anyone still around the clinic?"

"I think Dr. Which came by a while ago to get something."

"Good. Stacy, call Mr. Atwater downstairs in Maintenance. Then go find Dr. Which. I want the three of you to go find Maude and make sure she's all right—take her back to her room—and then ask Dr. Which to call me about giving her a sedative."

"Okay, Laura. Gee, she's sick, huh?"

"Hurry, Stacy, okay? And make sure I get a report."

"Betcha." Stacy hung up.

Replacing her phone, Laura went into the living room again. Pacing, she tried to remember what had happened in the back hallway when someone hit her on the head. For an instant her memory almost opened, giving her a feeling like the one she sometimes got when she wanted the name of someone out of the past, when she could see the person clearly and knew the name was *right there* at memory's gate, but staying maddeningly just beyond reach.

If she could remember, she thought again, everything might be done with. Despite her best intentions, she felt impatient with herself, furious.

Think of something else; that was what Dr. Hodges had suggested.

Okay: Maude and her clues. But they all sounded so silly, Laura couldn't maintain a steady focus on them. Vanlandingham had done more copying, Maude had said. She hoped he hadn't emptied the machine again. Mrs. Epperman was going to have a cow when she learned how much of her precious paper he had used up. She had said her hideously colored bargain buy would last through the first of the year. But Vanlandingham had put Laura into the stock of that puky pink stuff already. He must have run a thousand sheets of the almost unreadable green stuff, and now seemed intent on using up the pink as well.

Laura sat on the couch and thought about the awful-colored paper and Mrs. Epperman and all Vanlandingham's script revisions and notices. Her mind free-wheeled in no set pattern.

Then, all at once, the timing of some things leaped into sharp focus. She sat upright, tingling with the shock of discovery.

Was she right about this? *Think. Go slow. Think it through. All right, all right, go back through it in an organized way this time:*

She knew she had had at least two reams of the green paper left when George Vanlandingham first asked to use the machine, because she remembered his complaints about the color. He had completely reprinted a dozen copies of his script, however, and then later had forced her to break into other stock to give him enough sheets to print out revision pages on dif-

ferent colors. She had given him a few remaining dregs from
other boxes: She could remember some canary yellow and
some pale gray. Then, having still another revision page or
two to duplicate, he had gone in on his own and run about
forty pages on Timberdale letterhead loaded into the lower
tray, which would have sent Mrs. Epperman into orbit if she
had known about it.

But had there been any of the horrid pink stuff during that
time?—No. Laura quite clearly remembered struggling to get
the first twelve-ream carton of the stuff out of the cabinet.

That had been early this morning.

So the machine had not had any pink paper in it until today.

Maude had been all atwitter when she found the crumpled
note in an atrium chair. She had thought it was a clue in the
real murder.

George Vanlandingham had laughed and said it was a script
clue, which he later proved by displaying a script page—on
pink paper.

Laura's head ached as she raced back over the chronology.
On Friday the last script changes had been made; there was
green paper in the machine. On Saturday, pink paper went into
the copy-machine tray. The crumpled note was found. And
Vanlandingham had shown Laura a pink page to prove that
the note wasn't real.

The pink script page mentioning the note could not have
been produced before mid-morning on Saturday, Laura
thought—*after the note had been found*. Which meant that
Vanlandingham must have hurriedly produced and then duplicated that page while she was in session with her groups.

Why would he say a real clue was a script clue, and then
go to all that trouble to make it appear so? Laura began to
feel feverish. My God, was she starting to get as bad as
Maude? It wasn't time in her life yet to start needing extra
hormones. This was kind of embarrassing. But she still felt
she had just stumbled onto something incredibly important.

Was there some logical explanation she was overlooking?

She racked her brain and couldn't come up with one. George Vanlandingham had meddled with real evidence. That had to mean...

She sat very still in the quiet living room, going over and over other encounters and conversations since the actors had arrived, looking for anything else that might make more sense in the context of her new suspicions. Vanlandingham had been angry and resentful. The troupe hadn't been paid. He felt overworked, responsible for everything while Redwine took the credit.

It didn't seem like much to go on.

A small sound, the natural creaking of a wall or ceiling as night became more chill, came from the back bedroom. It startled Laura for an instant, but then she relaxed, decided she needed to clear her head, and went into the kitchen to make some instant coffee. She put a small pan of water on the electric stove and turned the burner on high, then got the instant coffee and a cup out of the cabinet. Going to the refrigerator, she rummaged around and found a chunk of Gouda wrapped in Saran Wrap. She remembered how recently she had eaten. Nervous hunger now, she thought glumly. If she gave in to it, she would start gaining weight again. She gave in to it, unwrapped the cheese, and munched on it.

Just think it through one more time before you start trying to track down Aaron, she told herself.

She stood by the stove and watched the water in the little pan begin to form bubbles at the bottom, then roil, then begin to steam. Why else would George Vanlandingham have gone to all the trouble of writing a found note into the murder mystery script, then duplicating that script? What if she had been smart enough at the time to ask others in the company about the alleged clue? Wouldn't they have said they never heard of it? Of course, but Vanlandingham could have said that he'd set it up, then decided against using it. A thin cover-up, but maybe an adequate one. And why should she ever have asked others in the cast about it anyway? There had already been the second pistol and the broken reading glasses. Unless—

She stopped, tingling.

Unless one or both of them had been real clues, too—covered up by script changes written in after the fact.

Good God.

She knew to reach for the telephone. The sheriff's office would know where Aaron was.

At that moment, another sound came from the back of the apartment. Something was being moved.

Laura's nervous system went wild. She knew instantly what she was hearing. Somebody was coming in through the back bedroom window. The earlier sound, she thought, mind racing, had to have been the flimsy window lock cracking, and what she had just heard now was the small table being pushed aside to let someone climb in.

Panicked, she snatched up her telephone and punched 911. The earpiece sounded funny.

It sounded dead.

She pushed the hang-up button in and out, but absolutely nothing happened. Tossing the receiver down, she turned to run to the front door.

George Vanlandingham, pupils crazy pinpoints, stepped into the doorway, blocking her way. She shrieked. He moved toward her. He had a length of white material—possibly a torn bedsheet—in his hands. His face had an expression of wild desperation and fear like nothing she had ever seen.

"I'm sorry," he moaned. "I don't have any choice now. I didn't want this to happen—any of it."

Backing up, Laura bumped against the stove counter. Her hand went behind her and knocked against the small pan of water, making some of it slosh, sizzling, onto the red-hot burner.

Vanlandingham lurched toward her.

She grabbed the handle of the pan and swung it around. The boiling water spewed in a glittering arc and cascaded into his face. He screamed and staggered backward, dropping the sheet, hands going to his eyes.

Laura rushed past him, into the living room, to the front door. Behind her, Vanlandingham was screaming in pain.

She flung the bolt back and pulled the door open and ran out onto the porch, screaming too.

TWENTY-SIX

"I SHOULDA BEEN HERE," Trissie whimpered, huddling closer against Laura's side on the couch. "I could've—I could've—done *something*."

"There, there, sweetie," Laura murmured, stroking her daughter's tangled hair. "It's fine. Everything is okay."

Aaron Lassiter, standing like a grim statue at Laura's other side, reached down and gave Trissie an awkward pat. "Your mom did just fine, Tris. She's safe now. Everything is over now."

Two Norman policemen stood in the kitchen, talking in low tones. Another was in the back bedroom, taking pictures. A fourth stood beyond the front door, which remained ajar; he was patiently telling the small crowd of curious neighbors that it was all over now, folks, and please just go on back home.

It had been an hour since Laura dashed the boiling water in George Vanlandingham's face and ran outside. Her screams had brought neighbors outside instantly, and someone had called the police. At Lassiter's request, one car was already only a block away, prowling the neighborhood. The police had been at Laura's side in a twinkling.

An hour had passed. But she still felt as if the quaking of her insides might make her bones crack.

"Do you want some coffee now?" Lassiter said solicitously.

Laura shuddered. "I don't know if I'll ever be able to look a cup of coffee in the face again."

"Maybe something stronger?"

She looked up at him. She knew she was all right now, but she yearned to go into the bedroom and pull the covers over her head and know he was right there beside her. The tears were still coming, too. "I'll get hold of myself in a minute. I'm sorry to be a boob."

His forehead instantly wrinkled. "You're not being a boob. The sucker was *after* you!"

"He has to have been the one, Aaron. He changed pages in the script to cover the note Maude found, and maybe—"

"I know, babe. I know. You've said all that."

"Have I?" Distracted, she thought about it. "Sure, I have. I know that. Damn, now my short-term memory is all out of whack."

The policeman on the porch poked his head in the door. "Ms. Michaels? Your friend from across the way wants to know if your daughter is going back over there, or what."

Laura glanced at Lassiter again. His sober expression tightened. "I want you to go by the ER and just make sure you check out fine."

"I told you, Aaron: he didn't touch me."

"I know that. But there needs to be a formal report."

"But he didn't touch me!"

"There needs to be a formal report."

Studying his dear, troubled face, she had no idea whether he was telling her the truth. But she knew him well enough to realize that he would make her have a checkup, to be certain, if he had to carry her back to the hospital.

She told the officer, "Trissie can go back over there right now."

"Mom!" Trissie protested, and snuggled tighter against her.

It took a few minutes, and everything else waited while Laura had Jill and her mother come in, and then the three of them worked on Trissie. Finally she was as calm as she would be this night. Laura walked to the porch with her, talking reassuringly, confident that it was better for the child to be back in the quiet confines of the neighbor's apartment. Finally Trissie gave in and went along reluctantly.

"Honey, we'll talk in the morning, and then we'll see if we can't go to Sunday school, okay?" She waited anxiously for her daughter's reaction to that.

Trissie, pretty pink in her flannel nightgown, made a glum face. "Mom, if everything is really all right—"

"It is, honey. Really."

"Then maybe we could go to Legends for their brunch instead of Sunday school. I feel like I've really had a bad scare. I really think some of their cinnamon rolls would make me feel a lot better."

Laura relaxed a little, hiding her smile. Trissie was going to be all right. "We'll decide in the morning, honey."

Back inside her own apartment, she met a police captain who had been outside at one of the cars.

"They're still treating him at the emergency room," the captain told her and Lassiter. He was a tall, lanky man with bushy black hair and a handlebar mustache. "They don't think he'll be permanently blinded, but he's in a hell of a mess at the moment."

"Has he been interviewed yet?" Lassiter asked.

"They tried a few preliminary questions, but he clammed up. The medics have him shot full of painkillers, so it's hard to tell if he's drugged or planning to try to stonewall it."

"What happens to him next?" Laura asked.

The mustache twitched. "Looks like he'll be in the hospital at least until tomorrow. He'll be guarded. Then charges filed Monday morning."

"Those being...?"

"First-degree burglary. Assault. Attempted murder, I'd say, for a start. From what you've said, the murder of this Redwine guy too, I imagine."

"What's Mrs. Redwine's condition?"

"Critical, but holding her own. They think she'll make it."

Lassiter asked, "Is she conscious yet?"

"She was for awhile."

"And she said...?"

"This guy Vanlandingham went to see her tonight. Seems she had told the cast that she was taking over the company. He waved papers at her, proving he had legal commitments from her husband or something. Threatened to sue hell out of her, hold up the cash found in her husband's room. Bad scene. He left, called back, made more threats. She cracked, took pills. He kept calling, I guess to yell at her some more. That's what alerted the desk, all his wild-ass—oops, sorry, ma'am—calls.''

Lassiter put a protective arm around Laura. "Now that you know he's the one, has it helped your memory any?"

She shook her head. "I wish I could say it had."

He shrugged. "It will come back quicker now, I imagine. Of course that shrink stuff is your bailiwick, not mine."

The captain said, "It will be tomorrow sometime before your phone line gets repaired, I think. We'll report it. You need to follow up on that. We've notified apartment management here, and they said they've got a guy on the way over to board up that back window until permanent repairs can be made on that." His eyes swiveled to Lassiter. "You're taking her by the hospital?"

"Right."

He looked back at Laura. "I'll come by there and take a formal statement from you while you wait."

"Sure. But I don't expect to be there more than a minute."

The captain's handlebars drooped. "You'll be there more than a minute. It takes them a lot longer than that to get around to you, no matter what your problem is."

LASSITER DROVE Laura to the hospital, where more serious emergencies took precedence. Beginning to sag badly in the aftermath of the scare and excitement, she actually found herself dozing on the chilly gurney in a screened-off examining cubicle when she was finally taken into the bustling, impersonal treatment area. Lassiter went away, came back, fumed, grew more and more angry, and went away twice more. She didn't know what he must have said the last time he went out, but she distantly heard his voice, loud and belligerent, and a doctor and a nurse bustled in immediately afterward. The doctor asked questions and did some routine examining, and notes were made on a form stuck on an aluminum clipboard. Then they took what seemed like a great deal of blood and carted her off to have X-rays. Then she waited some more, and finally the nurse came back to report that everything appeared within normal limits and Laura could go.

"Goddamned idiots," Lassiter muttered, bulleting the cruiser down deserted downtown streets toward her apartment complex.

Laura yawned. "It's okay, darling."

"It's *not* okay," he shot back. "You've been through enough. You shouldn't have to wait half the night."

"At the moment, I don't much care about that. I think I just want to get home and into my own bed."

He reached a big hand across the seat, groping for hers. "At least it's over. You're safe now."

"Yeah." She took a deep, shuddery breath. "I was really scared. He looked like a madman."

"He *is* a madman, killing Redwine."

"I'd just like to know why he did it the way he did, making it look like part of the play. The whole thing is crazy."

"We'll get the answers."

They reached the apartments, the parking lots and lawns vast and dark and totally normal again. He walked her to her door, went in ahead of her without a word, and made a quick, thorough inspection. "Everything shipshape. That back window isn't pretty, but the boards are secure."

She yawned again. All the strength seemed to have gone out of her. "I just want to sleep."

He glanced at his watch. "No wonder. It's past three."

She moved into his arms. "I'm lucky to have you around."

He muttered with regret, "I can't stay, babe. Now I've got to get down to the courthouse, fill out a report, check on Mrs. Redwine again—"

"That's fine, Aaron. Really."

He frowned down at her. "You're sure?"

"I'm sure."

He hesitated, clearly not wanting to leave her. "I'll be back in the morning."

"Good."

At the door, he looked down at her again.

"I'm *fine*," she told him, and gave him a quick, fierce little hug.

He returned her hug, looked down at her, then turned and strode off into the night. She closed the door, locked it, and set the bolt.

Going directly into the bedroom, she pulled off her clothes, padded into the bathroom, removed her little makeup, brushed her teeth, and ran a brush through her hair. The face that stared back at her from the mirror was pale, with a gaunt face and fear-stricken eyes. She took a deep breath and went gratefully back into the bedroom, leaving the lights on. She felt safe enough, but somehow she wasn't quite ready to sleep in the dark.

Tossing the bedcovers back, she groaned as she stretched out on the cool sheets. She felt totally exhausted yet not nearly as sleepy as she had been in the commotion of the emergency room. Her body was still scared, regardless of what her mind might know. She practiced deep breathing and relived the awful moment when Vanlandingham appeared in the kitchen doorway, his eyes filled with that insane, terrifying light. Shuddering, she rolled over and tried to think about other things.

Before she knew it, she had fallen into a light sleep. She began dreaming at once. But it was not a normal dream.

She was in the back hallway. Turning a corner. Looking ahead. A gurney stood in the middle of the hall. Someone on it—she went cold with shock as she saw the blood on J. Turner Redwine's chest—and then she saw the figure bending over Redwine, turning to stare at her with those same wide, insanely scared eyes. And then she heard the slight sound behind her and started to turn—

With a tremendous jolt she sat bolt upright in bed, her heart hammering, her body bathed in sweat.

The memory was back.

All of it this time—every terrifying instant.

She sat paralyzed by the images, incredulous that something so vivid and clear could have been totally lost.

Then, suddenly, she remembered Maude.

"Oh, God." Swinging bare legs out of bed, she hit the floor running. In the kitchen she snatched up the telephone and started to dial before the dead sound on the line reminded her the line had been cut.

She rushed back into the bedroom and grabbed the first clothes she saw: an old maroon nylon warmup suit. Pulling on panties and bra, she threw the warmups on and jammed her feet into running shoes without benefit of socks. It took only another few seconds to find her purse and car keys.

In the deep night the wind had stilled. Her shoes made crunching sounds on the dry grass as she ran, taking a shortcut to her car in the lot. Climbing in, she started the engine and backed out, making tires squeal.

The lights of the little convenience store glowed like an oasis in the darkness of the remote surburban street six blocks away. Pulling up beside the telephone booth outside, she hurried to the phone, dropped in coins, and punched in the familiar number.

Stacy Miller sounded sleepy when she answered the Timberdale call. She woke up fast when Laura started to talk.

"Laura? Gosh! We've been trying and trying to reach you! Your phone just rings and rings, no answer."

"It's out of order," Laura snapped. "Is Maude all right?"

"That's just it. We tried."

Alarm rose sharply. "What do you mean, you tried?"

"Well, we looked in her room and we looked around the first floor and even in the crafts room, but we didn't locate her."

"What did you do then?"

"I didn't know what to think. When you didn't answer, I got sort of shook up so I called Mrs. Epperman."

"Good! And she told you to...?"

"She said Maudie must be visiting someone else's room. No other explanation, she said. I was scared maybe Maudie had gone out and taken a walk and forgotten where she was. You know how Mr. Keen does that all the time, but—''

"Stacy, can it! What did Mrs. Epperman have you do?"

Stacy sounded vague. "Well…nothing."

"Nothing!"

"She said if Maudie isn't in her room, and didn't sign out, she must be playing cards late with somebody or something like that—''

"Maude doesn't play cards, dammit. She says no one has the analytical ability to keep up with her."

"Anyway, Mrs. Epperman said to tell you to speak to Maudie about it in the morning. She had me put a note on your desk."

"And Maude is still missing," Laura said despairingly.

"I guess so. Nobody's looked for a while now. Mrs. Epperman said to cool it. She said we need to—''

"Let me guess," Laura said, groaning. "'Reestablish normalcy,' or something like that."

"Gee! How did you—''

"Stacy, shut up and listen. I want you to call the sheriff's department. Tell them I called, and to tell Deputy Lassiter that I'm on the way to Timberdale, and to meet me there just as fast as he can get there. Have you got that?"

"I guess so." Stacy sounded dazed. "What—?"

"No time to talk now, Stacy. Just do it, okay?"

"Sure, but—''

Laura banged the pay phone back on its hook and ran to her car, the motor left running. She could only hope Aaron would be easy to find and would respond fast. In the meantime she couldn't wait for him. Maude Thuringer might already be dead. If she wasn't, every second counted.

Her newly discovered memory dancing like a VCR playback with tracking problems in her mind, she headed toward Timberdale. The back country road lay deserted and black. She drove like a maniac.

TWENTY-SEVEN

HER TOYOTA'S TIRES squealing in protest, Laura pulled around Timberdale's long, curving driveway and braked to a stop at the entrance canopy. Purse in hand, she ran to the front doors and almost broke her wrist trying to jerk them open. She had forgotten the night security locks that blocked entry from outside without assistance from the desk. She moved her aching hand to the doorbell button and pushed urgently on it.

Nothing happened. She pushed again, and still nothing happened.

Hopping from one foot to the other in frustration, Laura dug in her purse and found her outside key. The dim nightlights under the canopy provided just enough illumination for her to grope the key into the slot and turn it. The lock ratcheted open.

The atrium stood hugely empty and dim; no one was in sight. On the upper balconies nothing stirred. Timberdale seemed like a vast mausoleum. Laura could not find anyone at the reception desk, either. Only pizza wreckage, an opened sociology textbook, and an empty Dunkin' Donuts bag marked Stacy Miller's station.

Laura ran to the staff restroom. Stacy Miller stood at the large, bright mirror, applying lipstick in generous quantities. She whirled at Laura's entrance. "Wow! You made great time! I didn't expect—"

"Did you call the sheriff's office?" Laura demanded.

"Sure. The lady said she would deliver the message by radio right away."

"Good. Still no sign of Maude?"

"Gee, no. You look *awful*, Laura! Is something wrong?"

Laura turned and hurried back to the front desk. She saw no one. Nerves jangling, she went to the front doors, peered

out into the night. She could not see a sign of another car in
the driveway or headlights on the country road. She wanted
to wait. Her alarm was too great; she could not afford additional delay, in case Maude was still alive.

Stacy was just coming back to the reception desk. "Anything I can do, Laura? You look so shook up—"

"When Deputy Lassiter gets here, Stacy, send him right up
to Three East, okay?"

"But—"

"I expect to be in either Mr. Vanlandingham's room or
Miss Filmont's. Have you got that? Write it down."

"Sure." Stacy Miller reached anxiously for a pencil.
"But—"

Laura left her hanging and ran for the back elevator.

Somehow Maude had tumbled to the same clue she had
finally unraveled, she thought worriedly. Or possibly Maude
had found another one. She had *somehow* tumbled to *something;* otherwise she wouldn't be missing right now. Laura had
to find her at once in an effort to prevent more bloodshed. She
had to do that even if it meant walking in where angels would
have sent an excuse from the doctor.

The elevator finally reached the first floor. Laura stepped
inside and jabbed 3. The doors remained obstinately open,
taking their good old time. She punched the "door close"
button. The doors swept closed at a leisurely pace and the car
jolted softly into movement.

The memory picture was whole and clear in Laura's mind
now, and she was scared as hell to be doing this now. She
wanted to wait, but there was a chance Maude was still alive
and needed help instantly, not in five or ten minutes, or when-
ever Aaron Lassiter made it here. There was no choice.

She could not imagine how her mind had been able to hide
all details of what she had seen, and what had happened, back
there behind the activity room. Now that the defensive mental
trick had evaporated, she knew, she would never forget any
detail of the scene.

Watching the elevator's floor indicator blip "2," she relived the attack in an instant:

She turned the corner of the hallway, hurrying, and saw something ahead, just outside the rear door of the activity room. The wheelchair stood at an angle in the hallway, and in it slumped the figure of J. Turner Redwine, head lolling grotesquely to one side. She saw the bright, viscous blood.

She gasped. Standing beside the chair, bending over Redwine's figure, George Vanlandingham looked up in a spasm of alarm. He started to raise a hand and say something. At the same moment, however, Laura heard—or sensed—a movement at her back. She started to turn.

Behind her, face contorted in a grimace of desperation, the old character actress, Freddie Filmont, was already swinging some object toward Laura's face. She had just enough time to identify it—it was some kind of pistol, with a long barrel— and then the barrel collided with the side of her head and she felt sharp pain and nothing more but a sense of starting to fall....

Vanlandingham. And Filmont. It was unbelievable. She might even have doubted the veracity of her memory if the second unbelievable scene with Vanlandingham had not shocked her again just hours ago.

It didn't matter why or even how, she thought, watching the indicator light move to "3." Vanlandingham was in custody but Filmont was still free, and probably up here on the third floor. If Maude had stumbled into making an accusation, Laura's memory-picture left her no doubt that the old actress was capable of murder in the name of self-defense.

There was nothing to do but find Filmont and hope she hadn't already killed Maude.

The elevator lurched to a stop. The double doors started their leisurely trek to the open position. Laura was out and started down the hall of Three East long before they finished.

The carpet muffled her hurried footsteps, and only closed doors stared vacantly at her as she hurried along. At the corner alcove nearest the residents' rooms, she glanced behind the potted plastic plant, hoping against hope. Maude wasn't hiding there.

Freddie Filmont had been assigned to 326. The door stood closed like all the others. Laura took a breath. There was nothing to do but rush on in. She pressed the button beside the door and heard the chimes sound inside.

Several seconds passed, seeming longer. She pressed again.

The lock made a clattering sound, the knob turned, and Freddie Filmont's wide, startled eyes looked out at her. Although her hair hung in tangles and her face was a pasty gray without makeup, she had not been asleep: Wearing a gray skirt and shapeless matching sweater, she had a copy of a script in her hand. The metal fastener was pulled open and the cover sheet was clearly missing.

"You?" Filmont grunted in surprise.

"We have to talk," Laura said, and pushed her backward.

"Wait jush a minute!" But it was too late. Laura had already rushed past her into the narrow entry area of the apartment and toward the doors that led to the kitchenette, living room and bedroom.

All the lights blazed. The kitchen counters had coffee cups, empty highball glasses, and whiskey and vodka bottles—mostly dead soldiers—all over them. A glance into the bedroom revealed a messy bed with a suitcase opened on top of it, and clothes flung everywhere. Here in the living room, Filmont had pushed the coffee table back against the wall in order to clear a space on the carpet.

Scripts—at least ten of them—lay neatly arrayed in two rows of five. Each had had its metal fastener pulled open, the cover removed and laid aside, and several pages pulled loose for easy total removal. Beside the array of scripts, Laura saw two small stacks of pages—the ugly pink paper—evidently ready for insertion into each script copy.

"What do you want?" Freddie Filmont croaked, grabbing at Laura's arm. "You can't just barge in here like that!"

"Where is she?" Laura demanded.

"Where is *who*?"

"Maude. Where is she?"

Filmont's face twisted in disbelief. "Dunno wha' you're talking about. Get out of here."

Ignoring her, Laura hurried into the bedroom. There was no sign of Maude Thuringer, and no place a body could have been hidden. A glance into the tiny bathroom revealed nothing, and the single closet showed nothing either.

In the doorway, Filmont demanded angrily, "What *is* this? You bedder explain—explain yourself."

Laura brushed by her on the way back into the living room. She bent and glanced at the first of the two pink script pages on the floor. A line leaped out at her: "The crumpled note is to be found later."

Filmont grabbed at Laura again, catching her arm and almost toppling her onto the stacks of pages. "Geddout! Geddout!"

"What did you do to her?" Laura panted. "Where is she?"

"Who? I don' know what you're talkin' about."

Laura pulled free. Filmont staggered, and it was her turn to teeter, almost falling. Laura finally had time to register all the signs of heavy drinking: the old actress's tangled hair, smeared vestiges of makeup, slurry speech and bloodshot eyes.

"When did you 'stat all these extras?" she asked, pointing at the pages.

"What business ish that of yours? Thish ish outrageous."

"Did Vanlandingham give you this assignment before he headed to town?" Laura made a mental jump. "Don't you think it was a little strange that he hasn't come back yet?"

Filmont lurched against the doorway molding, steadying herself with a shaky hand. "Dunno what thish ish all 'bout."

Laura bent and snatched up one of the pages, thrusting it at Filmont. "Read this!"

Filmont reflexively took the page, frowned blearily at it, and held it at arm's length. "Why should I—"

"Hard to read something without the reading glasses that got broken downstairs?" Laura cut in. She felt a flush of triumph as another tiny bit of the puzzle fell into place. "He wrote *that* into a script change, to cover for you, just like he wrote the note in later, right?''

Filmont's face began to dissolve into tears. ''Whadda you know? Whadda you care? Wasen any money—he'd already gone to town 'n' cashed the check, cheatin' us again, was gonna fire me, cheated George out of havin' part ownership, lied about that, too, screwin' aroun' with Deena 'n' Janis both—''

''So you and George killed him,'' Laura said.

Tears made black mascara tracks down Filmont's face. Suddenly she looked far, far older, a shaking old hag on the brink of total loss of control. ''You don' *unnerstan'*. He'd done all of us wrong. Taken money for thish gig all for himself—lash straw. Proof he'd tricked poor George outta hish part—lash straw. Gettin' ready fire me—lash straw. Then Rebecca called, talked to George. He tol' her we'd sue for joint property, pay us what was owed. She laughed at him. She *laughed*. Said no joint property—said Reddy'd screwed us again. George went nuts—passed me note downstairs—we met, decided have it out with him right then 'n' there—threaten not to finish play if we don't get money right now.''

''And then you killed him,'' Laura said.

''Didn' mean to.''

''But you did.''

''Yes! Yes! But didn' mean to! Awful mad. Went back there, have it out with him right now, thish instant. Downstairs. Storage room. Told us get lost, he wash star, didn' need us. I had gun shtole from old fart—wanted scare him—he jush laughed. He *laughed!* Tried to hit him, he hit me, broke my glasses—I had gun—I jush pointed it an' pulled the trigger an' shot him.''

Behind Filmont, the corridor door swung open in a burst and Aaron Lassiter, sweating and pale, burst in. Filmont half-turned, saw him, and sagged more heavily against the wall.

Laura shot him a warning glance and kept her focus on Filmont. ''Why the gurney? Why the whole thing of putting him on the gurney for the next scene? Why all that?''

Sobbing, the old actress slowly slid down the wall, knees buckling, to end up sitting with her legs folded up against her chest. ''Scared—didn' know what to do—put him upstairsh, maybe confushe ever'thing, hide when it happened, where it happened. Then you came—awful—didn' have any more time, finish hidin' things. Hauled you downstairsh, time used up, hadda run for it, get set for scene—not thinkin'.'' Filmont raised crazy, accusing eyes. ''You were *dead!* No pulse. No breathing.''

Lassiter said, ''How did you get the colonel's gun?''

Filmont stared, evidently struggling to focus on him. ''Outa cabinet, I mean table.''

''When?''

''He was givin' me a drink. He hadda go pee. I'd noticed the guns right away. Never intended use it. Thought, 'If I hadda gun, I could scare the son of a bitch into paying us.' Colonel went to pee. I tried the lock on the table. It wash unlocked. I just reached in, grabbed firs' gun laid hands on, shoved it in my purse.'' Filmont grimaced. ''Poor colonel, came back, wanted to show me guns, went over, saw it missing. Thought he'd faint. Almost tried to put it back.''

''But instead you killed Redwine with it.''

''Never *meant* to! Jush wanted...scare him.''

''You did more than that.''

Filmont began to cry brokenly. ''He hit me—broke my glasses—laughed at me, said I wash old drunk, he's gettin' new actress. I jush lost it. Jush held the gun up in front of me 'n' pulled trigger.''

''Very good aim,'' Lassiter said grimly.

She shuddered.

Lassiter came to Laura's side and gave her his keenest look. ''You're okay?''

Laura nodded.

On the floor, Filmont choked, ''George can...'splain. Went to talk to Rebecca, make her unnerstan'. Oughta be back.''

''He's not coming back,'' Lassiter told her.

''Wha'?''

"Come on, now," he said, reaching down with his right hand to help her to her feet. With his left, he unsnapped the handcuffs from their usual place on the back of his belt.

Something drew Laura's attention toward the thinly draped windows. Out beyond them somewhere, swift flashes of red and blue had appeared. She hurried to the draperies, parted them an inch or two, and looked down into the curving front driveway three stories below. A car with red-and-blue strobe lights on its top rack had just pulled up. She saw two men bail out and run under the canopy and out of sight.

Lassiter looked up from handcuffing Freddie Filmont. "I didn't know what the hell was going on. I called for backup."

Laura sank to the edge of the couch. All strength seemed to have gone out of her. She started shaking. "I can't find Maude."

FREDDIE FILMONT shook her head violently and denied seeing or hearing from Maude Thuringer. One of the Norman policemen took her to the patrol car and stayed there with her while the other one helped Laura and Lassiter start a search.

Maude's room checked before, was still quiet and vacant. No one was to be found in places checked earlier: the mailroom, both activity rooms, the hall waiting bench outside the locked clinic, the arts-and-crafts room, the sauna and exercise area. Although the Norman police car hadn't used its siren, it had created enough commotion to rouse a few residents. Word spread by telephone or that magical gossip apparatus that never let anything remain a secret at Timberdale for more than six minutes, and by the time Laura had frantically started searching less obvious places for Maude, several slipper-and-robe-clad residents had joined in.

"She can't just have vanished," Laura nervously told Lassiter.

"We'll have to wake the other actors," he said. "Look in their rooms."

"How can they sleep through all this?"

"For one thing, babe, it's almost four o'clock in the morning. For another, they don't seem to have had somebody else calling them with the news, the way all your regular folks here did."

"God, when we start telling them, it will be more chaos."

"Chaos is the least of my problems right now. How about going to the switchboard or your office and starting to give them the calls?"

Reluctantly she led the way out of the kitchen area where their futile search had taken them. As she started through the empty dining room, she heard the first sounds of the commotion somewhere beyond.

"That sounds like One East," she said, hurrying.

The Castles and Judge Emil Young stood in the east alcove on the first floor, the point where the hallway split into two shorter ones. Down on the floor in the corner of the alcove, where she had been hidden behind a pair of dracaenas and a monstrous rubber plant, Maude Thuringer looked dazed and scared.

"The judge found her," Stoney Castle told Laura.

Lassiter bent to pull the huge rubber plant farther to one side. Maude, hunkered down against the wall in her pajamas and robe, looked up at him with stricken eyes.

"I was watching for stuff," she chirped. "I must have dozed off."

Lassiter's mouth set grimly. "Do you want to get up now, please?" He held out his hand.

Maude stirred, winced, and sank back against the wall. "I *can't.*"

Lassiter's tone showed his patience was going fast. "What do you mean, you can't?"

Maude whined. "My dad-blamed knees won't work."

TWENTY-EIGHT

THE DISTANT SOUND of a jangling something hauled Laura out of a sleep as deep as the Grand Canyon. She tried to ignore it. It kept clamoring somewhere.

She sat up with a violent start, fully awake in the tumbled covers of her own bed, and managed to focus on the bedside clock. It said nine o'clock. Daylight made her draperies bright gray. Her nerves were racketing louder than the sound, which she now recognized as the telephone in the kitchen.

My God, now what? Memories of everything that had happened only a few hours ago rushing through her mind, she tumbled hurriedly out of bed and staggered down the hall to the kitchen.

She grabbed up the phone. "Yes?"

A deep male voice said, "Just checking your line from outside, ma'am. Your service has been restored."

"Oh, crap."

"Beg pardon?" The repairman sounded startled.

"Nothing. Thank you." Laura hung up, shambled back down the hall, and tumbled into bed again.

Almost instantly the telephone started in again, impossible to ignore. She was fully awake now anyway.

"Look," she snapped into the mouthpiece, once she had completed the hall trip again, "I *said* thank you. It's fine. Good-bye."

"Laura? Is that you, dear girl?"

With a feeling of despair, Laura sank to the bar stool at the kitchen counter. "Good morning, Mrs. Epperman."

Timberdale's manager sounded as worked up as she had the first time she revealed that she had established a clear psychic channel to Pocahontas. "Where are you, Laura? Don't you know you should be here? The old dears are all absolutely beside themselves with excitement! We need all hands on deck. Haven't you any idea what's happened?''

"I was there for it," Laura said thickly, getting back off the stool to fumble in the cabinet for the jar of instant coffee.

"Well. I realize that, of course. But at a time like this, your presence is certainly required. I can't handle all this confusion by myself, and Francie is busy making plans for that trip she's taking later this week. How soon can you be here, Laura? We need to be much in evidence, answering questions, providing reassurance. With all the family visitors arriving for Sunday luncheon, I can't do everything by myself, as usual. I believe it might be well for you to come at once, perhaps even set up one of your little therapy sessions. Don't you?''

Laura got water on the stove, using the same small pan she had dashed into George Vanlandingham's face...when? My God, had that been just last night? She felt a hundred years old.

"Dear girl?''

Well, hell. "I'll be there in forty minutes or an hour, Mrs. Epperman."

"Please hurry, dear. That's a good girl. This is serious.''

Back in the bedroom, muttering to herself, Laura stripped and stepped into the shower, letting the hot water beat against her face and body, and to hell with her hair. By the time she stepped out, dripping on the beige tile, she felt almost alive again.

She was halfway dressed when Trissie called, wanting to come home. Trissie sounded considerably put out when Laura said she had to go to work for a while. No sooner had she hung up from that call, when the telephone rang yet again.

"Yes!" she barked, answering.

"Hey." Lassiter sounded sharply concerned. "Are you all right?''

"I guess. But Mrs. Epperman called and I've got to go back over there—try to help her keep everybody from flying into outer space with rumors and excitement.''

"Dammit, doesn't that woman have any mercy?"

"Hey, that isn't in her job description. What's going on?"

Lassiter quickly filled her in. "I'll check again and then come on out to Timberdale to wrap up a few things, all right?"

"Great. I'll see you there."

The coffee tasted like something out of the bottom of the urn at a 7-Eleven, but she got it down along with a couple of Pepperidge Farm cookies. When she went out to her car, she saw that the sky had cleared and thin autumn sunlight streamed down. The windless day promised to be considerably warmer. Ordinarily that would have cheered her up.

Now, she thought, wearily driving toward Timberdale, at least the danger was past. They could start trying to get back to normal, whatever that was.

Most of the guest parking places had already been taken when she drove in twenty minutes later. Finding a spot on the side of the complex in the employee area, she started for the front entrance, which looked entirely normal.

Still Bill Mills, raking a few leaves in one of the front flower beds, straightened up painfully at her approach. "Morning!"

"Working on Sunday, Bill?" she asked.

"Miz Epperman called," he told her glumly, reaching for a cigarette in the front pouch of his bib overalls. "Said she wanted all hands on deck."

"She's feeling very nautical today," Laura muttered.

"Well, maybe she's right. I can usually perceptuate people's feelings, and everybody is pretty stirred up in there to-day...real abdicated."

"See you later, Bill."

"Yep."

In the atrium, the scene was almost like a normal Sunday morning, younger couples and a number of small children standing around with their elders who were residents here, and the large silver coffee service in place along the north wall, with the remnants of what had been a big spread of cookies about thirty minutes ago. Laura's antennae picked up the undercurrent of tension at once, however, and she saw dozens of heads turn and follow her as she hurried toward her office.

Mrs. Epperman, hustling out of the dining room, where the preparations for brunch appeared to be on schedule, intercepted Laura in the hallway. The manager's Sunday-best suit, a purple military-style number with brass buttons, had cookie crumbs on it. Her five-inch-red-green-and-purple glass brooch—it depicted a fairy riding a butterfly—seemed to have gotten turned somehow: the fairy had stalled out into an inverted spin. "Laura! You're here at last!"

"Sorry I'm late."

The irony was entirely lost. "Everyone is positively *spastic* over all the recent events, dear. This is a superb opportunity to demonstrate some of our little extra services. You can set up a special little therapy talk session right after brunch, can't you? Good! I'm going to make the announcement right away."

"But—"

Mrs. Epperman turned, big black shoes clumping, and rushed to the PA amplifier station behind the desk. Pushing Paula Burwell out of the way, she flipped a row of switches and grabbed the microphone. Her voice boomed through the building as she spoke. "Your attention, please, your attention? Mrs. Michaels will hold a special joint meeting of her discussion groups in the main activity room immediately following brunch. Guests may attend. Thank you."

She looked happier as she clomped back to where Laura stood. "There, won't that be nice! Why are you looking so tense, dear? It's not as if you had to do anything. All you have to do is go in and listen to them talk, right? And you're really lucky to have all these chances to practice without having to pay for it, aren't you?"

"I just hope we don't have a mob scene."

"Nonsense! It will probably be a lot like your usual get-togethers. After all, most of our visitors are like me—don't think all this so-called talk therapy is worth a flip. But it will be a nice public-relations touch."

Laura nodded and started to turn toward her office.

Mrs. Epperman caught her arm. "No, no. You need to circulate now, dear. I can't—I have to write a memo to Pierre,
immediately. Two families have complained to me already this
morning. They say he's serving meals with too much fat and
cholesterol in them. Can you imagine? I wonder what the families would think if we served dried toast and oatmeal at the
Sunday brunch instead of knocking ourselves out with eggs
and ham and custard dessert. You'd think when you were
eighty years old you would just appreciate having fine French
cuisine, not gripe to your family members about cholesterol.
Well, I'll mention it to him. Very carefully, of course; you
know how temperamental he can be, the sweet man. But I
suppose if they want more boiled broccoli he can humor them.
Go on now, dear, go on. Be friendly. You know how important
that is."

HAVING A SPECIAL joint meeting of her discussion groups was
just about the last thing Laura wanted to do. While she circulated among the residents and guests, being so sunny and
charming she almost gagged herself, she tried to think of a
decent excuse that would get her out of it.

Joint meetings like the earlier one were difficult under the
best of conditions because every group quickly formed its own
distinct personality; one might be dynamic and crackling with
argument, like the Wednesday Breakfast Club, while another
could be quiet, passive, and resistant, like the Friday group.
Members tended to get somewhat comfortable with others in
their own group, but could instantly tense up—and close up—
with outsiders.

Add to that, Laura thought, the prospect of a few family
members poking their heads in the door out of idle curiosity—
or worse, an impulse to prove to Aunt Minnie that these things
were balderdash—and you had a recipe for a session that
might do far more harm than good.

As she circulated, however, and later as she sipped coffee

and observed Pierre Motard's latest bombardment of fat and cholesterol, she had to admit that a session might be in order.

"They're really uptight, some of them," she told Dr. Fred Which and nurse Kay Svendsen at the staff table in the corner of the big dining room.

Which, his skinny neck rattling around inside his stiff white dress-shirt collar, looked around the room. "No problem. Just send them down anytime before two o'clock and we'll load 'em up with tranquilizers and antidepressants."

"I'd rather get them to talk about what's bugging them, and see if we can't suggest changes in attitude," Laura countered.

"Sometimes," Which sniffed, "I think you'd try talk therapy on stuff as obviously physical as old Maude's knees."

It was Laura's turn to crane her neck. "Where is Maude, anyway?"

Svendsen's pretty eyes sparkled with mixed sympathy and amusement. "Resting down in the clinic."

"I drained water off both knees and shot her full of cortisone," Which said. "She's going to be hobbling for a while."

Laura considered the news. "Maybe it's for the best. We might have a lot of issues to look at in this session I'm going to have in a few minutes. Maude would try to take over. Her knees will keep her away."

Svendsen studied her with ironic good humor. "Wanna bet?"

When the time came for the special session, it looked at first like Kay Svendsen had been wrong. Standing behind the reception counter and watching residents drift into the big activity room, Laura saw no sign of Maude Thuringer. Several of her regulars from each group went in, along with two young couples and a lone younger man, then a single younger woman: adult children of residents she recognized but couldn't match with a name. Maude might be gone, but this was going to be tough.

The old grandfather clock bonged twice, and Laura gathered up notebooks and ballpoints and crossed the atrium, her stuff clutched to her chest. More conversation than usual racketed around the room. She had two semicircles of chairs full of people, and another half-dozen in chairs dragged up at random behind them. Two bratty children were chasing each other around the front area, and had already succeeded in knocking over her chair that faced the others. Laura set her chair back up. One of the younger women came up and made cutesy apologetic noises while trying to corral the little boy, who kicked her repeatedly in the shins. Dad came up and grabbed both kids and dragged them outside. The boy's yelps of angry protest echoed back.

"I just don't know what got into them," the mother gasped. "They're always so well-behaved. What's a body to do?"

Stoney Castle, sitting in the middle of the front row, adjusted the lapel of his red-checked sport coat and leered at her. "Might try beating their ass."

Laura intervened instantly, raising her voice. "Okay, everybody. We all seem to be here. Shall we get started?" Her voice was lost in the general rumble of conversation. She tried even louder: "Can we get started, please?" The side conversations continued, people unaware of her. "We need to get under way, so if you could come to order, please?" No discernible response.

Well, hell. She raised two fingers to her mouth, depressed her tongue, and blew. The resulting ear-piercing whistle startled everyone into instant attention.

"Thanks," she said with a grin. "Glad to see so many of our discussion group regulars here—good morning, Ellen, good morning, Sada—and welcome to our guests. This is a pretty free-wheeling thing we have here, so don't feel like you have to hold your hand over your mouth if there's something you feel you really would like to say. Now guys, we've had a lot of excitement around here the last few days. It's hard to cope with. Maybe we ought to talk about that. If there's anything about what's happened that I can fill you in on, I would certainly be glad to try. Now, who would like to start?"

Several hands went up. Laura hesitated, looking around.

One of the visitors, a porridge-faced man wearing an expensive dark suit, spoke up from the back: "I'd like to know what these things are supposed to prove."

Heads turned; some faces looked curious, a few irritated. Laura was careful to smile and be friendly. "That's a good question, and there isn't any easy answer. We—"

"My aunt isn't a regular," the man broke in, an edge of belligerence in his voice. "She comes sometimes."

"Your aunt is...?"

"Rose. Mrs. Davilla Rose."

"That's not true," Davilla Rose piped up in the second row. "I come all the time. Be quiet, Archie, for heaven's sake!"

Her nephew flushed. "Maybe I should have said she *shouldn't* come all the time. If you ask me, these things just keep her stirred up. She used to...you know...accept her lot in life. Now she writes all this poetry and has pictures of Gertrude Stein and some other weirdo in her apartment, and wants to go to *Paris*. How come Timberdale has these sessions if all they do is make old folks dissatisfied with their lot in life?"

"Archie," Davilla Rose groaned.

Laura hung in there, the smile pasted on. "We don't try to make people dissatisfied. What we hope is that members will talk about problems, get to know themselves a little better, perhaps be happier—"

"She was happy enough before you started these things. Hell, she never used to give us any trouble. Now, every time we come by, she's yelling about wanting to take over control of her own trust fund, stuff like that. It looks to me like your job here ought to be to keep people in line, accepting stuff, not causing trouble."

"Archie—" Laura started.

"Oh, Archie—" Davilla Rose began simultaneously.

Stoney Castle's voice boomed over both of them. "That's a bunch of horse manure, buddy."

Archie stared, eyes bulging. "What did you say, old-timer?"

Castle got to his feet, ignoring his wife's frantic efforts to tug him back down by his coattail. "Don't call me an old-timer, you officious little jerk. We've got things to talk about here. Be quiet and listen, and maybe you'll learn something."

Archie's fleshy face worked. He managed a phony smile, and his voice changed to the false-kindly, wheedling condescension Laura had heard so often when people spoke to their elders. "Okay, okay, I'm sorry. I know you senior citizens like to gossip, but—"

"And don't call me a goddamned senior citizen," Castle yelled. "I don't need that kind of crap. You don't call me a senior citizen and I won't call you a junior Republican, okay? We ain't senior citizens here, we're people who've gotten old. We don't need funny-bunny labels from people who look down their noses at us. If the judge, here, walks with a cane, that don't make him 'physically challenged' or some such baloney; it makes him a little *lame,* or even *crippled.* And if Maude or somebody forgets stuff sometimes or acts a little strange, that don't make them 'differently abled'; it makes them a little cuckoo. Goddammit, don't come in here and start throwing around these insulting labels, boy, and don't start shooting off your mouth before your brain is loaded. Just shut up, and maybe you'll learn something."

A deathly silence fell. Laura fought to keep a straight face when she felt like cheering. "Thank you, Stoney," she murmured.

Archie had gone pale. "I don't like being talked to that way," he said, struggling with the words and his temper. "I am a very important person down at Sooner Bowling Lanes—"

"Oh, Archie," Davilla Rose cut in, looking considerably brighter and more animated, "will you just please can it?"

The door of the room swung open. Maude Thuringer hobbled in on crutches. Someone scrambled to provide her a chair on the end of the second row. The interruption allowed Davilla's besieged nephew to sit down, fuming. Maude sat with an audible "ouch."

"What happened to *you?*" Ellen Smith demanded.

"Knees flared up," Maude said through set teeth.

"It is widely known," Judge Emil Young rumbled, "that your current debilitation stems directly, at least in part, from your midnight reconnaissance in One East."

"Well, maybe so," Maude said, grimacing. "But it paid off, didn't it? I cracked the case."

The back doors opened again and Colonel Roger Rodgers, stiff-backed, dense gray hair glistening with water, strode in. He was still wearing the clothes he had been arrested in, but his ramrod posture made the wrinkles in them seem to be standing at parade rest.

"I heard—" he began.

Someone started clapping, and then everyone joined in. The applause filled the room. Somebody whistled, and a woman Laura didn't spot in time to identify let out one of those orgasmic cowgirl whoops always heard from the audience at talk shows when someone you never heard of is introduced. The colonel reddened and marched up to the front row. Julius Pfeister, moving with surprising speed, hauled a chair over from the pile against the wall and set it up for him.

"Colonel," Laura said as the clapping subsided, "it's great to see you."

"Hey!" Ken Keen yelped. "They let you out, did they?"

Stoney Castle snarled, "Hell no, Ken. He's still in jail. Can't you see that?"

"Huh?"

The colonel stood at attention beside his chair. He was trying very hard to be stern, but he couldn't keep the grin from tugging at his mouth. "Cleared and released, and a ride back in a sheriff's car. Observation confirms I missed noon chow. Thought I would show here for the roster count, then check the mess hall for possible leftover rations."

A dozen silver bracelets clamored as Ellen Smith waved at him. "Colonel, I intended to make this a surprise, but I can't keep it a secret. I've already started a painting—a masterpiece—to honor you!"

The colonel studied her with puzzled eyes. "Say again?"

"I plan to present it to Timberdale as soon as it's completed, and I just know it will be permanently displayed in a prominent position, where everyone can see how it honors you. It's a picture of a battle. You're General Custer in it—heroic, gallant, wonderful!"

"I believe," Colonel Rodgers said, frowning, "it's an honor I could do without—"

"Too late! I've already painted the background sky and some of the marauding Indians."

Judge Young intervened, "Having just peregrinated from the courthouse, Colonel, perhaps you would be willing to provide a situational updating."

The colonel's eyes bulged slightly. "Say again?"

"What's the latest on the case?" Maude Thuringer chirped.

"Oh. Yes." Rodgers scowled. "Mrs. Redwine, I am informed, will live. She is much improved this morning. Vanlandingham has been released from the hospital, transported to the Cleveland County jail. Put in the same cell I had. The Filmont woman is there, too. The assistant district attorney told me Filmont has confessed everything. My weapon will be returned to me eventually. Damned woman stole it out of the table in my room. Details in re that episode not important." He glared around the room, daring a challenge.

When no one spoke, he went on: "Sheriff is notifying the others in the acting company now that they're free to go. The Cadillac will be impounded. Papers on the van show it registered to that Raddell chap. Actors planning to leave pronto, I'm told."

Maude groaned. "Then we'll *never* see the rest of the play!"

"Madam—"

The back doors rattled, starting to open yet again. Laura began to feel like someone trying to conduct business in the middle of a street. This time it was Mrs. Epperman, reading glasses bouncing on her bosom. She beamed and waved and romped up to the front of the room, edging Laura to one side.

"Good afternoon, everyone! I won't take a minute of your

wonderful session. I just want to make sure you all understand that Laura will continue to hold your regular little meetings, and if any of you are nervous or anything as a result of the events of recent days, the clinic will be specially open today until five o'clock, and Dr. Which will dispense medication, if you think you might need it.

"All of us *deeply* regret the interruption of our routine in the last few days, but all that is behind us now and we can get back to enjoying the easy-paced, friendly atmosphere that Timberdale is so noted for, isn't that so? Now I'll let you get back to your conversation, or whatever you do in here. But don't forget, anyone—meringues and tea in the atrium at four."

Mrs. Epperman marched out, Hannibal after crossing the Alps, Patton at the Rhine. Laura took a deep breath, trying to think of a way to get anything back on track.

Maude Thuringer's voice carried shrilly over the slight murmur of comment that had started up: "There's just one more thing I need an answer to, here."

Better Maude than nothing, Laura thought. "Yes, Maude?"

"Who got into J. Turner Redwine's room? What did they do that for?"

The question that had nagged at the back of Laura's mind was back again, and she had no answer for it. Leave it to Maude, she thought tiredly, to uncover a loose end that spoiled everything.

TWENTY-NINE

AT THREE-THIRTY, only a few minutes after the group session had finally broken up, Laura was standing in the atrium, dutifully visiting with a resident's children and their family, when she saw Aaron Lassiter come in the front door. His gaze found her. He looked unaccountably grim.

Laura diplomatically broke away and walked over to meet him in the front entryway.

"Are you okay?" he asked, studying her intensely.

"Sure. Fine. Has something happened? You look worried."

He looked past her toward the reception desk, where Mrs. Epperman was twittering with a handful of guests. "Is there someplace we can talk a minute?"

Laura thought a moment. "This way."

The supply room, with a now-silent duplicating machine, was far enough away from the atrium to be deserted and silent. Flicking on the overhead light, she took him inside and closed the door. "What is it, Aaron?"

His frown became a scowl. "The damned break-in, or whatever it was, of Redwine's room at the time of the murder."

"Maude just brought that up in the session a while ago, and I didn't have a clue. Have you found out something more about it? Did one of them finally confess to doing that, too?"

"No. That's just it. I was just down there. They've both cracked wide open, telling us everything. But both of them insist they don't know a damned thing about that."

Laura groaned. "I've been trying to convince myself it wasn't important anymore. But if they really didn't do it—"

"—then who the hell did?"

Laura thought furiously. "One idea I had—has anyone

asked Mrs. Redwine? She might have been spooking around. Maybe she was looking for papers or—''

''No. We thought of that, too. She denies it, says she was still in town. And nobody saw her around here that early. And if she had gotten in that way, why was she so insistent on getting permission to be allowed in later, after our search? I just don't think she did it.''

''Then George Vanlandingham or Freddie Filmont had to have done it,'' Laura said, groping.

Lassiter shook his head. ''They've given us a few more details. See, Vanlandingham had been thinking revenge ever since he found out in Dallas that Redwine had never filed the papers giving him a legal interest in the company. Then—still in Dallas—he got into Redwine's room and searched his files, trying to find out who else might have been screwed. Instead, he found contract papers proving Redwine was going to dump Filmont and bring in a new lady to take her place. He told Filmont about it and she went bonkers. It turns out *she* also had invested money in the company—she now says fifteen thousand bucks—with a promise of good parts and a return on her investment.

''They confronted Redwine. He said it was all a big mis-understanding, et cetera, and told them how he planned to bug out, report his wife missing, and get an easy divorce as a result, on the basis of her mental instability. He said they had some expensive joint property, and he could get it after he won the divorce settlement on the basis of her condition. Then, he said, he would pay Vanlandingham and everybody else.

''I guess they bought that story temporarily. Vanlandingham even told Sweete about it. She was sort of flirting with him then. He—and she, too—thought Redwine might be getting ready to dump her in favor of Mahafey, and so Sweete looked like a natural ally. But then Vanlandingham says he saw Sweete sneak into Redwine's room and spend the night, the first night the three of them got here. That made him more paranoid—be looking for another double-cross.

''*Then* after they were all here, and the play was already in progress, Vanlandingham found out Redwine had already cashed the Timberdale check and had lied about that, too. Another cheat. Right on the heels of that, Mrs. Redwine found out where the company was, called for Redwine, and got put through to Vanlandingham again. He made some crack about the divorce and joint property, and she told him he was nuts, they didn't have a thing, not a dime. That was the last straw.

"You remember the note Maude found. Vanlandingham says he passed it to Filmont out there in the atrium. I guess he was out of his tree, he was so sick of being jerked around. The two of them slipped away and compared notes in the back hall somewhere. They decided they couldn't wait a minute to confront Redwine, they were so piss—angry, and maybe if they hit him up right now, they could threaten to stick the whole production right in the middle of this performance if he didn't pay up from the cash he evidently had in his room someplace.

"Trouble was, Redwine was running around planting a couple of fake clues for the play, and making sure everything was all set backstage. Vanlandingham had to hunt him down. Filmont had to get dressed up for the four o'clock scene before joining him. In her room, she got the bright idea of taking the colonel's gun to maybe scare Redwine—show him she meant business. They met up in the back. You know what came down after that."

"But why did they go to all the trouble of hauling Redwine upstairs, putting him on that gurney, all the rest of it? It's crazy!"

"Not so crazy, after all. I admit they must have been in a panic. I don't think either of them intended anything like a murder. So here you've got those two shocked people with a body on their hands. They've got to do *something* with it. If they leave it where it fell, somebody might come in anytime. They think fast, and in a weird way come up with the only logical place to stash it."

"The set in the activity room? That's *logical?*"

"Try to put yourself in their position. The set was ready

and the lights had been turned out. The front doors were locked, and Vanlandingham knew he wouldn't open them until four o'clock.''

"I get it now. If they haul the body upstairs and leave it in the darkened room on the gurney, just as called for in the script—"

"Nobody can find it for at least thirty minutes, so they have that much time to be seen elsewhere, and patch up their alibis."

Laura thought about it. It made sense, but a new problem cropped up. "Why didn't they do something like that with me, too?"

Lassiter smiled grimly. "You weren't in the play."

"Oh."

"Also, you made them use up some of their precious time. They had to improvise a lot quicker and dirtier with you."

Laura rubbed her eyes, trying to make sense of the snarl. "What about his extra room key?"

"They say they didn't take it."

"Then who did?"

"If we knew that, we'd know everything, wouldn't we?"

Laura stared at the beautiful little copy machine, with its tray of incriminating pink paper. "I thought we had it all," she admitted ruefully.

"We've got the murders and we've got the scenario, screwy as it was," Lassiter agreed. "Maybe the room question will never be answered. But damn! I hate to have a thread hanging like that."

Laura studied his expression. "Because...?"

"Isn't it obvious? What if they're protecting somebody, for reasons we can't begin to figure out? I mean, what if it didn't all happen exactly as they say it did? What if there's a third person involved in this thing somehow?" Lassiter's teeth clicked together in a wolfish snap. "How do we say this thing has been 'cleared' when we've got a hole you could drop a truck through? *Who the hell rifled his room, and why?*"

THEY RETURNED to the atrium. Two of Pierre Motard's minions had brought out trays of multihued meringues, along with what looked like sand tarts and butter cookies in case anyone wanted more cholesterol. Kay Svendsen, looking unhappy, had been pressed into service pouring tea from the giant urn, along with Paula Burwell. Despite this, many of the visitors had already departed, and others could be seen making their farewells out under the canopy. Family devotion seldom could be strained beyond three or four hours.

Lassiter bleakly surveyed the scene. "I'm going out back. The actors are supposed to load up back there. They said they're going to stick together right now...at least try to play the date in Guthrie for some spending money. I need to make sure none of them has any final questions, then get forwarding addresses, just in case."

"I'll circulate," Laura told him. "If I don't, Mrs. Epperman might have a tizzy."

"I'm parked out at the side. After I check with the company, I've got to get back to town." He studied her with concern. "You're okay? You look beat."

"I am, but no problem."

"Can I call you tonight?"

"If you don't, there might be another murder. Yours."

He grinned, bent close to snatch the briefest kiss, and strode away. She watched him go. He had to be the nicest-looking, dearest man in the world.

She took a deep breath and launched herself across the room to be friendly some more.

IT WAS ALMOST an hour later when the crowed had thinned enough to allow her to slip away. Her legs aching from fatigue, she went out the back way, through the kitchen pantry area, to see if Lassiter might still be around. Out back, in the bright, now-slanting rays of the sun, she found Tad Raddell loading the last box into the back of the van while Deena Sweete, Janis Mahafey, and Franklin Pierce Lord stood by waiting for him to finish.

She walked over to them.

"My dear lady," Lord greeted her, removing his long cigarette holder from his teeth. "The time has come for a fond farewell. I regret that our visit resulted in such turmoil and suffering for everyone, but especially for you."

"The four of you are going to play the date in Guthrie," Laura said.

"Indeed yes." Lord gave a theatrical sigh. "It will be difficult, but I am confident in my ability to revise an existing script. I have already made telephone inquiries, and we audition local players in that fair community tomorrow afternoon. We hope to fill two temporary positions by using locals. Perhaps we can even turn such an eventuality into a plus for us, publicitywise. Local players onstage with us might improve our audience draw."

Deena Sweete, aglitter in DayGlo nylon pants and jacket, tapped a gold high-heeled pump. "Just as long as we remember who the female lead is, Frankie."

Lord rolled his eyes. "Yes, Deena. Of course, Deena."

Janis Mahafey, in dramatic black blouse and slacks, looked at her rival with narrowed eyes. "We're a democracy now. We're all stars."

"Some," Sweete replied smugly, "more than others. After all, talent *will* tell."

"Ladies, ladies," Lord intoned. "We have all agreed upon a truce, remember?"

Tad Raddell slammed the back doors of the van. In blue sweater and running shorts that bared his athletic legs, he looked happier than Laura had seen him before. "Ready, gang? Let's shag outta here."

"Thank heavens, Tad," Lord said, "you retained legal ownership of the van."

"The only smart thing I did with Reddy," the youthful actor muttered.

"He was a wonderful man," Sweete said quickly.

"He was a bastard," Mahafey said.

"He was an actor's actor," Lord added.

"Can we just *go?*" Raddell asked.

Lord turned again to Laura and clasped one of her hands in his. "Perhaps we shall meet again. Your law officer has our permanent addresses, and we have been instructed to maintain contact. When there are hearings or trials, all of us may be required to return to testify."

The others came over to shake hands. Sweete's dark red lipstick made her mouth almost like a thespian's mask as she beamed down at Laura. "It's been grand." Mahafey shook hands glumly, saying nothing. Raddell gave her a quick, easy hug and brushed his lips on her cheek Hollywood-style.

They all turned to the van.

At that moment, things clicked for Laura. She was by no means sure, but an instinctive little flush made her skin go hot. *It won't hurt to try.*

"Deena?" she said, not taking time to think it through.

Sweete turned. "Yes?"

"I forgot something," Laura ad-libbed. "Can you come back inside with me real quick?"

"What is it?"

Laura beamed her best smile. "One sec. Please. Okay?"

Frowning, Sweete started back.

"Hurry it up," Raddell said impatiently.

Nerves whanging discordantly, Laura maintained her smile as she held the back door for the tall blond actress. Puzzled and irritated, Sweete went through the door first. Laura followed, closing it behind them. They were in the dim-lit back hall behind the kitchen.

"Now what?" Sweete demanded. "We've got to be on the road, honey!"

Laura took a breath. "It was you, wasn't it?"

"It was me *what?*"

"You were the one who got into Redwine's room immediately after the murder."

"You're crazy!" Sweete reached for the door.

"It was your lipstick on his dresser," Laura said quickly before she could escape.

"Sure! I explained that to the sheriff. Reddy let me keep some cosmetics and a brush in there because his room was closer to all the scenes than mine, and—"

"Deena, give me a break. You had spent the night with him right after you both got here. One of his keys was missing. You had it. Was that so you could slip back in for an encore later?"

Sweete's face twisted. "You're nutty."

Oh, God, I guessed wrong. But she hid the spasm of uncertainty. "You used the extra key to his room to get back in there right after he was found dead, before anyone else could organize a search. What did you have to look for? You didn't even take time to grab your cosmetics, but you were looking for *something*. The money was practically in plain view, but you didn't take that, either. What was it? A contract? A letter?"

Sweete's mouth twisted, and suddenly the pretense had vanished. When she spoke, her voice came out flat and bitter. "Pictures."

"Pictures?" Laura was almost stunned with relief to know she had guessed right. But she didn't understand. "Of—?"

"Reddy liked to take…nudes."

Laura remembered the explicit photos of Janis Mahafey. "You…?"

"I couldn't let someone go in there and find all those pictures of me, or—God forbid!—some of those he took with a timer of him and me together. What would Rebecca do with something like that? She could leak them to the press or something—ruin me. They would have made me a prime suspect, too. I had to get them."

"And you did," Laura said, seeing.

"I *just* did. Your deputy or Mrs. Epperman or somebody was coming up the far hall when I found them. I grabbed them and ran for it—just got out the back fire stairs in time."

Laura felt weary. "Did you know who killed him?"

"No! How could I?"

"Taking those pictures might be construed as obstruction of justice, Deena. I guess you know that."

Sweete's large, overmadeup eyes became dark and haunted. "Are you going to turn me in?"

Laura stopped dead, unable for a moment to speak. She knew she should. She also knew it would accomplish nothing. Redwine had victimized this big, beautiful, dumb blond just as he had victimized everyone else. Her frightened, battered expression hinted at how desperate he had made her, how badly she had been used.

Seeing it all, Laura hesitated. Shouldn't she tell Lassiter at once? On the other hand, what good would it do to run screaming that this woman had been tricked into posing for obscene pictures, too, and in some throwback to innocence had run to Redwine's room after his death to prevent people from gawking at proof of her victimization?

Laura had a moment's sense of dizzy disorientation, as if she had wandered through a doorway into a shadowland, a place where the certainties did not exist and decisions became phantoms that darted in and out of the surrounding darkness, first in one form, then in another.

Deena Sweete's eyes glistened.

"It was a dumb thing to do," Laura said sadly.

"I know. I did a lot of dumb things."

Was stupidity a punishable offense?

Laura decided without thought. "Tad is an impatient guy. You'd better hurry along or he might leave you behind."

Sweete stared, her eyes going wide again. Then she dashed the back of her hand against the tears and leaned forward, seizing Laura in a fast hug that almost hurt her. "Thanks!"

The door winked open and closed again. Laura stood there alone for a few seconds, appalled at what she had just done. Would she ever know if she had done the right thing? All she knew at this instant was that no one else would ever know, not even Aaron Lassiter. Perhaps especially not him.

Beyond the door came the sound of an engine starting. She opened the door and looked out. Tad Raddell was just pulling his big, ugly van away from the back dock. As it turned, she noticed for the first time that one of them had smeared some paint over the side panels, obliterating the Redwine Players identification. The van trundled to the end of the back lot, turned right, and went out of sight behind the building.

THIRTY

THE SUN WAS gone again Monday morning, another cold front blowing in, when Laura drove the country road back to Timberdale.

It had not been a good night. She had been a little crabby with Aaron in the evening, partly because letdown had finally left her feeling like she was about to cave in, partly because of the secret she was withholding from him. Then even with Trissie back in the apartment and things starting back toward normal, her fatigue had made her sleep jumpily. Now she had a headache and was not looking forward to the day.

How long would it be, she wondered, before she could stop second-guessing herself about helping Deena Sweete keep her secret? How long would it be before anything got back to normal, with her feelings or here at Timberdale?

She felt off-balance, out of kilter. She expected everyone and everything at Timberdale to be out of kilter, too...at best, uncomfortable for a while. If she understood anything about trauma and its aftermath, she might be walking on eggs around everyone for an indefinite time.

Reaching the retirement center, she parked at the side as usual. The north wind tugged at her as she hurried around toward the front, where she had already spied Still Bill Mills working in a flower bed.

Ken Keen, wearing bright red golf slacks and a yellow T-shirt, galloped out from under the canopy, starting his morning walk. They approached one another.

"Good morning, Ken," she said, sending him a bright smile.

At that moment, the wind caught her skirt and whooshed it

up to her hips. She almost dropped her attaché case, grabbed for her hem.

"Hey, babe," Keen yelped. "You did that just for me, right? You're really hot today, huh? Listen! Lemme go get my camera, then do it again."

Furious with herself for blushing, she hurried on toward the entrance. Still Bill Mills leaned on a shovel and awaited her arrival.

"Hi, Bill."

"Don't pay any account to Ken," he advised. "You got to remember, he's in his second childhood. He's about as mature as a tyke in kidney garden."

She entered the building. It was early, and the atrium stood deserted as it usually did at this hour. So far, she thought, so good. So far, so normal. But she didn't expect it to last.

She hurried past Stacy Miller, busy cleaning up pizza crumbs. To her surprise, lights blazed in Mrs. Epperman's office. Starting past, she saw to her even greater amazement that there were lights on in the far office. Was it possible that Francie Blake had actually come to work on time?

"Laura!" the big voice bawled out of Mrs. Epperman's office. "Come in, dear girl!"

Mentally sighing, Laura turned back. Mrs. Epperman sat hunched behind her desk, her small crystal ball and the day's newspaper crossword in front of her. The crystal ball was an ominous sign; Mrs. Epperman consulted it when in search of new wonderful ideas like the mystery weekend.

"To take everyone's mind off things," Mrs. Epperman told her, "I've been thinking about a special event. I'm going to call it Fairy Tale Weekend, and I'm going to put you in charge. What do you think, dear? Doesn't that sound jolly?"

Good God. "When were you thinking about it?"

Before Mrs. Epperman could answer, footsteps sounded in the hall. Pierre Motard, high white hat flapping like a wing, charged in.

"Oh, dear," Mrs. Epperman muttered, and looked down at her puzzle.

Motard waved a sheet of Timberdale stationery. "What is these memorandum I find, cholesterol? I always use best recipe, Paris best! Cholesterol no concern of mine, let people exercise more, run! How you think make eggs Benedict no cholesterol! You think French toast grow on trees? I am outrageous!"

Mrs. Epperman looked up from her puzzle. "Laura, please straighten this out with Pierre, that's a good girl. Now—"

Ellen Smith tore in behind Motard, paint-smeared smock flying. "Someone has been in the craft room! They've raised the cover on my painting and *looked at it!* Something has to change. I demand a private room where I can practice my art without the interference of philistines. How can I get General Custer right if people are spying on me?"

The telephone bleeped. Mrs. Epperman let her reading glasses fall to her bosom. "Get that, Laura, will you, dear?"

Laura's back cracked as she reached across the desk and picked up the phone from under Mrs. Epperman's elbow. "Yes?"

"Laura?" It was Still Bill Mills. "I just found the sprinkler system control valve out here ain't working. We need to have a convisitation about it."

"I'll be right out, Bill." She reached back to hang up the phone.

"Well?" Ellen Smith fumed.

"What is about these memorandum?" Pierre Motard demanded.

Francie Blake hurried in breathlessly, killer legs twinkling. "Laura! I just don't know what I'm going to do about all this *work* you left me! I mean, I came in early today, but how can I do all *this?* Did you forget I'm leaving tomorrow to go to Mexico City with Dirk?"

"What's an eight-letter word for calculating device?" Mrs. Epperman muttered.

Laura took a deep breath and started to relax. She saw that her worries about the emotional situation at Timberdale had been groundless. She didn't understand anything about the aftermath of trauma after all. Second thoughts about Deena Sweete might plague her for a long time. But things at Timberdale seemed back to normal already.

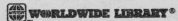

A MOST DEADLY
RETIREMENT

First Time in Paperback

A Laura Michaels Mystery

When one of Timberdale Retirement Center's residents makes a 6:00 a.m. run through the woods to the nearby convenience store to stock up on cigarettes, she never makes it back. Bludgeoned. But by whom?

Laura Michaels, the center's manager and social worker, is intent on doing something—at least stopping the media from sensationalizing the horror. But as more untimely deaths occur, it's clear that something terrible is happening and retirement has become most deadly.

JOHN
MILES

"The author...has created some real characters..." —*Sunday Oklahoman*

Available in October 1997 at your favorite retail outlet.

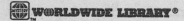